THE LAST
DAYS

Also by Scott Westerfeld

So Yesterday
Peeps

THE LAST DAYS

A NOVEL BY

SCOTT WESTERFELD

razor bill

The Last Days

RAZORBILL

Published by the Penguin Group
Penguin Young Readers Group
345 Hudson Street, New York, New York 10014, U.S.A.
Penguin Group (USA) Inc., 375 Hudson Street, New York,
New York 10014, U.S.A.
Penguin Group (Canada), 90 Eglinton Avenue East, Suite 700, Toronto, Ontario,
Canada M4P 2Y3 (a division of Pearson Penguin Canada Inc.)
Penguin Books Ltd, 80 Strand, London WC2R 0RL, England
Penguin Ireland, 25 St Stephen's Green, Dublin 2, Ireland
(a division of Penguin Books Ltd)
Penguin Group (Australia), 250 Camberwell Road, Camberwell, Victoria 3124,
Australia (a division of Pearson Australia Group Pty Ltd)
Penguin Books India Pvt Ltd, 11 Community Centre, Panchsheel Park,
New Delhi - 110 017, India
Penguin Group (NZ), Cnr Airborne and Rosedale Roads, Albany,
Auckland 1310, New Zealand (a division of Pearson New Zealand Ltd)
Penguin Books (South Africa) (Pty) Ltd, 24 Sturdee Avenue,
Rosebank, Johannesburg 2196, South Africa

Penguin Books Ltd, Registered Offices: 80 Strand, London WC2R 0RL, England

10 9 8 7 6 5 4 3 2 1

THE LIBRARY OF CONGRESS HAS CATALOGED THE HARDCOVER EDITION AS FOLLOWS:
Westerfeld, Scott.
    The last days : a novel / by Scott Westerfeld.
       p. cm.
    Summary: As an ancient evil stirs beneath the streets of New York City,
  infecting rats and people like a plague, five quirky teens come together to
  form a "New Sound" band whose music seems to have paranormal power.
    ISBN 1-59514-062-X (hardcover)
    [1. Bands (Music)—Fiction. 2. Monsters—Fiction. 3. Horror stories.]
  I. Title.
  PZ7.W5197Las 2007
  [Fic]—dc22

                                                              2006010418
Razorbill paperback ISBN: 978-1-59514-128-6

Printed in the United States of America

To Jazza
first reader and best friend

THE LAST DAYS

PART I

INFLUENCES

Ever hear this charming little rhyme?

Ring-around-the-rosy.

A pocket full of posies.

Ashes, ashes, we all fall down.

Some people say that this poem is about the Black Death, the fourteenth-century plague that killed 100 million people. Here's the theory: "Ring-around-the-rosy" was an early symptom of plague: a circular rash of red skin. In medieval times, people carried flowers, like posies, with them for protection against disease. The words "ashes to ashes" appear in the funeral mass, and sometimes plague victims' houses were burned.

And "we all fall down"?

Well, you can figure that one out for yourself.

Sadly, though, most experts think this is nonsense. A red rash isn't really a plague symptom, they say, and "ashes" was originally some other word. Most important, the rhyme is too new. It didn't appear in print until 1881.

Trust me, though: it's about the plague. The words have changed a little from the original, but so have any words carried on the lips of children for seven hundred years. It's a little reminder that the Black Death will come again.

How can I be so sure about this rhyme, when all the experts disagree?

Because I ate the kid who made it up.

NIGHT MAYOR TAPES:
102–130

1. THE FALL

I think New York was leaking.

It was past midnight and still a hundred degrees. Some kind of city sweat was oozing up through the sidewalk cracks, shimmering with oily rainbows in the streetlights. The garbage piled up outside the restaurants on Indian Row was seeping, leftover curry turning into slurry. The glistening plastic bags would smell jaw-droppingly foul the next morning, but as I walked past that night, they still gave off the perfumes of saffron and freshly thrown-out rice.

The people were sweating too—shiny-faced and frizzy-haired, like everyone had just stepped out of a shower. Eyes were glassy, and cell phones dangled limply on wrist straps, softly glowing, spitting occasional fragments of bubblegum songs.

I was on my way home from practicing with Zahler. It was way too hot to write anything new, so we'd riffed, plowing through the same four chords a thousand times. After an hour the riff had faded from my ears, like it does when you say the same word over and over till it turns meaningless. Finally, all I could hear was the squeak of Zahler's sweaty fingers on his strings and his amp hissing like a steam-pipe, another music squeezing up through ours.

We pretended we were a band warming up onstage, slowly revving the crowd into a frenzy before the lead singer jumps into the spotlights: the World's Longest Intro. But we didn't have a lead singer, so the riff just petered out into rivulets of sweat.

I sometimes feel it right before something big happens—when I'm about to break a guitar string, or get caught sneaking in, or when my parents are *this* close to having a monster fight.

So just before the TV fell, I looked up.

The woman was twenty-something, with fire-engine red hair and raccoon eyes, black makeup streaming down her cheeks. She pushed a television through her third-floor window, an old boxy one, its power cord flailing as it tumbled toward the sidewalk. The TV clipped a fire escape, the deep ringing sound swallowed seconds later by the crash on the pavement twenty feet ahead of me.

A spray of shattered glass skittered around my feet, glittering and sharp, tinkling like colliding chandeliers as shards rolled and skidded to a halt. Fragments of street-light and sky reflected up from them, as if the television had split into a thousand tiny screens, all still working. My own eye stared back at me from a Manhattan-shaped sliver. Wide and awestruck, it blinked.

The next thing I did was look straight up. You know, in case everyone was throwing out TVs that night, and I should roll under a parked car. But it was just her—she was letting out long, wordless screams now and throwing out more stuff:

Pillows with tasseled edges. Dolls and desk lamps. Books fluttering like crash-landing birds. A jar full of pens and pencils. Two cheap wooden chairs, smashed first against the window frame so they'd fit through. A computer keyboard that sent up a splash of keys and tiny springs. Silverware glittering as it tumbled, ringing on the pavement like a triangle when dinner's ready . . . a whole apartment squeezed out one window. Somebody's life laid bare.

And all the while she was shrieking like a beast above us.

I looked around at the gathering crowd, most of them getting out late from Indian Row, addled by curry. The rapt expressions on their upturned faces made me jealous. The whole time Zahler and I had jammed, I'd been imagining an audience like this one: flabbergasted and electrified, yanked out of the everyday by their ears and eyeballs. And now this crazy woman, with her rock-star hair and makeup, had them mesmerized. Why bother with riffs and solos and lyrics when all the crowd wanted was an avalanche of screams and smashed Ikea furniture?

But once the shock wore off, their rapture faded into something uglier. Soon enough, people were laughing and pointing, a gang of boys shouting, "Jump, jump, jump!" in rhythm. A camera flash popped, catching a satanic flicker in the woman's eyes. A couple of faces glowed with blue cell-phone light—calling the police, or nearby friends to come and join in? I wondered.

One of the spectators slipped into the impact zone, running half-crouched to snatch a black dress from under a rain of computer cables and extension cords. She backed away, holding it up to her body as if she'd pulled it off a rack. Another ducked in to snag an armload of magazines.

"Hey!" I yelled. I was about to point out that this wasn't exactly Dumpster diving—the woman might want her stuff back after this psychotic meltdown was over—but then the CDs started flying. Glittering projectiles spattered on the street like plastic hail, each one impelled from the window by a shriek.

The looters retreated—the woman was *aiming* now, and the CDs were deadly. I mean, compact discs don't hurt much, but these were still in their cases, giving them extra weight and corners.

Then I saw it: the neck of an electric guitar emerging from the window, then the whole instrument—a mid-seventies Fender Stratocaster with gold pickups and whammy bar, a creamy yellow body with a white pick-guard.

I took a step forward, holding one hand up. "Wait!"

The madwoman glared down at me, mascara smeared across her face like black blood, clutching the Stratocaster to her chest. Her hands found the strings, as if she was about to play, and then she let out one last terrible howl.

"No!" I shouted.

She let the guitar drop.

It spun in the air, delicate tuning hardware glittering in

the streetlights. I was already running, tripping on smashed plastic and tangled clothes, thinking that there were four hundred bones in my two hands, wondering how many of them that lacquered hardwood would break after a thirty-foot fall.

But I couldn't just let it smash. . . .

Then the miracle: the guitar snapped to a halt in midair. Its strap was caught on a corner of the fire escape, where it hung, spinning perilously.

I skidded to a halt, looking straight up.

"Over here!" someone shouted.

I glanced down for a split second: a girl my age, with short black hair and red-framed glasses, yanking something big and flat from under the clutter, sending silverware scattering in all directions.

"Watch out," I said, pointing up toward where the Strat was untangling itself. "It's about to fall."

"I know! Take the other side!"

I glanced back down at her, frowning. The girl was holding two corners of a blanket she'd rescued from the pile. She unfurled its plaid expanse toward me with a flick, as if we were making a bed. I grabbed for the other corners, finally understanding.

We stepped back from each other, pulling the blanket taut, looking up again. Above us, the guitar spun faster and faster, like a kid unwinding on a swing set.

"Be careful," I said. "That's a nineteen seventy-three . . . Um, what I mean is, it's really valuable."

"With gold pickups?" she snorted. "Nineteen seventy-five, maybe."

I looked down at her.

"Incoming!" she yelled.

The guitar slipped free, still spinning, hardware glittering, strap flailing. It landed heavy as a dead body between us, almost jerking the blanket from my fists. Its momentum pulled us both forward a few skidding steps, suddenly face to face.

But there was no awful thud; the Stratocaster hadn't struck pavement.

"We saved it!" Her brown eyes were glowing.

I looked down at the guitar, safely swaddled in plaid. "Whoa. We did."

Then the fire escape rang out again. Both of us flinched as we looked up. But it wasn't more stuff falling—it was a pair of human figures, six stories above, descending toward the crazy woman's window. They weren't climbing down the metal stairs, though—they were practically flying, swinging from handhold to handhold, graceful as headlight shadows slipping across a ceiling.

I watched them, awestruck, until the girl next to me shouted two terrifying words:

"*Toaster oven!*"

It was tumbling out the window directly over our heads, glass door hanging open, scattering crumbs. . . .

We bundled the Stratocaster into its blanket and ran.

2. TAJ MAHAL

"You know what the weird thing was?"

The cute guy frowned, still wide-eyed and panting. "*The* weird thing? I can't think of anything that *wasn't* weird about that."

I smiled, holding out both palms, weighing the weirdness. It was all relative, these days. You had to take your normal where you found it. People went crazy all the time; it was how they went crazy that mattered.

We'd taken the Strat and run around the corner—around a couple of corners, actually—until I'd led the guy to my street without saying so. My building was right across from us, but I wasn't sure I wanted him knowing where I lived—even if he was the sort of boy to consider catching a Fender Stratocaster with his bare hands. And I certainly didn't want my mom coming home late and finding me out on the front steps huddled with some random cute guy and a secondhand plaid bedspread. She might get the wrong idea. In fact, she would make a point of getting the wrong idea.

The stoop we sat on was darkened by scaffolding, protected from the streetlights, invisible. The Strat lay between us, still wrapped in its bedspread, partly to protect it and partly because the guy looked guilty, like he thought someone was going to chase us down and make us give it back.

Like who? Not that crazy woman: she was gone by now. I'd seen angels coming to collect her. That's what happens when you lose it these days: real-life angels, just like Luz had told me about, though I hadn't quite believed her until tonight.

But I didn't want to sound crazy myself, so I said, "Here's what was weird. That was girl's stuff she was tossing. The clothes coming out the window: dresses and skirts. *Her* stuff."

He frowned again. "Why wouldn't it be?"

"Because there's no *story* that way." I paused and pushed my glasses up my nose, which makes people focus on my eyes, which are dark brown and, frankly, fabulous. "I could understand if she was throwing all her boyfriend's crap out the window, because he cheated on her or something. That's more or less nonweird: people do that on TV. But you wouldn't throw your own stuff out like that, would you?"

"Maybe. Maybe not." He thought about it for a few seconds, frowning at someone laughing as she walked past, hands full of CDs in spiderweb-cracked cases. I thought he was about to tell me we should give back the guitar, but instead he said, "Girls have girlfriends too, you know. And roommates who don't pay the rent."

"Hmm," I said. I'd sort of thought the guy was thick, because he'd taken forever to understand my brilliant guitar-saving plan (the way firefighters used to save jumpers). But this answer demonstrated lateral thinking.

Cute *and* lateral. And he knew a Strat when he saw one.

"Maybe a girlfriend," I admitted. "But your roommate's stuff?" I'd never really had a roommate except my mom, which doesn't count. "Wouldn't you sell their crap on eBay?"

He laughed, dark eyes sparkling in the shadows. Then he got all serious again. "Probably. But you're right: I think it was hers. She was throwing her whole life away."

"But why?" I asked softly.

"I don't know, but right before she threw the Strat out she was holding it the right way. The way you really hold a guitar." He put his hands in air-guitar position, his left fingers playing delicate scales along an imaginary neck.

"Not like some model in a video," I murmured. "That drives me crazy."

"Yeah." He paused, then shrugged. "So it was her guitar. And she looked sad up there, not angry. Like someone losing everything she had."

Whoa. This guy was totally lateral, like he knew something he wasn't saying. "Wait. You're just guessing, right?"

"Yeah." He opened his hands and looked down at his palms. "Just looked that way to me."

"Well, then . . ." I put my hand on the plaid bundle between us. "If she *wanted* to throw it out, it's not like we stole it."

He stared at me.

"What?" I said. "You want to take it back and toss it on the pile?"

He shook his head. "No. Someone else would take it. And they'd carry it around unprotected, pretend they were playing it." He shuddered.

"Exactly!" I smiled. "What's your name anyway?"

"Moz."

I must have made an uncomprehending expression.

"Short for 'Mosquito,'" the guy said.

"Oh, of course." He *was* kind of small, like I am. Have you ever noticed that small people are cuter? Like dolls. "My name's Pearl. Not short for anything, despite its shortness."

Moz pulled his serious face. "So, Pearl, don't you think she might want her guitar back after she . . ." His voice drifted off.

"Comes back from wherever they lock her up?"

He nodded, and I wondered if he knew I didn't mean the generic "they" who lock crazy people up, but the two angels we'd seen on the fire escape. Did he understand what was happening to the world? Most people seemed to know even less than I did—all they saw were the garbage piling up and the extra rats, didn't even notice the rumbling underfoot. But this guy talked like he could sense things, at least.

"We could find out who she is," he said. "Maybe ask someone in her building."

"And hang on to it for her?"

"Yeah. I mean, if it was just some crappy guitar it wouldn't matter, but this . . ." His eyes got sparkly again, like the thought of a homeless Strat was going to make him cry.

And right then I had my brain-flash: the realization that had been screaming for my attention since I'd seen Moz running to catch the Stratocaster bare-handed. Maybe this was the guy I needed, a guy with raw heart, ready to throw himself under a falling Fender because it was vintage and irreplaceable.

Maybe Moz was what I'd been waiting for since Nervous System had exploded.

"Okay," I said. "We'll keep it for her. But at my place." I put my arm around the bundle.

"*Your* place?"

"Sure. After all, why should I trust you? You might go and pawn it. Three or four thousand dollars for you, when it was my idea to use the bedspread."

"But *I'm* the one who wants to give it back," he sputtered cutely. "A second ago you were all, 'It's not stealing.'"

"Maybe that's what you *want* me to think." I pushed my glasses up my nose. "Maybe that was just a cover for your devious plans." It hurt to see his wounded expression, because I was being totally unfair. Moz might have been lateral, but I could already tell that he was nine kinds of nondevious.

"But . . . you were just . . ." He made a strangled noise.

I hugged the Strat closer. "Of course, you could come over and play it anytime. We could play together. Are you in a band?"

"Yeah." His wary eyes didn't leave the bedspread. "Half a band anyway."

"Half a band?" I smiled, knowing now that my brain-flash had been right on target. "A band in need of completion? Maybe this is fate."

He shook his head. "We've already got two guitarists."

"What else?"

"Um, just two guitarists."

I laughed. "Listen, a drummer and a bass player is half a band. Two guitarists is just a . . ." He frowned, so I didn't finish. "Anyway, I play keyboards."

"You do?" He shook his head. "So how do you know so much about guitars? I mean, you called the year on that Strat when it was still in the air!"

"Lucky guess." And, of course, I *do* play guitar. And keyboards too, and flute and xylophone and a wicked-mean harmonica—there's practically nothing I don't play. But I figured out a while back not to say that out loud; everyone thinks we nonspecialists are amateurs. (Tell that to the nonspecialist currently known as Prince.) I also never show off my perfect pitch or mention the name of my high school.

His dark and gorgeous eyes narrowed. "Are you sure you don't play guitar?"

I laughed. "I never said that. But trust me, I absolutely play keyboards. How's tomorrow?"

"But, um, how do you even know we'd . . ." He took a breath. "I mean, like, what are your—?"

"Uh!" I interrupted. "Not that word!" If he asked me what my *influences* were, the whole thing was off.

He shrugged. "You know what I mean."

I sighed through clenched teeth. How was I supposed

to explain that I was in too much of a hurry to give a damn? That there were more important things to worry about? That the world didn't have time for labels anymore?

"Look, let's say you hated graves, okay?"

"Hated graves?"

"Yeah, detested tombs. Loathed sepulchers. Abhorred anyplace anyone was buried. Understand?"

"Why would I do that?"

I let out a groan. Mozzy was being very nonlateral all of a sudden. "Hypothetically hated graves."

"Um, okay. I hate graves." He put on a grave-hating face.

"Excellent. Perfect. But you'd still go to the Taj Mahal, wouldn't you?" I spread my hands in explanatory triumph.

"Um, I'd go where?"

"The Taj Mahal! The most beautiful building in the world! You know all those Indian restaurants around the corner, the murals on the walls?"

He nodded slowly. "Yeah, I know the one you mean: lots of arches, a pond out front, with kind of an onion on top?"

"Exactly. And gorgeous."

"I guess. And somebody's buried there?"

"Yeah, Moz, some old queen. It's a total tomb. But you don't suddenly think it's ugly, just because of its *category*, do you?"

His expression changed from tomb-hating to lateral-thinking. "So, in other words . . ." Brief pause. "You don't mind if you're in a band that plays alternative death-metal cypherfunk, as long as it's the Taj Mahal of alternative death-metal cypherfunk. Right?"

"Exactly!" I cried. "You guys can worry about the category. All the death metal you want. Just be *good* at it." I picked up the Stratocaster, wrapped it tighter. "How's tomorrow? Two o'clock."

He shrugged. "Okay, I guess. Let's give it a shot. Maybe keyboards are what we need."

Or maybe I *am*, I thought, but out loud I just told him my buzzer number, pointing across the street. "Oh, and two more questions, Moz."

"Sure?"

"One: do you guys really play death-metal cypherfunk?"

He smiled. "Don't worry. That was hypothetical death-metal cypherfunk."

"Phew," I said, trying not to notice how that little smile had made him even cuter. Now that we were going to jam together, it didn't pay to notice things like that. "Question two: does your half a band have a name?"

He shook his head. "Nope."

"No problem," I said. "That'll be the easy part."

3. POISONBLACK

The next day, Zahler and I saw our first black water.

We'd just met outside my building, on our way to Pearl's. A gang of kids across the street was gathered around a fire hydrant, prying at it with a two-foot wrench, hoping to get some relief from the early afternoon heat. Zahler stopped to watch, like he always did when kids were doing anything more or less illegal.

"Check it out!" He grinned, pointing at a convertible coming down the street. If the hydrant erupted in the next ten seconds, the unwitting driver was going to get soaked.

"Watch your guitar," I said. We were twenty feet away, but you never knew how much pressure was lurking in a hydrant on a hot summer day.

"It's protected, Moz," he said, but he stood the instrument case upright behind himself. I felt empty-handed, headed to a jam session with nothing but a few guitar picks in my pocket. My fingers were itching to play their first notes on the Strat.

We were sort of late, but the car was a BMW, its driver in a suit and tie and talking on his cell phone. Back when Zahler and I had been little, soaking a guy like that would have been worth about ten thousand fire-hydrant points. We could spare ten seconds.

But the kids were still fiddling as the convertible passed.

"Incompetent little twerps." Zahler sighed. "Should we give them a hand?"

"It's already after two." I turned and headed up the street.

But as I walked I heard the cries behind us change from squeals of excitement to shrieks of fear.

We spun around. The hydrant was spraying black water in all directions, covering the kids with a sticky, shimmering coat. A thick, dark mist rose into the air, breaking the sunlight into a gleaming spectrum, like a rainbow on an oil slick. The screaming kids were stumbling back, bare skin glistening with the stuff. A couple of the little ones just stood in the torrent, crying.

"What the hell?" Zahler whispered.

I took a step forward, but the smell—earthy and fetid and rotten—forced me to a halt. The dark cloud was still rising up between the buildings, roiling like smoke overhead, and the wind was shifting toward us. Tiny black dots began to spatter the street, closer and closer, like a sudden summer rain starting up. Zahler and I backed away, staring down at the pavement. The drops were as luminous as tiny black pearls.

The hydrant seemed to cough once, the gush of black water sputtering, and then the water turned clear. Above us, the cloud was already dissolving, turning into nothing more than a shadowy haze across the sky.

I knelt on the sidewalk, peering down at one of the black drops. It glimmered unsteadily for a moment, reflecting sunlight as the shadow from the cloud overhead faded. And then it boiled away before my eyes.

"What the hell *was* that, Moz?"

"I don't know. Maybe somebody's heating oil leaked into the pipes?" I shook my head.

The kids were staring at the hydrant warily, half afraid the water would turn black again, but also eager to wash themselves. A few stepped forward, and the oily stuff seemed to slide from their skin, dark stains disappearing from their soaked shorts and T-shirts.

A minute later they were all playing in the spray, like nothing weird had happened.

"Didn't look like any oil I've ever seen," Zahler said.

"Yeah. Probably just old water in the hydrant," I said, not wanting to think about it. It had disappeared so quickly, I could almost imagine it hadn't happened at all. "Or something like that. Come on, we're late."

Pearl's room looked like a recording studio had mated with a junkyard, then exploded.

The walls were lined with egg cartons, the big twelve-by-twelve ones that you see stacked outside restaurants. Sinuous hills rose between the egg-shaped valleys, curving like the sound waves they gobbled.

"Whoa, you've got a ton of gear!" Zahler exclaimed. His voice was echoless, rebounding from the walls with less bounce than a dead cat.

I'd always told Zahler that we could soundproof his room this way so that his parents would stop yelling at us to turn it down. But we'd never had enough motivation to make it happen. Or enough egg cartons.

The floor was covered with spare cables, effects boxes, all the usual fire hazards—we stepped lightly over the spaghetti-junctions of power strips, dozens of adapters squeezed into them, all labeled to show what was plugged in where. Two racks of electronics towered at one end of the room, the cables gathered with twist-ties. The modules were organized neatly into tribes: black and buttonless digital units; flickering arpeggiators; a few dinosaur synths with analog dials and needles, like old science-fiction movie props ready for takeoff.

Zahler was looking around nervously, probably wondering if his cheap little electric was going to get squashed under all that gear. I was wondering why Pearl, if she owned all this keyboard stuff, had risked falling toaster ovens just to save a vintage guitar.

"Where do you *sleep*?" Zahler asked. The bed was covered with scattered CDs, more cables, and a few harmonicas and hand drums.

"The guest room, mostly," Pearl said proudly. "I suffer for my art."

Zahler laughed but rolled me a look. Pearl wasn't exactly suffering. She hadn't showed us all of her mom's apartment, but what we'd seen was already bigger than his parents' and mine put together, the walls crowded with paintings and glass cases full of stuff from all over the world. Stairs led to more floors above, and we'd passed a pair of armed security guards down in the lobby. Pearl had probably seen the Taj Mahal in person.

So why had she contemplated helping herself to the Strat, when she could obviously afford to buy one of her own?

Maybe she was used to everything falling from the sky. She'd looked pretty annoyed when we weren't on time, like this was a job interview or something.

I sifted through the CDs on the bed, trying to peg her influences. What was Pearl really into, besides old Indian tombs, punctuality, and soundproofing? The discs left me clueless. They were hand-labeled with the names of bands I'd never heard of: Zombie Phoenix, Morgan's Army, Nervous System . . .

"Nervous System?" I asked.

Pearl groaned. "That's this band I was in. Bunch of Juilliard geeks and, um, me."

I glanced at Zahler: great. Not only did Pearl have lots of real gear, she also knew some real musicians, which meant she might not be too impressed with us. We weren't exactly into virtuosity—we hadn't taken any lessons since sixth grade. This jam session was going to be a bust.

"Did you guys play any gigs?" Zahler asked.

She shrugged. "We did, at their high school, mostly. But the System had no heart. Or it did, I guess, but then the heart exploded. You guys want to plug in?"

The Stratocaster soothed my nerves.

It swung from my shoulder featherlight, lacquered back

side cool against my thigh. The strings were six strands of spiderweb, with the easiest action my fingers had ever felt. I strummed a quick, unplugged E-major chord and was amazed to hear that even a three-story fall hadn't knocked the Strat out of tune.

Pearl pushed in the power button on a Marshall amp, a hulking old beast with tubes inside. (Why did a keyboardist have a guitar amp handy? Had it also fallen from the sky?) The tubes warmed up slowly, the hiss fading in like a wave breaking.

"You guys have to share this amp," Pearl apologized. "Nonoptimal, I know."

Zahler shrugged. "That's fool."

She raised an eyebrow. Zahler says *fool* instead of *cool*, which is kind of confusing. But at least he didn't mention that I'd never owned an amp, so we shared one over at his place too.

Pearl tossed us cords, and I plugged in—a sizzle-snap of connection, then the familiar hum of six open strings. I dampened five of them and plucked a low E. Zahler tuned up to it, booming through his strings one by one, setting off a little plastic chorus of CD cases shivering against one another on the bed.

The Marshall was set to 7, a volume we never dared in Zahler's room, and I hoped Pearl's egg cartons worked. Otherwise, her neighbors were going to feel us in their bones. But I was ready to risk someone calling the police. The Strat was squeaking impatiently as I slid my fingers along its neck, like it was ready too.

Finally Zahler nodded, and Pearl rubbed her hands

together, sitting down at the little desk jammed between the two racks of electronics. A computer waited there, cabled to a musical keyboard, the kind with elegant black and white keys instead of the usual jumble of letters, numbers, and symbol-junk.

She rested one hand on the keys, the other on a mouse. At her double-click, dozens of lights on the towers flickered to life. "Play something."

My fingers were suddenly nervous. It was important to get these notes right, to make a solid first impression on this accidental guitar. Pearl thought that "fate" had brought us together, but that was the wrong word for it. Fate hadn't made that woman go insane. People had been edgy this whole weird summer, what with the crime wave, the rat wave, and the crazy-making heat. That was bigger than Pearl and Zahler and me.

This guitar wasn't destiny. It was just another symptom of whatever bizarre illness New York City was coming down with, something strange and unexpected, like that spout of black water on the way over.

For a moment the Strat felt awkward in my hands.

But then Zahler said, "Big Riff?"

I smiled. The Big Riff went back a long time, as long as we'd been playing. It was simple and gutsy, and we didn't bother practicing it too much anymore. But the Strat was going to make it new all over again, like playing baseball with bottle rockets.

Zahler started up. His part of the Big Riff is low and growly, his strings muffled with the flesh of his right hand, like something trying to sizzle up out of a boiling pot.

I took a slow, deep breath . . . then jumped in. My part's faster than his, fingers roaming in the high notes halfway up the neck. My part skitters while his churns, blowing sparks from his embers. Mine darts and mutates, keeps changing, while Zahler's stays level and even and thick, filling in all the gaps.

The Strat loved the Big Riff, sliced straight into it. Its spiderweb strings tempted my fingers faster and higher, weightless against Zahler's firmament. If the Big Riff was an army, he was the infantry, the grunts on the ground, and the Strat had turned me into orbital ninjas dropping from the sky, black pajamas under their space suits.

Pearl sat there listening, fingers flexing, mouse twitching, eyes closed. She looked ready to pounce, waiting restlessly for an opening.

We kept going for ten minutes, maybe twenty—it's hard to tell time when you're playing the Big Riff—but she never jumped in. . . .

Finally Zahler gave a little shrug and let the Riff peter out. I followed him down, wrapping up with one last plunge from orbit, the Strat skittering into reluctant silence.

"So, what's the matter?" he asked. "You don't like it?"

Pearl sat silently for another few seconds, thinking hard.

"No, it's excellent. Exactly what I wanted." Her fingers stroked the keys absently. "But, um, it's kind of . . . *big*."

"Yeah," Zahler said. "We call it the Big Riff. Pretty fool, huh?"

"No doubt. But, uh, let me ask you something. How long have you guys been playing together?"

Zahler looked at me.

"Six years," I said. Since we were eleven, playing our nylon-string loaners from school. We'd electrified them with the mikes from his older sister's karaoke machine.

Pearl frowned. "And all that time, it's been just the two of you?"

"Um, yeah?" I admitted. Zahler was looking at me kind of embarrassed, maybe thinking, *Don't tell her about the karaoke machine.*

She nodded. "No wonder."

"No wonder what?" I said.

"There's no room left over."

"There's no *what*?"

Pearl pushed her glasses up her nose. "It's totally full up. Like a pizza with cheese, onions, pepperoni, chilies, sausage, M&M's, and bacon bits. What am I supposed to do, add the guacamole?"

Zahler made a face. "You mean it sucks."

"No. It's big and raw. . . ." She let out a hiss through her teeth, nodding slowly. "You guys made a whole band out of two guitars, which is very lateral. But if you're going to have a *real* band—like, one with more than two people in it—you're going to have to strip your sound way down. We have to poke some holes in the Big Riff."

Zahler glanced at me, eyes narrowed, and I realized that if I decided to blow this off right now, he would march out of there with me. And I almost did, because the Big Riff was *sacred*, part of our friendship from the beginning, and Pearl was talking about tearing it up just to make room for her towers of electronic overkill.

I glared up at all those winking lights, wondering how she was supposed to squeeze that much gear into anyone else's sound without squishing it.

"Plus, it's not really a song," she added. "More like a guitar solo that doesn't go anywhere."

"Whoa . . ." I breathed. "Like a *what*?"

"A guitar solo that doesn't go anywhere," Zahler repeated, nodding. I stared at him.

"I mean, you guys want to do *songs*, right?" Pearl continued. "With verses and choruses and stuff? Don't you think the Big Riff could use a B section?"

"Fool idea," Zahler said. Then he scratched his head. "What's a B section?"

4. NEW ORDER

-ZAHLER-

The new girl was intense. And kind of hot.

She could pull a tune apart like it was *nothing*. Not like Moz, who always talked in circles. Pearl could just hum what she meant, fingers waving little patterns, like she was *seeing* air-notes at the same time. I watched carefully, wishing my fingers could do that.

She was one of those girls who looked better in glasses—all smart and stuff.

The way she stripped down the Big Riff was totally fawesome. Like I knew would happen, she didn't touch my part. My part is basic, the foundation of the Riff. But Moz's jamming could get kind of random, like she'd said about pizza. You know when they have the sundae bar at school where you make your own sundae? I always add toppings until the ice cream disappears, and it winds up kind of disgusting. Give him enough room, and Moz's playing can get like that.

Don't get me wrong—the Mosquito's a

genius, a way better player than me, and there was some pretty fool stuff in his Big Riff zigzags. But it took Pearl to pick out his best threads and weave them back together in a way that made sense.

She explained that a B section was a completely different part of a song, like when the chorus has a different riff, or everything slows down or changes key. Me and Moz didn't do that too much, because I'm happy playing the same four chords all day long and he's happy buzzing around on top of them.

But when you think about it, most songs do have B sections, and we sort of hadn't noticed that ours almost never did. So the moral of the story is, you shouldn't be in a band with just two people for six years. Kind of saps your perspective.

Moz was all buzzy at first, like the Big Riff was his pet frog that Pearl was dissecting. He kept looking at me and making faces, but I eyeballed him into submission. Once he saw that I thought Pearl was okay, he sort of had to listen to her. It hadn't been my idea to drag my ax all the way down here, after all.

In the end, Moz was no idiot, and only an idiot would mind listening to a smart, hot girl telling him something that's for his own good. And for the good of the band, which is what the three of us were already turning into.

It was fawesome to watch. All the years Moz and I had been jamming, it was about adding *more* to the riffs. So it felt great to see stuff getting erased, to sweep away all the mosquito-droppings and get back to the foundation.

Which, like I said before, is where I'm happiest.

Once the Big Riff was cleaned up, Pearl started playing. I'd figured she was going to blow us away with some kind of thousand-note-a-minute alternafunk jazz, because she'd been in that Juilliard band. But everything she played was sweet and simple. She spent most of her time poking around with her mouse, diluting the tones flowing from her synthesizers until they were thin enough to sneak through the folds of the Big Riff.

In the end, I realized that Pearl was playing some of the lines she'd erased from Moz's part. Even though she'd simplified them, the whole thing wound up bigger, like an actual band instead of two guitarists trying to sound like one.

And then came the moment when the whole thing finally clicked, totally paranormal, falling into place like an explosion played backwards.

I yelled, "You know, we should record this!"

Moz nodded, but Pearl just laughed. "Guys, I've been recording the whole time." She pointed at the computer screen.

"Really?" Moz skidded us to a halt. "You didn't say anything about that."

I eyeballed him to calm down. The Mosquito is always afraid that someone's going to steal our riffs.

Pearl just shrugged. "Sometimes people choke when you press the red button. So I just keep my hard disk spinning. Here, listen."

She fiddled with her mouse, popping in and out of the last two hours, little snatches of us, like we'd already been turned into cell-phone ringtones. In a few seconds, she pinned down the one-minute stretch where the New Big Riff had somehow flipped inside out and become perfect.

We all sat there, listening. Moz's and my mouths were open.

We'd finally nailed it. After six years . . .

"Still needs a B section," Pearl said. "And drums. We should get a drummer."

"And a bass player," I said.

She looked at me. "Maybe."

"Maybe?" Moz said. "What kind of band doesn't have a bass?"

She shrugged. "What kind of band has only two guitarists? One thing at a time. You guys know any drummers?"

Moz shrugged.

"Yeah, they're hard to find," Pearl said, shaking her head. "The System had a couple of *percussionists* but no real drummer. That's part of why we sucked. But I know a few from school." She shrugged.

"I know this girl," I said. "She's great."

Moz looked at me, all buzzy again. "You do? You never told me about any drummer."

"You never told me we were looking for one." I shrugged. "Besides, I don't really know her, just seen her play. She's fawesome."

"Probably not available, then," Pearl said, shaking her head. "There's never enough drummers to go around."

"Um, I think she might be available," I said. What I didn't mention was that she didn't exactly have real drums and that I'd never seen her playing with a band, only in

Times Square, asking for spare change. Or that she might also be sort of homeless, as far as I could tell. Unless she *really* liked playing in Times Square and wearing the same army jacket and pair of jeans every day.

Totally fool drummer, though.

"Talk to her," Pearl said. She shot a mean look at the egg-carton-covered door to her room. "Listen, I think my mom's home, so maybe we should quit. But next time, we'll write a B section for the Big Riff. Maybe some words. Either of you guys sing?"

We looked at each other. Moz can sing, but he wouldn't admit to it out loud. And he's too genius a guitarist to waste in front of a mike.

"Well," Pearl said. "I know this really lateral singer who's free right now, sort of. And in the meantime, you can talk to your drummer."

I smiled, nodding. I liked how in a hurry this girl was, how she was motivating us. And she looked pretty hot doing it, all focused and in charge. Six years of jamming, and all of a sudden it felt like a real band was falling into place. I was looking at the posters on Pearl's wall, already thinking of album covers.

"Drums? In here?" Moz said.

My gaze swept across all the amps, cables, and synths. There was about enough room for us, all this crap, and *maybe* someone playing bongos. No way could a whole drum kit fit in here, even if they weren't exactly drums. And with egg cartons jammed into the windows, the place was already reeking of rehearsal sweat. I could imagine what a hardworking drummer would do to that equation.

That was another reason I'd never bothered to mention her to Moz before. Drummers are way too big and loud for bedrooms.

"I know a place where we can practice," Pearl said. "It's pretty cheap."

Moz and I looked at each other. We'd never paid to rehearse before. But Pearl didn't notice. I guessed she'd shelled out money to rehearse in lots of places. I just hoped she was paying for this one too. I had some money from my dog-walking gig, but Moz was the tightest guy I'd ever met.

"The other thing is, before we start adding a bunch more people, we need to figure out a name for the band," Pearl said. "And it has to be the right name. Otherwise, it'll keep changing every time someone new jams with us." She shook her head. "And we'll never figure out who we are."

"Maybe we should call ourselves the B-Sections," I said. "That would be fawesome."

Pearl looked at me, kind of squinting. "Fawesome? Do you keep saying *fawesome*?"

"Yeah." I grinned at Moz. He rolled his eyes.

She thought about it for a minute, then smiled and said, "Fexcellent."

I laughed out loud. This chick was totally fool.

5. GARBAGE

"One of those boys was rather fetching."

"Yeah, I noticed that, Mom. Thanks for pointing it out, though, in case I missed it."

"A bit scruffy, though. And that dirge you were playing was making the china rattle all afternoon."

"It wasn't *all* afternoon." I sighed, staring out the window of the limo. "Maybe two hours."

Getting a ride with Mom was nine kinds of annoying. But deepest Brooklyn was such a pain by subway, and I had to see Minerva right away. Her esoterica kept saying that hearing good news helped the healing process. And my news was better than good.

"Besides, Mom, 'that dirge' is totally fex-cellent."

"It's feculent?" She made a quiet scoffing sound. "Don't you know that feculent means *foul*?"

I giggled, reminding myself to tell Zahler

that one. Maybe we could call ourselves the Feculents. But that sounded sort of British, and we didn't.

We sounded like the kind of band that rattled the china. The Rattlers? Too country and western. China Rattlers? Too lateral, even for me. The Good China? Nah. People would think we were from Taiwan.

"Will they be coming over again?" my mother asked in a small voice.

"Yes. They will." I played with my window buttons, filling the limo's backseat with little bursts of summer heat.

She sighed. "I'd hoped that we were past all this band practice."

I let out a groan. "*Band practice* is what marching bands do, Mom. But don't worry. We'll be moving our gear to Sixteenth Street in a week or so. Your china will soon be safe."

"Oh. That place."

I peered at her, pushing my glasses up my nose. "Yes, full of musicians. How awful."

"They look more like drug addicts." She shivered a little, which made her icicles tinkle. Mom was all blinged out for some fund-raiser at the Brooklyn Museum, wearing cocktail black and too much makeup. Her being dressed up like that always creeps me out, like we're headed to a funeral.

Of course, I was creeped out anyway—we were in Minerva's neighborhood now. Big brooding brownstones slid past outside, all tricked out like haunted houses, turrets and iron railings and tiny windows way up high. My stomach started to flutter, and I suddenly wished it was both of us going to some dress-up party, everyone drinking champagne and being clueless, and next year's budget for the Egyptian Wing the big topic of consternation. Or, at worst, talking about the sanitation crisis, instead of staring out the window at it.

Mom detected my flutters—which she's pretty good at—and took my hand. "How's Minerva doing, poor thing?"

I shrugged, glad now that I'd scrounged a ride. Mom's minor annoyances had distracted me almost the whole way. Waiting for the subway, staring down at the rats on the tracks, would've totally reminded me of where I was going.

"Better. She says."

"What do the doctors say?"

I didn't even shrug. I wasn't allowed to tell Mom that there were no doctors anymore, just an esoterica. We stayed silent until the limo pulled up outside Minerva's house. Night was falling by then, lights going on. The brownstone's darkened windows made the block look like it was missing a tooth.

The street looked different, as if the last two months had sapped something from it. Garbage was piled high on the streets, the sanitation crisis much more obvious out here in Brooklyn, but I didn't see any rats scuttling around. There seemed to be a lot of stray cats, though.

"This used to be such a nice neighborhood," Mom said. "Do you need Elvis to collect you?"

"No. That's okay."

"Well, call him if you change your mind," Mom said as the door opened. "And don't take the train too late."

I slipped out past Elvis, annoyance rising in me again. Mom knew I hated the subway late at night, and that Minerva's company didn't exactly make me want to dally.

Elvis and I traded our funny little salute, which we've been doing since I was nine, and we both smiled. But then he glanced up at the house, lines creasing his forehead. Something skittered in the garbage bags by our feet—stray cats or not, rats were in residence.

"Are you sure you won't be wanting a ride home, Pearl?" he rumbled softly.

"Positive. Thanks, though."

Mom likes all conversations to include her, so she scooted closer across the limo's backseat. "What time did you get in last night anyway?"

"Right after eleven."

She pursed her lips the slightest discernible amount, showing she knew I was lying, and I gave her the tiniest possible eye-roll to show I didn't care.

"Well, see you *at* eleven tonight, then."

I snorted a little for Elvis. The only way Mom was coming home before midnight was if they ran out of champagne at the museum, or if the mummies all got loose.

I imagined old-movie mummies in tattered bandages. Nice and nonscary.

Then her voice softened. "Give my love to Minerva."

"Okay," I said, waving and turning away, flinching as the door boomed shut behind me. "I'll try."

Luz de la Sueño opened the door and waved me in quick, like she was worried about flies zipping in behind.

Or maybe she didn't want the neighbors to see her new decorations, seeing as how Halloween was more than two months away.

My nostrils wrinkled at the smell of garlic tea brewing, not to mention the other scents coming from the kitchen, overpowering and unidentifiable. These days, New York seemed to disappear behind me when I came through Minerva's door, as if the brownstone had one foot in some other city, somewhere ancient and crumbling, overgrown.

"She is much better," Luz said, ushering me toward the stairs. "And excited you are visiting."

"That's great," I said, but I hesitated for a moment in the foyer. Luz's take on Minerva's illness had always been a bit too mystical for me, but after what I'd witnessed the night before, I figured the esoterica was at least a little noncrazy.

"Luz, can I ask you a question? About something I saw?"

"You saw something? Outside?" Her eyes widened, drifting to the shaded windows.

"No, back in Manhattan."

"*Sí?*" Luz said. The intensity of her gaze was freaking me out as usual.

I usually understand where people fit, organizing them in my head, like arranging Mom's good china in its case. But I was totally clueless about Luz—where she came from, how old she was, whether she'd grown up rich or poor. Her English wasn't fluent, but her accent was careful, her grammar exact. Her unlined face looked young, but she wore these old-lady dresses, sometimes hats with veils. Her hands were calloused and full of wiry strength, and three fat skull rings grinned at me from her big-knuckled fingers.

Luz was all about skulls, but they didn't seem to mean to her what they meant to me and my friends. She was more gospel than goth.

"There was this woman," I said. "Around the corner from us. She went crazy, throwing all this stuff out the window."

"*Sí.*" Luz nodded. "That is the sickness. It is spreading now. You are still careful, yes?"

"Yep. No boys for me." I put my hands up. Luz believed everything was because of too much sex—part of her religious thing. "But it looked like her own stuff. Not like when Minerva broke up with Mark, hating everything he'd given her."

"Yes, but it is the same. The sickness, it makes the infected not want to be what they were before. They must throw away everything to make the change." She crossed herself—*the change* was what she was trying to prevent in Minerva.

"But Min didn't trash all her stuff, did she?"

"Not so much." Luz fingered the cross around her neck. "She is very spiritual, not joined to things. But to people, and to *la musica.*"

"Oh." That made a kind of sense. When Minerva had cracked up, she'd thrown away Mark and the rest of Nervous System first. And then her classes and all our friends, one by one. I'd stuck with her the longest, until everyone hated me for staying friends with her, and then she'd finally tossed me too.

That meant Moz had been right: the crazy woman had

been getting rid of her own stuff, throwing her whole life out the window. I wondered how he'd known.

I thought about the mirrors upstairs, all covered with velvet. Min didn't want to see her own face, to hear her own name—suddenly it all made sense.

Luz touched my shoulder. "That is why it is good you are here. I think maybe now, Pearl, you can do more than I."

I felt the music player in my pocket, loaded up with Big Riff. I couldn't do anything myself—I wasn't some kind of skull-wielding esoterica—but maybe this fexcellent music . . .

Luz started up the stairs, waving for me to follow.

"One more thing: I think I saw angels."

She stopped and turned, crossing herself again. *"Angeles de la lucha?* They were fast? On the rooftops?"

I nodded. "Like you told me to watch for around here."

"And they took this woman?"

I shrugged. "I don't know. I got the hell out of there."

"Good." She reached out and stroked my face, her fingers rough and smelling of herbs. "It is not for you, the struggle that is coming."

"So where do the angels take you?" I whispered.

Luz closed her eyes. "To somewhere far away."

"What, like heaven?"

She shook her head. "No. On an airplane. To a place where they make the change firm in you. So you can fight for them in the struggle." She took my hand. "But that is not for you—not for Minerva. Come."

The rest of the way up, there were lots of new decorations to check out. The stairway walls were covered with wooden crosses, a thousand little stamped-metal figures nailed into each one. The figures were nonweird shapes—shoes, dresses, trees, dogs, musical instruments—but the wild jumble of them made me wonder if someone had put normality into a blender, then set it on disintegrate.

And of course there were the skulls. Their painted black eyes stared down at us from the shadows, every floor a little darker as we climbed. The windows up here were blacked out, the mirrors draped with red velvet. Street noises faded as we climbed, the air growing as still as a sunken ship.

Outside Minerva's room, Luz bent to pick up a towel from the floor, sighing apologetically. "It is only me tonight. The family are more tired every day."

"Anything I can do to help?" I whispered.

Luz smiled. "You are here. That is help."

She pulled a few leaves from her pocket, crushing them together in her hands. They smelled like fresh-cut grass, or mint. She knelt and rubbed her palms on my sneakers and the legs of my jeans.

I'd always kind of rolled my eyes at her spells before, but tonight I felt in need of protection.

"Maybe you will sing to her."

I swallowed, wondering if Luz had somehow divined what I'd been planning. "Sing? But you always said—"

"*Sí.*" Her eyes sparked in the darkness. "But she is better now. However, to keep you safe . . ."

She pressed a familiar little doll into my hands, stroking its tattered red yarn hair into place. It stared up at me, smiling maniacally, one button eye dangling from two black threads, setting my stomach fluttering again.

The doll was the creepiest of Luz's rituals of protection. But suddenly it made sense. It had always been Min's favorite back when we were little, the only object she'd ever really been attached to, besides the ring she'd thrown at Mark in front of the whole System. I was glad to have the doll tonight, even if Minerva hadn't been violent since her family had given up on drugs and doctors and had switched to Luz.

I wondered how they'd found her. Were esotericas listed in the phone book? Was Esoterica a cool band name, or too lateral? Was the Big Riff in my pocket really a kind of magic—

"Don't be afraid," Luz whispered. Then she opened the door with one strong hand, the other pushing me into the darkness. "Go and sing."

6. MADNESS

-MINERVA-

Pearl was glowing. Her face shimmered as the door swung closed, setting the candle flickering jaggedly.

"You're shiny," I murmured, squinting.

She swallowed, licking her upper lip. I could smell her nervous saltiness.

"It's hot out."

"It's summer, right?"

"Yeah, middle of August." Pearl frowned, even though I'd been right.

I closed my eyes, remembering April, May . . . all the way up to graduation. Pearl was jealous because she had to go back to Juilliard next year, though everyone else in the Nerv—

The thing inside me flinched.

Zombie made a grumpy noise and rolled over on my belly. His big green eyes opened slowly, surveying Pearl.

"I have good news," she said softly. When I first got sick, I hated the sound of her voice, but not anymore. I was getting better—I didn't hate Pearl, or anyone human. All I hated now was the Vile Thing she brought every time she visited. It hung from her hands, one eyeball dangling, leering at me.

I tried to smile, but the lenses of Pearl's glasses caught the candlelight, bright as a camera flash, and I had to turn away.

She raised her voice a little. "You okay?"

"Sure. It's just a little bright today." Sometimes I blew out the candle, but that made Luz cross. She said I'd have to get used to it if I was ever going to leave this room again.

But my room was nice. It smelled like Zombie and me and the thing inside us.

"So I met these guys," Pearl said, talking fast now, forgetting to whisper. "They've been playing together for a while. They're nine kinds of raw, not like Nervous—"

I must have flinched again, because Pearl went quiet. Zombie *mur-row*ed and dropped heavily to the floor. He started toward her, winding his way through my old toys and clothes and sheet music, all the objects on the floor that crept closer every night while I slept.

"We weren't so bad," I managed to say.

"Yeah, but these guys are fawesome." She paused, smiling at herself. Pearl always liked silly, made-up words. "They're sort of New Sound, like Morgan's Army, but more raw. Like when we started, before you-know-who messed up your head. But without six composers trying to write one song. These two guys are much more . . ."

"Controllable?" I said.

Pearl frowned, and the Vile Thing in her hands glared at me.

"I was going to say *mellow*."

Zombie had tiptoed up behind Pearl, like he'd been planning to wind through her legs. But he was slinking close to the floor now, sniffing at her shoes suspiciously. He didn't like the smell of anyone but me these days.

"But I was thinking, and maybe this is stupid." Pearl shifted her weight from one foot to the other. "If these guys work out, and you keep getting better—"

"I'm already better."

"That's what Luz says. The three of us aren't ready yet, but maybe by the time we are . . ." Her voice wavered, sounding fragile. "It would be great if you could sing for us."

Her words made me close my eyes, something huge moving through my body, half painful, half restless. It took a moment to recognize, because it had been gone for so long.

To twist and turn, spreading out and surrounding people, drowning them—my voice seething, boiling, filling up the air.

I wanted to sing again. . . .

A slow sigh deflated me. What if it still hurt, like everything else that wasn't Zombie or darkness? I had to test myself first.

"Could you do something for me, Pearl?"

"Anything."

"Say my name."

"Crap, no way. Luz would kick my ass."

I smelled Pearl's fear in the room and heard Zombie's

soft footfalls retreating from her. He jumped up onto the bed, warm and nervous next to me. I opened my eyes, trying not to squint in the candle-brightness.

Pearl was sweating again, pacing like Zombie does because Luz never lets him go outside. "She said that singing might be okay. But your name? Are you *sure*?"

"I'm not sure, Pearl. That's why you have to."

She swallowed. "Okay . . . Min."

I snorted. "Shiny, smelly Pearl. Can't even do the whole thing?"

She stared at me for a long moment, then said softly, "Minerva?"

I shuddered out of habit, but the sickness didn't come. Then she said the name again, and nothing swept through me. Nothing but relief. Even Luz had never managed that.

It felt outlandish and magnificent, as naughty as a cigarette after voice class. I closed my eyes and smiled.

"Are you okay?" she whispered.

"Very. And I want to sing for your band, Pearl. You brought music, didn't you?"

She nodded, smiling back at me. "Yeah. I mean, I wasn't sure if you . . . But we have this really cool riff." She reached into her pocket for a little white sliver of plastic, then began to unwind the earphones wrapped around it. "This is after only one day of practice—well, six years and a day—but there's no chorus or anything yet. You can write your own words."

"I can do words." Words were the first thing I'd gotten back. There were notebooks full of scrawl underneath the bed, filled with all my new secrets. New songs about the deep.

Pearl had an adapter in one hand. She was looking around for my stereo.

"I broke it," I said sadly.

"Your Bang and Olufsen? That's a drag." She frowned. "Say, you didn't throw it out the window, did you?"

I giggled. "No, silly. Down the stairs." I reached out my hand. "Come here. We can share."

She paused for a moment, glancing back at the door.

"Don't worry. Luz went downstairs already." She was working in the kitchen now, preparing my nighttime botanicas. I could hear the rumble of water through the pipes and smell garlic and mandrake tea being strained. "She trusts you enough not to listen in."

"Oh. That's good, I guess." Pearl put the adapter back in her pocket and took a step closer, the Vile Thing leering at me from her hand.

"But you have to put that *thing* down," I said, waving one hand.

She paused, and I could smell her start to sweat again.

"Don't you trust me, shiny Pearl?" I squinted up at her. "You know I would never eat you."

"Um, yeah." She swallowed. "And that's really non-threatening of you, Minerva."

I smiled again at the sound of my own name, and Pearl smiled back, finally believing how much better I was. She knelt, placing the Vile Thing carefully on the floor, like it might explode.

Taking a deep breath, she began to cross the room with measured steps. Zombie padded away as she grew closer, and I smelled the catnip on Pearl's shoes. That's why he was being so edgy. She smelled like his old toys, which he hated these days.

He went over to sniff the Vile Thing, which suddenly had turned into just some old doll. It looked lifeless and defeated there on the floor, not nearly as vile as it had been.

More relief flowed through me. Just the thought of singing was making me stronger. Even the shiny candle-light didn't seem so jagged.

Pearl sat next to me on the bed, the music player in her hand glowing now. I saw the apple shape on it and flinched a little, remembering that I *had* thrown something out the window—eighty gigs of music that smelly boy had given me.

Pearl reached across, pushing my hair back behind one ear with trembling fingers. I realized how greasy it was, even though Luz made me shower every single Saturday.

"Do I look horrible?" I asked quietly. I hadn't seen myself in . . . two months, if it was August.

"No. You're still beautiful." She grinned, putting one earphone in her own ear. "Maybe a little skinny. Doesn't Luz feed you?"

I smiled, thinking of all the raw meat I'd eaten for lunch. Bacon cold and salty, the strips still clinging together, fresh from between plastic. And then the chicken whose neck I'd heard Luz wring in the backyard, its skin still prickly from being plucked, its living blood hot down my throat. And still I was hungry.

As Pearl leaned forward in the Apple glow, I saw the pulse in her throat, and the beast inside me growled.

Mustn't eat Pearl, I reminded myself.

She gave the other earphone to me, and I put it in. We looked into each other's eyes from a few inches away, tethered by the split white cord. It was strange and intense—no one but Luz had dared get this close to me since I'd bitten that stupid doctor.

I could smell coffee on Pearl's breath, the clean sweat of summer heat, the separate scent of fear. Her pupils were huge, and I remembered that to her eyes, my room was dark. My life was spent in shadows now.

There was a hint of moisture between her upper lip and nose, in that little depression the size of a fingertip. I leaned forward, wanting to lick it, to see if it was salty like the bacon had been. . . .

Then she squeezed the player, and music spilled into me.

It started abruptly—a rough edit, not even on the downbeat—but the riff was too gutsy to care. One guitar rumbled underneath, simple as a bass part, someone playing with three untutored fingers. Another guitar played up high, full of restless and cluttered energy, seductively neurotic.

Neither was Pearl, I could tell.

Then she entered on keys, spindly and thin but fitting perfectly. She was even leaving room for me, laying low, like she never had back in the System.

That thought made me jealous—little Pearl growing up a bit while I'd been lying here in shadows. Suddenly, I wanted to get up and put on clothes and sunglasses, go out into the world.

Soon, I thought, still listening. The music had me humming, venturing into the spaces Pearl had left open, finding lines to twist and turn. She was right—it was New Sound–ish, like all those indie bands we'd loved last spring. But less frantic, as smooth as water. My whole body wanted to jump into this music.

But when my lips first parted, only random curses spilled out, verses from the earliest, most unreadable scrawl in the notebooks under my bed. Then they sputtered to a halt, like the fading geyser from a shaken beer bottle, and I gradually gained control. I began to murmur a jagged, wordless song across the music.

For a few moments it was beautiful, a savage version of my old self, though with new spells in it. The sound of my own singing made the beast inside me burn, but clever Pearl had cheated it for a few moments: I could only hear myself with one ear. The other was filled with the riff, a dense and splendid protection.

But soon enough the sickness closed my throat, the song choking to a stop. I looked at Pearl, to see if I'd imagined it. Her eyes, inches from mine, glowed like her music player's screen.

Catching my breath, I concentrated on the riff again, listening. She was right: They were way outside the System, this oddball pair of guitarists. They had pulled something out of me, slipped it right past the beast.

"Where did you find them?"

"Sixth Street. Totally random."

"Hmm. The one who can really play, he sounds . . ." I swallowed.

"Yeah," Pearl said. "He's lateral and raw, like I always wanted Nervous System to be. No lessons, or at least not many, and *no* theory classes. He fills up whatever space you give him. Almost out of control, but like you said, controllable. He's the Taj Mahal of random guitarists."

I smiled. All those things were true, but I hadn't been thinking them.

To me, he sounded more like . . . *yummy.*

PART II

AUDITIONS

The Plague of Justinian was the first time the Black Death appeared.

Fifteen hundred years ago, the emperor Justinian had just embarked on his greatest work: the rebuilding of the Roman Empire. He wanted to reunite its two halves and place the known world under Roman rule once more.

But as his vast war began, the Black Death came. It swept across the eastern Mediterranean, leaving millions dead in its wake. Thousands died daily in the Byzantine capital of Constantinople, and Justinian was forced to watch his dreams crumble.

Oddly, historians aren't certain what the Black Death was. Bubonic plague? Typhus? Something else? A few historians suggest that it was a random assortment of diseases brought on by one overriding factor: an explosion of the rat population fostered by the Roman army's vast stores of grain.

That's close, but not quite.

Whatever caused it, the Black Death's effects were clear. The Roman Empire slipped into history at last. Much of the mathematics, literature, and science of the ancients was lost. A dark age descended on Europe.

Or, as we said back then, "Humanity lost that round."

NIGHT MAYOR TAPES:
142–146

7. STRAY CATS

-ZAHLER-

My dogs were acting paranormal that day, all edgy and anxious.

The first bunch seemed fine when I picked them up. In the air-conditioned lobby of their fancy Hell's Kitchen building, they were full of energy, eager to be walked. Ernesto, the doorman, handed over the four leashes and an envelope stuffed with cash, my pay for that week. And then—like every Monday, Wednesday, and Friday—I headed one block uptown to pick up three more.

I got the idea of being a dog walker from an old trick of mine. Whenever I was totally bummed, I'd go over to the Tompkins Square Park dog run—a big open space that's just for dogs and owners—and watch them jumping on one another, sniffing butts and chasing balls. Huge dogs and tiny ones, graceful retrievers and spastic poodles were all jumbled together and all fawesomely ecstatic to get out of their tiny, lonely New York apartments and into a chase, a growling match, or a mad dash to nowhere in particular. No matter how depressed I was, the sight of scrappy puppies facing off with German shepherds always made me feel much better. So why not be paid to get cheered up?

You don't make much per dog per hour, but if you can handle six or seven at a time, it starts to add up. Most times it's easy money.

Sometimes it's not.

Straight out the door, the heat and stink seemed to get to them. The two Doberman brothers who usually kept order were nipping at each other, and the schnauzer and bull terrier were acting all paranoid, zigzagging every time a car door slammed, too jittery even to sniff at piles of garbage. As we battled down the street, their leashes kept tangling, like long hair on a breezy day.

Things only got worse when I picked up the second pack. The doorman realized that the owner of the insanely huge mastiff had forgotten to leave money for me and buzzed up to ask her about it. While I waited, the two packs started tangling with each other, nipping and jumping, their barking echoing off the marble walls and floor of the lobby.

I tried to unwind them and restore order, one nervous eyeball on the elevator. It would be totally unfool for my costumers to see their dogs brawling when they were supposed to be getting exercise. So when nobody answered the doorman's buzzing, I didn't stick around to complain, just hauled them out of there and back into the heat.

I was already wishing I hadn't been in such a hurry to show Moz our possible drummer. A trip to the anarchy of Times Square was exactly what my unruly dog pack didn't need.

Here's what I've learned about dogs:

They're a lot like pretty girls. Having one or two around makes everything more fun, but when you get a whole bunch together, it turns into one big power struggle. Every time you add or subtract from the pack, everything gets rearranged. The top dog might wind up number two or fall all the way to the bottom. As I watched the Doberman brothers trying to stare down the mastiff, I was starting to wonder if being in a band was pretty much the same thing—more Nature Channel than MTV.

And really, all the jostling was a big waste of time, because Pearl was clearly the right girl to run things.

Don't get me wrong, the Mosquito was my oldest and best friend. I would never have picked up a guitar if it hadn't been for him, and he was the fawesomest musician I'd ever seen. But Moz wasn't cut out to be in charge. Of *anything*. He'd never held on to even the crappiest job, because any kind of organized activity—waiting in line, filling out forms, showing up on time—made him all buzzy. There was no way he could keep five or six unruly musicians on their leashes and pull them all in the same direction.

As for me, I thought the little dogs had the right attitude. The schnauzer didn't really care whether the mastiff or the Dobermans took charge: he just wanted to sniff some butt and get on with the walk.

He just wanted the struggle to be over.

Today, though, nobody was in control—certainly not me. The seven leashes in my hand didn't mean squat. Each time we got to an intersection, I'd try to pull us toward Times Square, but the pack kept freaking out about every stray scent, surging off in random directions. I'd let them wander a bit until they got it out of their system, then pull them back toward the way I wanted us to go. We weren't going to set any crosstown speed records, but at least there was plenty of time before we were supposed to meet Moz, who, like I just mentioned, was probably going to be late anyway.

The weird thing was how much the vacant lots scared them. Even the mastiff was slinking past open spaces, when normally she would have charged straight in for a run.

How weird was that? A creature the size of a horse who'd been cooped up in a Manhattan apartment all day, and all she wanted to do was cling to me, shivering like a wet poodle.

In this mood, the commotion of Time Square was going to turn my pack into a portable riot. It seemed like Moz and I might have to see my drummer some other day.

Then we passed the mouth of a dark alley, and things really got paranormal.

The bull terrier—who always has to pee on every-thing—took advantage of the anarchy to pull us all in. He trotted to the piss-stained wall, cocked his leg halfway, then suddenly froze, staring into the darkness. The yapping of the other dogs choked off, like seven muzzles had been strapped on all at once.

The alleyway was full of eyes.

Hundreds of tiny faces gazed up at us from the shadows. Behind me trucks rushed past, and I could feel the warmth of sunlight on my back, the reassuring pace and movement of the real world. But in the alley everything was frozen, time interrupted. The bulbous bodies of the rats were motionless, huddled against garbage bags, their teeth bared, heads poking out of holes and crannies. Nothing moved but a shimmer of whiskers as a thousand nostrils tested the air.

In the farthest corner, a lone cat was perched high on a leaking pile of garbage. It stared down at me, unimpressed by my small army of dogs, offended by my presence in the alley. I felt tiny under its arrogant gaze—like some street kid who'd stumbled into a five-star restaurant looking for a place to pee.

The cat blinked its red eyes, then yawned, its pink tongue curling.

This is totally unfool, I thought. If my Dobermans spotted that cat, they'd go after it, dragging me and the whole pack deep into the alley. I could imagine myself returning seven rat-bitten, half-rabid canines to the doormen and never seeing another dime of dog-walking money again.

"Come on, guys," I murmured, gently pulling the fistful of leashes backward. "Nothing to see here."

But they were paralyzed, transfixed by the galaxy of eyes.

The cat opened its mouth again, letting out a long, irritated *mrrr-row*. . . .

And the Dobermans ran like scaredy-cats.

They both leaped straight up, twisting around in midair, and charged past me toward the sunlight. The others followed in a mob, wrapping their leashes around my legs and dragging me stumbling into the street.

It was all I could do to stay on my feet as the mastiff charged ahead, opening up into her full gallop. She pulled the rest of us straight out onto the road, where a yellow flash of taxi screeched past dead ahead of us. A squat little delivery van squealed around us, horn blaring, scaring the mastiff into a sharp left turn.

We were headed down the middle of the street now, a garbage truck thundering along in front of us, the delivery van behind. We were *in traffic*, as if I'd decided to take a dog-powered chariot out for a little spin.

Unfortunately, I'd sort of forgotten to bring the chariot, so I was stumbling and staggering, seven leashes still tangled around my legs. And if I fell down, I knew the mastiff would keep going, galloping along until my face had been rubbed off completely on the asphalt. Even if my face friction somehow brought the pack to a halt, the pursuing delivery van would squash us all flat.

It was still blaring its horn, because that was *clearly helping*, and the two guys on the back of the garbage truck were laughing, pointing their giant-gloved fingers at me. A pair of bike messengers shot past in polka-dotted Lycra, me and my dogs just another bunch of clowns at the rodeo.

The whole procession swerved around some street work ahead, and suddenly my feet were slipping across an expanse of loose sand. I spotted an abandoned pizza box and planted my sneakers on it. Then I was skidding, my free hand in the air, riding the box like it was a boogie board at the beach.

Just when it was getting fun, the garbage truck began to slow, pulling up in front of a big apartment building with long, turd-shaped garbage bags piled outside. The truck filled the whole street, leaving nowhere for the pack to go.

Our momentum stalled, and the pack's energy wrapped itself into a tightly wound bundle of nipping and barking. By now the little dogs could hardly even stand, reduced as they were to a spaghetti mishmash of leashes and legs. Even the mastiff was tired out, her long, curving tongue lapping at the air.

One of the garbage guys swung himself down to work a big lever on the side of the truck, its huge maw opening in front of us with a metal screech. The other jumped off and shouted at me through the din.

"Hey, boss! You didn't take those pooches into that alley back there, did you?" He pointed over my shoulder, but I knew which one he meant.

"Um, yeah?"

He shook his head. "Bad idea. Even we don't go down there no more. Not worth it."

I blinked, still trying to catch my breath. "What do you mean?"

"Didn't you hear about the crisis? Way things are going, you got to be respectful. Let the rats have some of the city back, you know?" He laughed, patting the rumbling metal expanse with his gloved hand. "Especially if you don't got a big truck to protect you. Bunch of pooches isn't enough these days."

He turned to the pile of bags behind him and kicked one viciously. Waiting for a second to make sure no tiny creatures scattered from it, he shouldered the bag and began to feed its length into the giant steel maw.

I blew out a slow breath, knelt down, and started to untangle my dogs, wondering what they and the Sanitation Department knew that I didn't. Moz had said some paranormal stuff about the woman who'd tossed him her guitar—that she was part of something bigger— and I'd read there was a crime wave now, to go along with the heat and the garbage.

But wasn't it always like this in the middle of every long summer, brains beginning to zigzag in the fawesome temperatures?

Of course, the day before, Moz and I had watched that black water spraying out of a fire hydrant, as if something old and rotten had been dredged up beneath the city. Despite the heat bouncing off the asphalt, I shivered, thinking about what I'd seen back in that alley. That cat was *in charge* of all those rats, one glance had told me. Like my dogs, those glowing eyes were one big pack, but the feline had total control, no jostling or butt-sniffing required, like they were all family. And that just wasn't natural.

The delivery truck guy blared his horn at me one more time—like it was me in his way and not the garbage truck—so I gave him the finger. On the other side of his glass, his face broke into a smile, as if a little disrespect was all he'd been looking for.

Before the garbage truck was done, I got the pack unwound and back onto the sidewalk. We headed across town, toward the bottom end of Times Square, where we were supposed to meet Moz.

Maybe we could see my drummer after all. The hundred-yard dash had finally worn my dogs out, and the mastiff trotted ahead, tail high, having taken over through the mysteries of dog-pack democracy. Maybe it was because she'd led us down the street to safety, or because the Dobermans had fled first from the rat-infested alley.

Whatever. At least it was all decided now, and someone other than me was in charge.

8. CASH MONEY CREW

Times Square was buzzing.

Even in broad daylight, the battery of lights and billboards rattled me, rubbing my brain raw. Huge video screens were wrapped around the curving buildings over my head, shimmering like water in the rain, ads for computers and cosmetics flickering across them. News bites scrolled past on glittering strips, punctuated by nonsense stock-ticker symbols.

I was an insect in a canyon of giant TVs, mystified and irrelevant.

And penniless.

I'd never felt poor before, never once. I'd always thought it was moronic to ogle car ads and store windows, but now that I needed it, I saw money everywhere—in silver initials on thousand-dollar handbags, woven like gold threads into suits and silk scarves, and in the flickering images overhead. On the subway coming up here, I'd coveted the dollars invisibly stockpiled in magnetic strips on MetroCards, even the change rattling in beggars' paper cups.

Money, money, everywhere.

I couldn't go back to my piece-of-crap guitar after that Stratocaster. I had to own that same smooth action, those purring depths and crystal highs. Of course, maybe it didn't have to be a '75 with gold pickups. In the music stores on Forty-eighth Street, I'd found a few cheaper guitars I could live with, but I still needed to scrape together about two thousand bucks before the crazy woman returned.

Problem was, I had no idea how.

I'm not lazy, but money and me don't mix. Every time I get a job, something always happens. The boss tells me to smile, pretending I want to be at work when I'd rather be anywhere else. Or makes me call in every week to ask for my hours, and it turns into a whole extra job finding out when I'm supposed to be at my job. And whenever I explain these issues, someone always asks me the dreaded question, *If you hate it so much, why don't you just quit?*

And I say, "Good point." And quit.

In that flickering canyon of advertising, two thousand dollars had never seemed so far away.

Zahler was waiting at the corner where he'd said to meet, seven dogs in tow.

He was panting and sweaty, but his entourage looked happy—gazing up at the signs, sniffing at tourists passing by. It was all just flickering lights to them.

No jobs, no money. Lucky dogs.

"How much you get paid for that, Zahler?"

"Not enough," he panted. "Almost got killed on the way down here!"

"Yeah, sure," I said. One of the little ones was nibbling me, and I knelt and petted him. "This guy looks deadly."

"No really, Moz. There was this alley . . . and this cat."

"An alley cat? And you with only seven dogs." One of which was gigantic, like a horse with long, flowing hair. I stroked its head, laughing at Zahler.

Still panting, he pointed his free hand at one of the little ones. "It's all his fault, for peeing."

"Huh?"

"It was just—never mind." He frowned. "Listen, you hear that drumming? It's her. Come on."

I grabbed the monster-dog's leash from Zahler, and then two more, pulling the three of them away from a pretzel cart whose ripples of heat smelled like seared salt and fresh bread. "So, you think Pearl will approve of this drummer?"

"Sure. Pearl's all about talent, and this girl is fexcellent."

"But she plays on the street, Zahler? She could be homeless or something."

He snorted. "Compared to Pearl, you and me are practically homeless. Didn't you see that apartment?"

"Yeah, I saw that apartment." I could still smell the money crammed into every corner.

"*And* there were stairs. More floors than we even saw."

"Sure, Pearl's insanely rich. And this is supposed to

convince me she can deal with a homeless drummer?"

"We don't know that this girl's homeless, Moz. Anyway, all I'm saying is that if Pearl can deal with you and me, she's no snob."

I shrugged. *Snob* wasn't the word I would've used.

"Are you still bummed because of what she did to the Riff?"

"No. Once I got used to the idea of flushing all those years of practice down the toilet, I got over it."

"Dude! You *are* still bummed."

"No, I mean it."

"Look, I know it hurts, Moz. But she's going to make us *huge*!"

"I *get* it, Zahler." I sighed, angling my dogs away from a hot-dog cart. Of course, practicing yesterday had hurt— but so did getting a tattoo, or watching a perfect sunset, or playing till your fingers bled. Sometimes you just had to sit there and deal with the pain.

Pearl had rubbed me raw, but she knew how to listen. She could hear the heart of the Big Riff, and she hadn't done anything I wouldn't have if I'd been listening. I'd had six years to figure out what she'd recognized in six minutes. That's what made me cringe.

That and the whammy she'd put on Zahler. He wouldn't shut up about how brilliant Pearl was, how she was going to make us big, how things were finally going to happen. Like all those years with just the two of us had been a waste of time.

Zahler had a total crush on Pearl—that was obvious. But if I said so out loud, he'd just roast me with his death stare. And talk about wasting time: girls like her were about as likely to hook up with boys like us as Zahler's dogs were to pull him to the moon.

"Okay, I thought you said she was a drummer."

"What?" Zahler cried above the rumble. "You don't call that drumming?"

"Well, she's got drumsticks. But I thought drummers were to supposed to have *drums*." I shook my head, trying to keep my three curious dogs from surging into the rapt crowd of tourists, Times Square locals, and loitering cops surrounding the woman.

"Yeah, well, imagine if she did have drums. Listen to how much sound she's getting out of those paint cans!"

"Those are actually paint *buckets*, Zahler."

"What's the diff?"

I sighed. Painting had been one of my shorter-lived jobs, because they just gave you the colors to use, instead of letting you decide. "Paint cans are the metal containers that paint comes in. Paint buckets are the plastic tubs you mix it up in. Neither of them are drums."

"But *listen*, Moz. Her sound is huge!"

My brain was already listening—my mouth was just giving Zahler a hard time out of habit and general annoyance—and the woman really did have a monster sound. Around her was arrayed every size of paint bucket you could buy, some stacked, some upside down, a few on their sides, making a sort of giant plastic xylophone.

It took me a minute to figure out how a bunch of paint buckets could have so much power. She'd set up on a subway grate, suspending herself over a vast concrete echo chamber. Her tempo matched the timing of the echoes rumbling up from below, as if a ghost drummer were down there following her, exactly one beat behind. As my head tilted, I heard other ghosts: quicker echoes from the walls around us and from the concrete awning over-head.

It was like an invisible drum chorus, led effortlessly from its center, her sticks flashing gracefully across bat-tered white plastic, long black dreadlocks flying, eyes shut tight.

"She's pretty fool, Zahler," I admitted.

"Really?"

"Yeah. Especially if we could rebuild this chunk of Times Square every place we played."

He let out an exasperated sigh. "What, the echoes? You never heard of digital delay?"

I shrugged. "Wouldn't be the same. Wouldn't be as big."

"Doesn't have to be as big, Moz. We don't want her playing a gigantic drum solo like this; we want her smaller, fitting in with the rest of the band. Didn't you learn *any-thing* yesterday?"

I glared at him, the anger spilling out from the place I thought I'd had it tucked away, rippling through me again. "Yeah, I did: that you're a total sucker for every chick who comes along with an instrument. Even if it's a bunch of *paint buckets*!"

His jaw dropped. "Dude! That is totally unfool! You just said she was great. And you know Pearl's fexcellent too. Now you're going to get all boys-only on me?"

I turned away, thoughts echoing in my brain, like my skull was suddenly empty and lined with concrete. Between the Stratocaster that wasn't mine, the other guitars I couldn't afford, Pearl's demolition of the Big Riff, and now the thought of *paint buckets*, it'd been too many adjustments to make in forty-eight hours.

I almost wished it was just Zahler and me again. We'd been like a team that was a hundred points behind—we weren't going to win anything, so we could just play and have fun. But Pearl had changed that. Everything was up in the air, and how it all came down *mattered* now.

Part of me hated her for that and hated Zahler for going along so easily.

He kept quiet, wrangling the dogs while I calmed myself down.

"All right," I finally said. "Let's talk to her. What have we got to lose?"

We waited till she was packing up, stacking the buckets into one big tower. Her muscles glowed with sweat, and a few splinters from a stick she'd broken rolled in the breeze from a subway passing underneath.

She glanced at us and our seven dogs.

"You're pretty good," I said.

She jutted her chin toward a paint bucket that was right side up and half full of change and singles, then went back to stacking.

"Actually, we were wondering if you wanted to play with us sometime."

She shook her head, one of her eyes blinking rapidly.

"This corner is mine. Had it for a year."

"Hey, we're not moving in on you," Zahler spoke up, waving his free hand. "We're talking about you playing in our band. Rehearsing and recording and stuff. Getting famous."

I cringed. "Getting famous" had to be the lamest reason for doing anything.

She shrugged, just a twitch of her shoulders. "How much?"

"How much . . . what?" Zahler said.

But it was obvious to me. The same thing that had been obvious all day.

"Money," I answered. "She wants money to play with us."

His eyes bugged. "You want *cash*?"

She took a step forward and pulled a photo ID card from her pocket, waved it in Zahler's face. "See that? That's from the MTA. Says I can play down in the subway, legal and registered. Had to sit in front of a review panel to get that." As she put the card away, a little shiver went through her body. "Except I don't go down there any-more."

She kicked the upturned paint bucket, the pile of loose change clanking like a metallic cough. "Seventy, eighty bucks in there. Why would I play for free?"

"Whoa, sorry." Zahler started to pull his dogs away, giving me a look like she'd asked for our blood.

I didn't move, though, staring at the bucket, at the bills fluttering on top. There were *fives* in there—it probably totaled a hundred easy. She had every right to ask for money. The world was all *about* money; only a lame-ass bunch of kids wouldn't know that.

"Okay," I said. "Seventy-five a rehearsal."

Zahler froze, his eyes popping again.

"How much for a gig?"

I shrugged. "I don't know. One-fifty?"

"Two hundred."

I sighed. The words *I don't know* had just cost me fifty bucks. That's how it worked with money: you had to know, or at least act like you did. "Okay. Two hundred."

I held out my hand to shake, but she just passed me her business card.

"Are you crazy, Moz? Pearl's going to freak when she finds out she has to pay for a drummer."

"She's not paying anyone, Zahler. I am."

"Yeah, right. And where are you going to get seventy-five bucks?"

I looked down at the dogs. They were staring in all directions at the maelstrom of Times Square, gawking like a bunch of tourists from Jersey. I tried to imagine rounding up customers, going door-to-door like Zahler had, putting up signs, making schedules. No way.

My plan was much better.

"Don't worry about it. I've got an idea."

"Yeah, sure you do. But what about the Strat? You can't save up for a guitar if you're paying out seventy-five bucks two or three times a week."

"I'll figure that out when its owner shows up again. If she shows up."

Zahler let out his breath, not sure what to make of this.

I looked down at the card: *Alana Ray, Drummer*. No address, just a cell-phone number, but if she could make a hundred bucks a day in cash, somehow I doubted she was homeless.

It had been so simple hiring her, a million times simpler than I'd imagined. No arguing about influences, getting famous, or who was in charge. Just a few numbers back and forth.

Money had made it easy.

"Moz, you're freaking me out. You're, like, the tightest guy I know. You never bought your own amplifier, and I've only seen you change your strings about twice in the last six years."

I nodded. I'd always waited until they rusted out from under my fingers.

"And now you're going to pay out hundreds of dollars?" Zahler said. "Why don't we find another drummer? One who's got real drums and doesn't cost money."

"One who's that good?"

"Maybe not. But Pearl said she knew a few."

"We don't have to run to her. We said that we'd handle this. So I'll pay." I turned to him. "And don't tell Pearl about the money, okay?"

Zahler groaned. "Whoa, now I get it. You want to pay this girl so she owes you, right? You want her to be *your* drummer, not Pearl's." He shook his head. "That is some dumb-ass logic at work, Moz. We're supposed to be a band."

"Pearl's already paying for rehearsal space."

"Which is no big deal for her. You're getting into a spending contest with a girl who lives in an apartment that has *stairs*. Whole other *floors*!"

I looked down at my tattered shoes. "It's not a contest, Zahler. It's just business."

"Business?" He laughed. "You don't know jack about business."

I looked up at him, expecting to feel the death stare, but he was just confused. I didn't understand myself, not completely, but I knew I had to get some part of this band under control. If I let Pearl decide everything and pay for everything, Zahler and I would wind up just a couple of sidekicks along for the ride. "Just don't tell her about the money, okay?"

He blinked, his dogs winding around his feet in disarray. I saw him wondering if I'd gone insane, wondering if I was going to screw this whole thing up, and knew I was right on the edge of losing him.

Which was fine, if he really thought I was that hopeless. Maybe it was better to walk away now than later.

But finally, he exhaled. "Okay. Whatever. I won't tell Pearl you're paying. I guess I can pitch in some of my dog money too."

I shook my head. "I've got it covered."

"But maybe we should warn Pearl . . . before we all show up for rehearsal."

I frowned. "Warn her about what?"

"Um, that our new drummer drums on paint buckets . . ."

9. FEAR

I took the subway to Brooklyn, so Mom wouldn't find out from Elvis.

Skittering sounds wafted up from the tracks as I waited for a train, the shuffling of tiny feet among discarded coffee cups and newspapers. The platform was empty except for me, the tunnels murmuring with echoes. The subways sounded wrong these days, almost alive, like there was something big down here. Something breathing.

I hated facing the subway on Sunday mornings, with no rush-hour crowds to protect me, but we didn't have much choice about when to rehearse. Minerva said that church was the only thing that kept Luz away till after noon.

This would all be much easier when we didn't have to sneak Minerva out of her room, but she needed to join the band *now*. Lying around in bed all day was never going to cure her. She had to get out of that dark room, meet some new people, and, most of all, sing her brains out.

Moz, Zahler, and I had rehearsed together four times now—we had a B section for the Big Riff and two more half-formed songs. We were better every time we played, but we needed structure: verses and choruses, a drummer too. We didn't have time to wait for Min to get completely well. The world was in too much of a hurry around us.

Except for the F train, of course. Ten minutes later, it still hadn't come, and I hoped it wasn't broken down again. The subways were having some kind of weird trouble this summer. Minor earthquakes, they said on TV—Manhattan's bedrock settling.

That was also the official explanation for the black water infecting the pipes. They said it wasn't dangerous, even if they didn't know exactly *what* it was—it evaporated too quickly for anyone to find out. Most people were drinking bottled water, of course. Mom was bathing in Evian. I wasn't sure I believed any of it, but in any case, I didn't have time for earthquakes today. The rehearsal space was reserved in my name, on my credit card—the others couldn't get in without me. If I was late getting up to Sixteenth Street, everything would fall apart.

I fished out my cell phone. It searched for a signal, until a tremulous 7:58 A.M. appeared. One hour to get to Brooklyn and back.

Still hovering on the screen was the last number I'd called the night before—Moz's—to remind him again about this morning.

Lonely and nervous on the empty platform, I pressed send.

"Yeah?" a croaky voice answered.

"Moz?"

"Mmm," came his annoyed grumble. "Pearl? Crap! Am I late?"

"No, it's only eight."

"Oh." He scratched his head so hard I could hear it over the cell-phone crackle. "So what's up?"

"I'm on my way out to Brooklyn to pick up Minerva. I was wondering if . . . you wanted to come."

"To *Brooklyn*?"

That's how he said it: *Brooklyn?* Like I wanted to drag him to Bombay.

I should have given up. For two weeks now I'd been trying to connect with Moz, but he always kept his distance. If only I hadn't messed up that first rehearsal, the one where I'd pulled the Big Riff apart. I should have gone slowly, respecting what had been conjured between us when the Strat had fallen from the sky. But instead I'd decided to dazzle him with nine kinds of brilliance. *Clever, Pearl.*

Eight A.M. was probably not the best time to break my losing streak, but for two seconds I'd imagined that maybe this morning—the morning we became a real band—might be different.

I kept talking, trying to make it sound fun. "Yeah. I didn't explain this before, but it's kind of a ninja mission, getting her out of there."

"Kind of a *what*?"

"Kind of tricky. Her parents have this thing about . . ." Insanity? Abduction? "Well, let's just say I could use your help."

I hadn't said much about Min to anyone yet, except what a lateral singer she was. It wouldn't hurt if Moz got used to her weirdness before she met the rest of them. And it would be nice just having someone beside me on the way out there, even if he only waited outside while I snuck in to get her.

"Look, uh, Pearl . . ." he said. "I just woke up."

"I sort of figured that. But I'm at the F station down from your house. You could get here in five minutes."

Silence crackled in my ear; a breeze stirred newspapers on the tracks.

I sighed. "Look, it's no big deal. Sorry to wake you up."

"That's okay. My alarm's about to go off anyway. See you at nine."

"Yeah. You're going to love Minerva. And a drummer! It's going to be fawesome, huh?"

"Sure. Totally."

I felt like I was supposed to say more, something to get him revved up for our first real rehearsal. "Don't forget your Strat."

"It's not mine. But yeah, see you soon." Click.

I slipped the phone back into my pocket, letting another sigh slip through my teeth. I'd let him take the Stratocaster home after the second rehearsal, but that hadn't changed anything between us. I was still Boss Pearl.

The newspapers stirred on the tracks again, one rolling

over restlessly. I felt the platform rumbling under my feet, and my stomach tightened. As the sound steadily grew into a roar, it pushed all the thoughts from my head, thundering across me as if something huge was about to burst from the tunnel, overpowering all my plans.

But it was just the F train pulling in.

In the past two weeks, Minerva's block had gotten worse. The garbage had been massed into a few huge, leaking mountains. Like how you deal with snow: push it into piles, then wait for the sun to make it go away.

Except garbage doesn't melt, and snow doesn't smell bad.

It was more than weird. Mom always bitched about this or that neighborhood going to seed, but I'd figured that took decades, longer than I'd been alive anyway. Until this summer, New York had always looked pretty much the same to me. But this part of Brooklyn seem to change every time I saw it, like someone dying of a disease before my eyes.

Luz always talked about "the sickness" like it wasn't just Minerva but the whole city—maybe the whole world—that was afflicted, all of it a prelude to the big struggle. Only she never said what the struggle was actually about. Good versus evil? Angels versus demons? Crazy versus sane?

Crazy Versus Sane. Now *there* was a band name that fit us like a glove.

The early morning shadows stretched down the block, sunlight spattering the asphalt through the leaves, dancing with the breeze. I crept past the garbage mountains, trying not to listen to the things inside them and wishing I didn't have the Taj Mahal of hearing. No people were on the street, not even any dogs. Just the occasional red flash of cats' eyes watching me from overgrown front yards.

The front-door key was where Min had told me her mom kept it, under an iron boot-wipe by the door. It was covered with grime and stained my fingertips a red-brown rusty color when I tried to wipe it off. But it fit smoothly into the lock, the bolt sliding across with a soft *click*.

The door swung open onto a silent audience of skulls.

I took slow, careful steps into the darkness, listening for any noise from the wooden planks underfoot. According to Minerva, her parents were deep sleepers— her little brother, Max, was the one we had to worry about. I just hoped Min was awake and dressed, not surfing some nightmare that would make her scream when I opened her door.

I took the stairs slowly, my soft-soled fencing shoes pressing on the edges of the steps, not in the creaky middles. As a little kid, I'd once gotten up at midnight and pushed down every key of our baby grand from top to bottom, pressing so delicately that the hammers never struck the strings, making not a whisper of sound the whole way. Once you've managed that, you can pretty much do anything without waking the grown-ups.

The house creaked and settled around me, like a huge old instrument in need of tuning. I passed the blenderized-reality crucifixes, her parents' room, my slow, trembling steps carrying me silently to Min's door. Staring at the heavy sliding bolt that locked her in, I suddenly wished I didn't have to touch the scrollwork symbols carved into the bolt: cat's eyes and centipedes, worms with eyes and spindly legs, and, of course, more skulls.

I swallowed as my fingertips grasped the cool metal, then slid the bolt slowly across. I opened the door and slipped inside.

Minerva was still under the covers, still asleep.

"Min!" I hissed.

A cold hand fell on the back of my neck.

10. THE MUSIC

-MINERVA-

Pearl was shiny, glistening, smelling of fear. There was lightning in her eyes—like Zombie when you rub his fur the wrong way hard.

She made sputtering noises, so I put a finger to my lips. "Shhh, Pearl. Mustn't wake Maxwell."

"Jesus, Min!" she hissed. "You scared the *crap* out of me!"

I giggled. I'd been giggling for half an hour, waiting in that corner to make her jump. That was the first thing being sick taught me: it's fun to scare people.

"Look!" I pointed at the Min-shaped bundle in my bed. "It works like magic."

"Yeah, nine kinds of supernatural." As her breathing slowed, Pearl's eyes swept up and down me, still flashing. I was dressed in cocktail black and dark glasses, more Saturday night than Sunday morning, but it felt fantastic to be in real clothes after months of pajamas. The dress squeezed me tight, shaping my body, embracing me. My four thickest necklaces lay tangled against my breasts, and my nails were painted black.

I shook my head, making my earrings tinkle.

"Cute," she whispered. "You look like an Egyptian princess crossed with a twelve-year-old goth."

I stuck my tongue out at her and snapped for Zombie. He scampered over and jumped into my arms. "Let's go. I want to make music."

Pearl glared at him, still pissy. "You can't bring a *cat* to rehearsal, Min!"

"I know, silly." I giggled softly, stroking Zombie's head. "He's just going out to play."

She frowned. "But Luz says he's not supposed to go out."

"We can't leave poor Zombie in here. He'll be all lonely." I stared into his eyes and pouted. "What if he starts scratching on my door and yowling? Could wake up Daddy."

Pearl pushed her glasses up her nose, which she does when she's being bossy. "Luz will freak if she sees him outside."

"Luz is mean to Zombie," I said, pulling him closer to kiss his little triangular cat-forehead.

"She'll be even meaner to me if she figures out I took you into Manhattan."

"She won't. It'll be okay, Pearl. We'll bring him in when we get back. He'll come when his mommy calls." I smiled.

Her breath caught. My teeth had gotten pointy lately. Certain things kept happening, no matter what Luz did to stop them.

"I just don't see how Zombie escaped that whole throwing-things-away bit," Pearl muttered. "You got rid of your boyfriend, your band, your fexcellent German stereo, and me—but not your stupid *cat*?"

"Not stupid." I turned Zombie around and looked into his eyes. He knew things. Big things.

Pearl was being pissy at her phone now. "Crap. It's past eight-thirty. I don't suppose there are any taxis around here on Sunday morning?"

"No taxis ever." I frowned. "Daddy says they won't bring him home from work anymore."

Pearl swore under her breath, closing her eyes. "I'm going to have to call Elvis, or we'll be late." She looked at me, all serious. "Can you try to act normal in front of him?"

"Of course, Pearl. No need to get all shiny."

"Are you sure you're ready for this?"

I smiled my pointy smile and turned to face my desk. "Watch this. . . ."

I leaned across to blow out the candle, and smoke poured up, sandalwood turning instantly to the smell of ashes. Reaching out with my free hand, I tugged at one corner of the fabric draped across the mirror, and velvet flowed down onto the desk like water.

"*Minerva!*" Pearl hissed.

There was my face, trapped inside the mirror frame, but it didn't make me scream. I didn't faint or suddenly want to throw Zombie out the window.

Luz had put the beast inside me to sleep, and everything was easier now.

My skin was pale and flawless, glowing softly in the candlelight. Two months uncut, my dark hair flowed raggedly around my features. Cheeks, chin, brow—everything was sharper and finer now, as if my flesh had tightened. When I pulled off my sunglasses, my eyes were radiant and wide, stuck in an expression of bewilderment and wonder.

Zombie purred softly in my arms.

"Still pretty," I whispered. And something more than pretty now.

I hadn't told Luz yet that I could do this: look at my own reflection. It would make her too happy, like she was winning. Luz wanted to strip away my new senses, file down my pointy teeth, turn me back into the boring old Minerva.

But Pearl was going to help me stop that from happening—Pearl and her music. I slipped my glasses back on and, Zombie's weight shifting in my other arm, lifted the notebooks from the desk. Inside them were secrets, ancient words I'd heard in the worst of my fever. Singing the old mysteries would keep me the way I was: not crazy anymore, but so much more than boring.

Halfway cured was best.

Pearl was talking on her phone, wheedling Elvis until he promised not to mention this little trip to her mom.

When she hung up I pouted. "But I wanted to go on the subway." Luz had told me never, ever to go down in the earth again. But I could feel it calling me, rumbling underfoot. It wanted me.

"There's no time for a train," shiny Pearl whispered,

opening the door. "Come on. And try to be quiet on the stairs."

Stairs, I thought happily. Finally, I was headed down, out of this attic prison and down toward the earth. I wanted to go down into basements, into tunnels and chasms and excavations. I wanted to sing my way down to the things waiting there for me.

"Ah, *la musica*," I whispered. "Here I come."

II. SOUND DIMENSION

-ALANA RAY-

I got there early, just to watch.

I'd been to the Warehouse plenty of times. It's an old factory building in Chelsea, hollowed out and loaded up with rehearsal spaces, foam spread across the walls to kill the echoes, forty-eight power plugs in every room. There's a recording studio in the basement—sixty dollars an hour, one dollar a minute—but it's full of junk and strictly for the kids.

I watched the place fill up, random guitar chops and drumbeats filtering out, bouncing up and down the block. Sixteenth isn't a narrow street, over fifty feet from wall to wall, so it takes a tenth of a second for sound to cross over and jump back. At 150 beats per minute, that's a sixteenth-note lag.

I clapped my hands and listened to the echo, then drummed softly on my jeans in tempo as I watched.

From the stoop of the empty FedEx office

down the block, I could catalog all the faces going in, concentrating so I'd remember the new people I was meeting upstairs. I always try to see people before they see me, same way as animals want to be upwind, not down.

At the school I went to, where we all had special needs, some of the other kids couldn't recognize faces very well. They learned to identify people by their posture or their walk, which seemed like a good idea to me. I can understand faces just fine, but I don't trust people till I've seen the way they move.

A long gray limousine slid up in front of the Warehouse. A big Jamaican guy in a gray uniform got out and glanced up and down the block, making sure it was safe. But he didn't see me.

The bulge of a shoulder holster creased his jacket. Times Square was getting more like that every day, armed guards appearing at the entrances of the big stores. More policemen too.

Satisfied, the driver opened the limo's door for two girls.

They looked about the same age as the boys who'd hired me nearly two weeks ago, seventeen or eighteen, but I figured these limo-girls couldn't possibly know them. Those dog-walking boys didn't have limo money—not even *taxi* money.

Also, the boys hadn't been druggies, and one of these girls definitely had a problem. Skin pale as an oyster, she unfolded from the limousine and stood there holding on to the door, shaky from the ride. Though her long arms were thin and wiry, her muscles were almost as defined as mine.

What kind of junkie works out? I wondered as she made her way around the car to the entrance of the Warehouse. Her movements were slow and pointy, articulated in the wrong spots. I couldn't take my eyes off her: it was like watching a stick insect walk along a branch.

A minute later the two dog-boys showed up, and it turned out they did know one another—or at least the boys knew the other girl, the little one with eyeglasses. She introduced them to the junkie girl; then they all went inside except the boy who'd hired me. He waited outside, like he'd said he would.

His name was Moz: M-o-z. I remembered that because I'd written it down.

I watched him wait, doing a nervous little dance, never putting his guitar case down. His fingers ran through practice patterns, flickering against his thigh, and I matched his tempo for a while on my knees.

I wondered how they'd come together: a junkie, a rich girl, two scruffy boys, all of them younger than me, probably too young to be serious about their music. Maybe they were *all* rich, and the boys had dressed down just to hire me cheap.

That was a dirty trick if they had, and I don't play with people who trick me. But I wasn't sure yet.

When my watch said sixteen seconds left, I picked up my duffel bags and crossed the street.

"Hey, Alana," he said. "You made it."

"Alana Ray," I corrected him. "Nine o'clock on Sunday morning."

"Yeah. Pretty messed up, huh?" He shrugged and rolled his eyes, like the time had been someone else's idea. Someone annoying.

"You got my eighty bucks?" I asked, still drumming two fingers against the strap of one duffel bag.

"Sure . . . um, eighty?" His eyes narrowed a bit.

I smiled. "Seventy-five. Just messing with you."

He laughed in a way that said five bucks meant something to him, and the money came out of his pockets in crumpled singles and fives, even ten dollars' worth of quarters rolled by hand.

I relaxed a little. This boy was dirt poor. There wasn't any kind of rich person who'd go to that much trouble to trick me.

"Those all your drums . . . um, buckets?" he asked, staring at the duffel bags.

"Don't take up much space, do they?" I said. But really I hadn't brought everything, not for the first time. No sense hauling forty-two pounds of gear if all these kids wanted was a drum machine with dreadlocks.

"Must be easier to carry than a real set."

I nodded. I've never carried a real drum set, but it seemed like it would be hard.

He counted up to seventy-five, which seemed to clean his pockets out. I felt a little bad about my eighty-dollar trick, and my feet started tapping.

"Um, there's one thing," he said, shouldering his guitar and screwing up his face, nervous and flickering again. He was kind of cute, all uncomfortable like this. I felt myself worrying about him, like a kid walking down the street with one shoelace untied.

"What is it?" I said.

"It'd be better if you didn't mention the money to Pearl."

"Who's Pearl?"

"She's the . . ." He frowned. "Just don't mention it to anyone, I guess. Okay?"

"Fine with me." I shrugged. "Money's the same, whoever gives it to you."

"Yeah, I guess it is." He nodded, his face serious like I'd said something profound instead of simply logical. That was the *point* of money, after all: crisp and clean or wrinkled or disintegrated into quarters—a dollar was always worth a hundred cents.

We headed on in.

Upstairs was like every practice room: distracting. Four walls and a ceiling of undulating foam, the pattern shimmering in the corners of my vision. The disconcerting tangle of cables on the floor. The stillness hovering around us, the air robbed of echoes.

The small girl with eyeglasses took over, introducing me to everyone.

"This is Zahler. He plays guitar." The big burly dog-boy smiled broadly. He hadn't wanted to pay me, I remembered.

"And Minerva. It's her first time too. She's going to sing for us."

The junkie girl took off her dark glasses for two seconds, squinting in the fluorescent lights, and smiled at me.

She was wearing a long black velvet dress, as shiny as the streets after it rains, a tangle of necklaces, and dangling earrings. Her long black nails glistened, dazzling me like the undulating ceiling.

"She's a singer?" I asked. "Huh . . . I'd have figured she was a roadie."

They all laughed at my joke, except for Minerva, whose smile curled tighter. Her teeth sent a little shiver toward me. I touched my forehead three times, blinked one eye, then the other to still the air.

"And I'm Pearl: keyboards," the other girl said. "You're Alana, right?"

"Alana Ray. One name," I said, my voice tremulous from Minerva's stare.

"Cool," she said. "Hyphenated?"

I grinned. I'd known the little rich girl was going to ask that. It bugs some people, me having two first names that are invisibly stuck together.

"No. *Carbon*ated. Just a little bubble of air."

No one laughed, but no one ever does. That joke was just for me.

Setup was quick. The boys just had to plug in and tune, and Pearl had only one small keyboard. She balanced it on the room's mixing console, where she could control everyone else's sound. The junkie girl adjusted her microphone stand higher, then fiddled with the light switches, her movements still jerky and insectlike. Even though she was still wearing those dark glasses, she turned down the lights till I could hardly see.

I didn't complain, though. Her glare had made me shiver once already.

I set up in one corner, two walls of foam padding at my back, twenty-one paint buckets arranged before me, the stacks growing taller from right to left, one to six buckets high. $(6! = 21)$

I pulled out six contact microphones, my own mixer and effects boxes, and went to work. I don't like rehearsal spaces or recording studios as much as the open air—but at least I can bring my own echoes.

Pearl watched me clip the mikes to my stacks of plastic, run their cables into the mixer, then route them out through the effects.

"Paint cans, huh?" she asked.

"Paint buckets," I corrected, and saw Moz smile for the first time.

"Uh, sure. How many channels you need?" she asked, fingering the sliders on the mixing board. "Six? Twelve?"

"Just two. Left and right." I handed her the cables.

Pearl frowned as I turned away from her. This way, she couldn't control my mix from her board. It was like she wanted me to give her my eggs, my cheese, and my chives all in separate bowls. But instead I was handing her the whole omelet, cooked just the way I liked it.

She didn't argue, though, and I saw that Moz was still grinning.

"Everybody ready?" Pearl asked. Everyone was.

Minerva swallowed and walked up to grasp her mike with one pale hand. The other held a notebook, which I could see was open to a page of chaos, like the hand-writing of the unluckiest kids back at my special school.

Moz just nodded, not looking up at Pearl, flicking his cords around on the floor with one toe.

The burly boy (whose name I'd already forgotten; should have written it down) was the only one who smiled. He leaned his head down to stare closely at his strings, setting his fingers carefully. Then, concentrating hard, he began to play. It was a simple riff, thick and dirty.

Pearl did something on the board, and the sound softened.

I listened for a moment, then tuned my echoes to ninety-two beats per minute. Moz started playing, high and fast. I thought it was a strange way to start, too complicated, like a guitar solo bursting out of nowhere. But then Pearl entered, playing a gossamer melody that wrapped a shape around what he was doing.

I listened for a while, not sure what to do. I had a lot of choices. Something simple and lazy, to give the music more backbone? Or should I swing the beat, a little off-kilter, to loosen it up? Or follow Moz's superquick fluttering, like rain against the roof?

I always relished this moment, right before starting to play. It was the one time my fingers didn't tremble or drum against my knees, when I could hold my hands out steady. No reason to hurry.

Also, I didn't want to make a mistake. There was something fragile about this music, as if it would fly apart if pushed in the wrong direction. Pearl, Moz, and the other boy thought they knew one another already, but they didn't yet.

I began carefully, only a downbeat at first, building the

pattern one stroke at a time—simple to complicated, less to more. Then, just before it got too crowded, I slipped sideways, subtracting one stroke for each I added, gradually shifting the music around us, but leaving it still tenuous, directionless.

For a moment I thought I'd made a mistake. These were just kids. Maybe they needed to be pushed in one direction or another, or maybe they'd wanted a drum machine, after all.

But then the junkie girl came in.

There were no words, though she held one of the notebooks open in front of her. With the microphone pressed close to her lips, she was humming, but the melody emerged from the speakers sharp-edged and keening, cutting through the mass of intricacies we'd built.

Suddenly the music had focus, a beating heart. She wrapped the rest of us around herself, piercing my gradual shadows with a single ray of light.

I smiled, having a rare moment of absolute comfort in my own skin, every compulsion satisfied, the clockwork of the whole world clicking into place around my drumming. Even if they were young and flawed, these four had something. Maybe a happy accident was happening here, like the first time I'd ever noticed the echoes from the street matching my footsteps. . . .

Then the strangeness began, something I hadn't seen since I was little. The air started to glitter wildly, my eyelids fluttering. This was more than ripples of heat from summer asphalt, or the shimmers I saw when someone was angry at me.

Shapes were forming on the cable-strewn floor, and faces materialized in the patterns of the soundproofing: I glimpsed expressions of hurt and fear and fury at the edges of my vision, as if my medication was failing.

I imagined dropping my sticks, reaching into my pocket, and spilling out my pills to count them. But I was positive I'd taken one that morning, and the labels always warned that they built up slowly in the bloodstream: weeks to take effect, weeks to fade away. Never stop, even if you think you don't need them anymore.

Minerva was glowing, her pale skin luminous in the darkness. Her movements had smoothed out, no longer insectlike. She was singing now, teeth jammed close to the microphone, her incomprehensible song sputtering for a moment as she turned a page of the notebook.

The practice room was seething, phantasms filling up the spaces between objects, demons with long tails riding the sound waves in the air.

I was afraid, but I couldn't stop. I couldn't bring my drumming to a halt any more than I could smother the tapping of my foot or the twitches in my face. I was trapped here, caught in the pattern I'd helped shape.

Then reality shifted once more, like the sprockets of a film finally catching, and I saw something I'd almost forgotten . . . *what music looked like.*

Moz's guitar notes were scattered like Christmas lights across the ceiling, shimmering in and out, Pearl's sinuous melody linking and electrifying them. The dog-boy's riff spread out underneath, solid and steady, and my drumming was the scaffolding that held it aloft, all of it pulsating at ninety-two beats per minute, alive and connecting us.

I stared at the apparition, awestruck. This was the way I'd been born to see music, before the doctors had taught me to separate my senses, to grab objects and faces and hold them in place. Before they'd cured me of these visions with therapy and pills.

How had this other reality returned? Every sense conjoined, complete and undivided . . .

But then my eyes dropped to the floor, and I saw Minerva's song.

It was tangled around our feet, twisting its way through cords and cables, plunging in and out of the floor, like loops of Loch Ness monster in the water. It was a worm, blind and horned, its rippling segments pushing it through the earth, rearing up a hungry maw teethed with a ring of knives.

And suddenly I knew that Minerva's curse was something a thousand years older than heroin or crack.

I let out a gasp, and she turned her head toward me, *saw* me seeing it. She dropped the notebook and pulled off her glasses in one brittle motion, her song dissipating into a long, furious hiss. The architecture of the music shattered overhead, my drumsticks spinning from my hands.

The rest of them stumbled to a halt. Pearl was staring at her friend, alarmed. Moz was staring at Minerva too, and for a moment his expression was unmistakable: the boy was dripping with desire.

"Why'd you two stop, man?" the burly dog-boy cried. "That shit was *paranormal*!"

I blinked, looking down at empty hands. No trembling, just like after any good session. I felt no need to tap my feet or touch my forehead. There was nothing in the air but the hiss of amplifiers, a barely visible ripple in the corners of my eyes.

But I still felt it in the soles of my feet, the beast we'd been playing. Something was rumbling in the earth, deeper than six stories below. Answering Minerva's song.

"You can smell it too, can't you?" she whispered to me.

"No . . . not smell. But sometimes I see things I shouldn't." I swallowed, clutching at my pill bottle through my jeans, by reflex spilling out the speech they made us memorize at school, in case the police ever thought we were on drugs: "I have a neurological condition that may cause compulsive behavior, loss of motor control, or hallucinations."

Minerva raised an eyebrow, then curled back her lips in a sneer that showed too many pointed teeth. "*Spasticus . . . autisticus.*"

I nodded. That was more or less me.

But what the hell was she?

12. THE TEMPTATIONS

Her uncovered face was radiant, shining with a brilliance that liquefied me.

She'd worn her shades until that moment—a total poser, I'd figured. But I could see now that she *had* to wear them, not for her protection, but for ours, to shield us from her eyes.

What she had wasn't beauty, it was something a thousand times scarier, something that gnawed at my edges. I'd already heard it in the music, felt it in the way she'd wrenched us all into her wake—the whole band sucked up and totaled by her magnetism, or whatever you'd call it. Something *charisma* was too small a word for.

Something overriding, bottomless.

Suddenly, this was *her* band, not mine or Pearl's. And just as suddenly, I didn't mind.

Minerva put her sunglasses back on.

I picked up her notebook from where it had fluttered to the floor.

What covered the open pages wasn't writing, more like the scroll from a lie detector, or one of those machines that inscribes the shapes of earthquakes. Ragged black lines undulated in impenetrable columns, smeared and spattered with drops of water. A few smudges were rusty brown, like old blood.

I offered it to her, but Minerva was still staring at Alana Ray—*glaring*, her gaze dangerous even through dark glasses. I felt like I should say something to calm her down, since I'd brought Alana Ray here and Minerva was angry at her about . . . something.

Because Alana Ray had dropped her sticks? But Minerva had freaked out before the Big Riff had broken down. I opened my mouth but found myself silenced by the memory of Minerva's naked eyes.

"Min?" Pearl said.

I closed my mouth. Let Pearl handle this.

"You okay, Min?"

"Yeah, sure." Minerva leaned across to take the notebook from my hand, pressed it close against her chest. "Sorry about that. Didn't mean to have a hissy fit. I was just kind of . . . into that song."

"I'm sorry too," Alana Ray said quietly. "My condition sometimes leads to performance complications."

I swallowed, trying to remember what Alana Ray had confessed about herself . . . something wrong with her brain? All of a sudden, she was talking funny, with microscopic pauses between her words. Little twitches traveled across her body as she stared back at Minerva, as if her nervous system was unraveling inside. I opened my mouth again to say something.

"Hey, no problem," Zahler said first. "You were fawesome. We were *all* totally paranormal!" He turned to Pearl. "Right?"

"Yeah," Pearl said softly. "We were." She gave me a questioning look.

I held her gaze, something I hadn't done in two weeks.

It had all clicked—our music, this band. Pearl's strange, electric friend had pulled us together and forged us into something as brilliant as she was.

"That was great," I said, nodding at Pearl. "Good going."

Her face brightened in the dark practice room. "Well, okay, then." She turned to Alana Ray. "You need to take a break?"

Alana Ray blinked one eye, then the other, then shook her head like she had water in her ear. "No. I'd rather keep playing. I think my . . . complication is over. But maybe a different song? Sometimes the same stimulus can provoke the same reaction."

"Uh, sure," Pearl said, then shrugged. "How about Piece Two?"

Zahler and I just nodded, but Minerva smiled, pulling the microphone closer to her mouth. Low, soft laughter, touched with reverb, scattered about the room.

"No problem, Alana Ray," she whispered, opening her notebook. "I've got about a million stimuli to go."

Nobody freaked out for the rest of rehearsal.

We played Piece Two, a long jam wrapped around a looped sample from an old vinyl record of Pearl's, then our third song, which didn't even have a working title yet. Alana

Ray never stumbled again, just accompanied us with psychic comprehension. With every new section she'd follow along for a while, then slowly start to build us up, adding structure and form, staring at invisible sheet music hovering in the air, somehow *seeing* what we needed her to do.

I didn't catch a single word Minerva sang, but every time she opened her mouth, she injected us with brilliance. Her voice had an uncanny magnitude, as if her notebooks were full of incantations for making the ground beneath us rumble. I couldn't take my eyes off her, except when I closed them and listened hard.

Between songs, I kicked myself for not having gone out to Brooklyn that morning. I finally saw how stupid the struggle between Pearl and me had been. Neither of us were rock stars—we were backups, sidekicks, allies. Good musicians, maybe, but Minerva was luminous.

The anger that had been dogging me the last two weeks was spent, leaving nothing but contentment. I had an awesome band, a place to rehearse with no one yelling, "Turn it down!" and a 1975 Strat with gold pickups in my hands. I'd even cracked the money thing and was saving a few bucks for myself every day. I couldn't remember why being miserable had seemed so important.

Minerva had changed everything.

After an hour and a half, we'd played every song we knew as many times as we could and ground to a reluctant halt.

"Hey," Zahler said. "We need some new tunes, don't we?"

"Yeah." I looked at Pearl. "We should get together soon. Work on some more stuff for next Sunday." Suddenly I had fragments of a million songs in my head.

Pearl smiled happily. "More tunes? No problemo."

Minerva frowned. "*Problem*a. *Pero masculino.*"

"Huh?" I said, glancing at Pearl.

"Um, Min's been studying Spanish, sort of." Pearl pulled out her cell phone and frowned at it. "Speaking of which, I think we need to get back to Brooklyn for your, um, lesson."

"You're studying Spanish?" Zahler said, grinning. "*Mas cervezas!*"

"*Prefiero sangre*," Minerva said, her teeth glimmering in the darkness.

"Yeah, okay." Pearl turned to Alana Ray. "Listen, it was great to meet you. You were brilliant. I mean, especially for paint cans."

"Paint buckets," Alana Ray said. "It was good to meet you too."

"So . . . you want to play with us again?"

Alana Ray looked at me, and I nodded—at seventy-five bucks she was a bargain. She smiled. "Yes. This was very . . . involving."

"That's us. Involving." Pearl swallowed. "Sorry that Min and I have to run, but you've got the room until eleven. If I go reserve it for next week, can you guys handle breaking down?"

"What about your mixing board?" Zahler said.

"They keep it locked up downstairs. Here's my key." She threw a glittering chain across the room to Zahler and grabbed Minerva's hand. "Come on, Min. We really have to motor."

Zahler shouted goodbye, but Pearl was already pulling Minerva out of the door, yanking her along like a five-year-old who didn't want to leave the zoo.

I followed them into the hall, running ahead to stab the elevator button.

"Thanks," Pearl said. "Sorry to leave you guys to clean up. It's just . . ." Her voice faded into a sigh.

"Smelly Spanish lessons," Minerva said. From all around us, the mutterings of bands leaked out, the thump of drums, muffled stabs of feedback.

"Don't worry about it." I wondered what their mysterious rush was really all about. Not Spanish lessons, obviously. I tried to remember what Pearl had said on the phone that morning. Something about *ninjas*? "You've done everything so far, Pearl. It won't kill us to put some stuff away."

"Not everything. You guys found Alana Ray. She's incredible."

"Yeah, I guess she is." I smiled. "Listen, I'm sorry I was so sleepy when you called this morning. Next time, I'll be glad to help out . . ." I glanced at Minerva. "With whatever."

"Oh, cool," Pearl said softly, her smile growing. She was staring down at the floor. "That's great."

The elevator came, and when they stepped on, I did too, wanting a few more seconds with Minerva. "I'll come down with you guys, if you don't mind, and then ride back up."

"We don't mind," Minerva said.

It was quiet in the big freight elevator, the walls padded with movers' blankets to protect them from the ravages of dollies, amps, and drums.

I cleared my throat. "Listen, Pearl, I've been kind of a dickhead."

"About what?" Pearl said, and Min's eyebrows rose behind dark glasses.

"About everything; about you. But this band is finally coming together, and I feel kind of stupid about the way I've been acting. So . . . I'm okay now."

"Hey, Moz. It's my fault too." Pearl turned to me, her face a little pink, almost blushing. "I know I can be sort of bossy."

"She's got a point there," Minerva said.

I laughed. "Nah. You just know what you're doing." I shrugged. "So me and Zahler should come over tomorrow? Get some new tunes worked up before next Sunday?"

Pearl nodded, still grinning. "Perfect."

"You coming?" I asked Minerva. "I mean, you're the singer and everything." I pointed at the notebooks she still clutched to her chest.

"Um, probably not," Pearl said. "She's kind of—"

"It's very *intensive* Spanish," Minerva said.

"Oh. Sure."

The elevator doors opened, and we stepped out into the lobby, Pearl still pulling Minerva along. A couple of guys were rolling a dolly full of turntable decks into the building, negotiating the bump between stairway ramp and marble floor with extreme care.

Pearl stepped up to the front desk, pulling out a credit card and talking to the guy about next week.

Minerva turned to me and said softly, "See you next week."

I nodded, swallowing, suddenly glad she was wearing those dark glasses. I wondered how many fewer stupid things I'd have said in my life if all pretty girls wore them. "I'll totally be there."

Okay, maybe not that many.

But Minerva just laughed and reached out with the hand Pearl wasn't holding. Hot as a freshly blown-out match, her fingertip traced my arm from wrist to elbow. Between her parted lips, I could see teeth sliding from left to right against each other, and then she mouthed a silent word.

Yummy.

She turned away from my shiver, back to Pearl just as she finished up and flicked open her phone.

"Elvis? We're ready." Pearl snapped the phone shut and looked at me. "See you guys tomorrow. Call me?"

"Yeah. I'll tell Zahler." My breath was short, the line Minerva had traced along my arm still burning. "See you."

They waved, and I watched them walk through the door and out, then make their way toward a huge gray limo—a *limo*?—that slid into view. Minerva's mouthed word still echoed in my head, so unexpected, more like a daydream than something that had actually *happened*. My brain couldn't get hold of it, like a guitar lick I could hear but that my fingers couldn't grasp.

But she turned back toward me just before she ducked

into the car and stuck her tongue out. Then her smile flashed, wicked and electric.

The limo slid away.

I swallowed, turned, and ran back to catch the elevator's closing doors. The guys with turntables were piled inside, leaving just enough space for me to squeeze in. As we rode up, I was rocking on the balls of my feet, humming one of the strange fragments Minerva had left in my brain, bouncing off the blanketed wall behind me.

I glanced over at the two guys and noticed they were watching my little dance.

"Fresh tunes?" one said, grinning.

"Yeah, very." I licked my lips, tasting salt there. "Things are going *great*."

PART III

REHEARSALS

The Black Death had a distant twin.

At the same time the Plague of Justinian was raging across the Roman world, a great empire in South America, that of the Nazca, was also disappearing. The Nazca temples were suddenly abandoned, their cities emptied of life. Historians have no clue why this vast and sophisticated culture, thousands of miles away from plague-ridden Rome, vanished at exactly the same historical moment.

Most people haven't heard of the Nazca, after all. That's how thoroughly they disappeared.

It wasn't until the 1920s that the outside world discovered their greatest legacy. Airplanes flying over the arid mountaintops of Peru spotted huge drawings scratched into the earth. Covering four hundred square miles were pictures of many-legged creatures, vast spiders, and strange human figures. Archaeologists don't know what these drawings mean. Are they images of the gods? Or of demons? Do they tell a story?

Actually, they're a warning.

It is often noticed how they were built to last, cut into mountaintops where rain hardly ever falls and where there's almost zero erosion. Amazingly, they're still clearly visible after fifteen hundred years. Whatever they're trying to say, the message is designed to last across the centuries.

Maybe the time to read them is now.

Night Mayor tapes:
282–287

13. MISSING PERSONS

-PEARL-

The halls of Juilliard seemed wrong on that first day back to school.

This was my fourth year here, so the place was pretty familiar by now. But things always felt strange when I returned from summer break, as if the colors had changed slightly while I was gone. Or maybe I'd grown some fraction of an inch over the last three months, shifting everything imperceptibly out of scale.

Today I couldn't get used to how empty the hallways felt. Of course, it made sense. All my friends in Nervous System (or *ex*-friends, really, thanks to Minerva's meltdown) had graduated last year, leaving the school full of acquaintances and strangers. That was what I got for hanging out with so many seniors when I was a junior.

I picked up my schedule from the front office and checked over the signs saying which classes and ensembles had been canceled due to lack of interest. No baroque instruments class this year. No jazz improv group. No *chamber choir*?

That was kind of lateral.

But all my planned classes were still scheduled. They made you take four years of composition and theory, after all, and my morning was full of required academics: English, trig, and the inescapable advanced biology.

So it wasn't until lunch that I began to see how much had really changed.

The cafeteria was the biggest room at school. It doubled as a concert hall, because even fancy private schools like Juilliard couldn't take up infinite space in the middle of Manhattan. My third-period AP bio class was just next door, prime real estate for getting to the front of the food line. Walking in ten seconds after the lunch bell, I was happy to see all the vacant tables. The familiar floury smell of macaroni and cheese *à la Juilliard*, one of the nonfeculent dishes here, made me smile.

Even if the System was gone, it was good to be back.

I got a trayful and looked around for anyone I could sit with, especially someone with useful musical skills. Moz and I might want to bring in backup musicians one day.

It only took a few seconds to spot Ellen Bromowitz all alone in the corner. She was in my year and a fawesome cellist, first chair in the orchestra. We'd been temporary best friends in our early freshman days, back when neither of us knew anyone else.

I took a seat across from her. Cellos could be cool, even

if Ellen sort of wasn't. Besides, there was hardly anyone else there.

She looked up from her macaroni, a little puzzled. "Pearl?"

"Hey, Ellen."

"Didn't expect to see you here." She raised an eyebrow.

"Well . . ." I wasn't quite sure what she meant. "Haven't seen you in a while. Just thought I'd say hi."

She didn't answer, just kept looking at me.

"How's it going?" I asked.

"Interesting question." A wry little smile played across her face. "So, you don't have any friends to sit with either?"

I swallowed, feeling more or less busted. "I guess not. The rest of Nervous System were seniors. All your friends graduated too, huh?"

"Graduated?" She shook her head. "No. But no one's back yet."

"Not back from where?"

"Summer." She looked around the cafeteria.

The place still hadn't filled up. It seemed so quiet, not like the lunchtime chaos I remembered. I wondered if it had always been this spacious and peaceful in here, and if this was just another of those little summer-shifted perceptions making everything feel wrong.

But that didn't quite make sense. Things seeming smaller every year, I could understand. But *emptier*?

"Well, it was a pretty feculent summer," I said. "Between the sanitation crisis and the rats and stuff. Maybe not everyone's back from Switzerland or wherever else they escaped to."

Ellen finished swallowing some mac and cheese. "My friends don't go to Switzerland in the summer."

"Oh, right." I shrugged, remembering how scholarship students always hung out together. "Well, Vermont, or whatever."

She made a little sighing sound.

"Still, it's great to be back, huh?" I said.

Her eyes narrowed. "You're in an awfully good mood. What's that all about? Got a new boyfriend or something?"

I laughed. "No boyfriend. But yeah, I'm really happy. The weather's finally cooler, the subways are working this week, and I'm getting another band together." I shrugged. "Things are going great, I guess. And . . ."

"And what?"

"Well, *maybe* there's a boy. Not sure yet if it's a good idea, though."

I felt an embarrassingly nonsubtle grin growing on my face.

True, I wasn't sure whether it was a good idea at all, but at least the downright feculence between me and Moz had finally ended.

Having a band had wrung all the resentment out of him. He never complained about our early Sunday morning rehearsals anymore, just showed up ready to play. Moz could be so amazing when he was like this—like my mom said, totally fetching—focused when he played, intense when he listened to the rest of us.

So maybe sometimes I imagined distilling that concentration down to just the two of us, putting his newfound focus to work in other ways. And maybe, writing songs in my bedroom, I occasionally had to remind myself that it wasn't cool to jump the bones of your bandmates.

Mark and Minerva had shown me how much trouble that could cause. I'd heard he'd cracked up completely over the summer. Must be tough, losing your girlfriend and your band on the same day.

So I bit my tongue when Moz starting looking really intense and fervent, reminding myself it was for the good of the band, which was more important to me than any boy.

But that didn't mean I never thought about it.

The band had changed Minerva too. She could be nine kinds of normal these days. Maybe she still wore dark glasses, but the thought of going out in the sun didn't terrify her anymore. Neither did her own reflection—mirrors were her new best friends. Best of all, she loved dressing up and sneaking out to rehearsals. Her songs evolved every time we played, the formless rages slowly taking shape, bent into verses and choruses by the structure of the music.

One day soon, I figured, the words might actually start making sense.

The funny thing was, Alana Ray seemed to help Min the most. Her fluttering patterns wrapped around Minerva's fury, lending it form and logic. I suspected that Alana Ray was guiding us all somehow, a paint-bucket-pounding guru in our midst.

I'd gone online a few times, trying to figure out what exactly her condition was. She twitched and tapped like she had Tourette's, but she never swore uncontrollably. A disease called Asperger syndrome looked about right, except for those hallucinations. Maybe Minerva had called it during that first rehearsal, and Alana Ray was a little bit autistic, a word that could mean all kinds of stuff. But whatever her condition was, it seemed to give her some special vision into the bones of things.

So now that we had a drummer-sage and a demented Taj Mahal of a singer, the band only had two problems left: (1) we didn't have a bass player, which I knew exactly how to fix, and (2) we *still* didn't have a name. . . .

"How does Crazy Versus Sane sound to you?" I asked Ellen.

"Pardon me?"

"For a band name."

"Hmm," she said. "I guess it makes sense; you're going to be all New Sound, right?"

"Sort of, but better."

She shrugged. "It's a little bit trying-too-hard; the word *crazy*, I mean. Like in *Catch-22*. Anyone who tells you they're crazy really isn't. They're just faking, or they wouldn't know they were crazy."

"Okay." I frowned, remembering why hanging out with Ellen could be a drag sometimes. She had a tendency toward nonenthusiasm.

But then she smiled. "Don't worry, Pearl. You'll think of something. You playing guitar for them?"

"No, keyboards. We've got one too many guitarists already."

"Too bad." She pulled up an acoustic guitar case from the floor, sat it in the chair next to her. "Wouldn't mind being in a band."

I stared at the guitar. "What are you doing with that?"

She shrugged. "Gave up the cello."

"What? But you were first chair last year!"

"Yeah, but cellos . . ." A long sigh. "They take too much infrastructure."

"They do what?"

She sighed, rearranging the dishes on her tray as she spoke. "They need infrastructure. Most of the great cello works are written for orchestra. That's almost a hundred musicians right there, plus all the craftsmen to build the instruments and maintain them and enough people to build a concert hall. And to pay for that, you're talking about thousands of customers buying tickets every year, rich donors and government grants. . . . That's why only really big cities have orchestras."

"Um, Ellen? You *live* in a really big city. You're not planning to move to Alaska or something, are you?"

She shook her head. "No. But what if big cities don't *work* anymore? What if you can't stick that many people together without it falling apart? What if . . ." Ellen's voice faded as she looked around the cafeteria once more.

I followed her gaze. The place still was only two-thirds full, with entire tables vacant and no line at all for food. It was like nobody had been scheduled for A-lunch.

It was starting to freak me out. Where the hell *was* everyone?

"What if the time for orchestras is over, Pearl?"

I let out a snort. "There've been orchestras for centuries. They're part of . . . I don't know, *civilization*."

"Yeah, civilization. That's the whole problem. . . ." She touched the neck of the guitar case softly. "I was so sick of carrying that big cello around, like some dead body in a coffin. I just wanted something simple. Something I could play by the campfire, whether or not there's any civilization around."

A weird tingle went down my spine. "What happened to you this summer, Ellen?"

She looked up at me and, after a long pause, said, "My dad went away."

"Oh. Crap." I swallowed, remembering when my parents had divorced. "I'm really sorry. Like . . . he left your mom?"

Ellen shook her head. "Not right away. You see, someone bit him on the subway, and he . . . got different."

"*Bit* him?" I thought of the rumors I'd heard, that some kind of rabies was spreading from the rats—that you could see people like Min on the streets now, hungry and wearing dark glasses.

She nodded, still stroking the guitar case's neck. "At least I'm still on a full scholarship. So I can switch to guitar before—"

"But you're a great *cellist*. You can't give up on civilization yet. I mean, New York City's still around."

She nodded. "Mostly. There are still concerts and classes and baseball games going on. But it's kind of like the *Titanic*: there's really only enough lifeboats for the first-class passengers." She scanned the room. "So when I see people not showing up, I sort of wonder if those passengers are already leaving. And then the floor's going to start tilting, the deck chairs sliding past."

"Um . . . the what?"

Ellen turned to me with narrowed eyes. "Here's the thing, Pearl. I bet your friends are already off in Switzerland, or someplace like that."

I shrugged. "They mostly just graduated."

"I bet they're in Switzerland anyway. Most people who can afford it are already gone. But *my* friends . . ." She shook her head, then shrugged. "They don't have drivers or bodyguards, and they have to ride the subway to school. So they're in hiding, sort of."

"You're here."

"Only reason is that we live around the corner. I don't have to ride the subway. Plus . . ." She smiled, touching the case in the seat next to her. "I really want to learn to play guitar."

We talked more—about her father, about all the stuff we'd seen that summer. But my mind kept wandering to the band.

Listening to Ellen, it had occurred to me that bands like ours needed a lot of infrastructure too, as much as any symphony orchestra. To do what we did, we needed electronic instruments and microphones, mixing boards and echo boxes and stacks of amplifiers. We needed nightclubs, recording studios, record companies, cable channels that showed music videos, and fans who had CD players and electricity at home.

Crap, we *needed* civilization.

I couldn't exactly see Moz and Min jamming around a campfire, after all.

What if Luz's fairy tales were true, then, and some big struggle was coming? And what if Ellen Bromowitz had it right, and the time for orchestras was over? What if the illness that had ripped apart Nervous System was going to bring down the infrastructure that made having our kind of band even possible?

I straightened up in my chair. It was time to get moving. I had to quit patting myself on the back just because Moz was happy and Minerva was relatively noncrazy and rehearsals were going well.

We needed to become world-famous soon, while there was still that kind of world to be famous in.

14. THE REPLACEMENTS

We churned out one fawesome tune after another—me, Moz, and Pearl, meeting two or three times a week at her place. After we'd used up all our old riffs, we started basing stuff on Pearl's loopy samples, and the Mosquito didn't even buzz about it. Ever since the band had gotten real—with a drummer, a singer, even separate amps for Moz and me—he'd finally realized that this wasn't a competition.

What he hadn't realized was how hot Pearl was or that she had a major crush on him.

All I could do was shake my head about that last part. The problem for Pearl was, she'd really given Moz something. She'd stripped away his shell, had shown him a way to get everything he really wanted, had helped him find a focus that he'd been too lame to discover for himself.

He was never going to forgive her for that.

Me, I still thought Pearl was hot. But for

now, there was nothing I could do about it. And actually, I was happy with things the way they were. My best friend and the foolest girl in the world had finally quit fighting, the music was fexcellent, and Pearl loved the band, which meant she wasn't going anywhere without me tagging along.

It was all going so good, I should have known something was about to explode.

We were working on the B section of one of the new tunes, called "A Million Stimuli to Go." It was totally complicated, and no matter how hard I tried, I just couldn't play it. Moz kept showing me how on his Strat, but for some reason it didn't work on my fingers.

At least, it didn't until Pearl jumped in. She swept aside the CD cases and a harmonica scattered across her bed and sat down next to me. Unhooking the strap of my guitar, she pulled it over into her lap.

"Let me, Zahler," she said.

Then, like it was no big deal, she started playing the part.

Normally, sitting that close to her would have been pretty fool. But at that moment I was too dumbfounded to appreciate it.

"See?" she said, her fingers practically smoking as they cruised across the strings. "You've just got to use your pinky on that last bit."

Moz laughed. "He hates using his pinky. Says it's his retarded finger."

I didn't say anything right then, just watched her play,

nodding like a moron. She was dead on about how to make the part work, and now that I could see it from behind the strings, it didn't even look that hard. When Pearl handed me back my guitar, I managed to get it right the first time.

She stood up and went back to her keyboards, tweaking her stacks while I ran through it a dozen more times, pushing the riff deep into my brain.

I didn't say anything more about it till later, when it was just me and the Mosquito.

"Moz, did you see what happened back there?"

We were wandering through late-night Chinatown, surrounded by the clatter of restaurant kitchens. The thick sweat of fry-cooking rolled along the narrow streets, and the metal doors of fish markets were rumbling down, the briny smell of guts lingering in the air.

It was pretty quiet at night since the pedestrian curfew had been imposed. Moz and I always ignored the curfew, though, so it was like we owned the city.

"See what?" Moz twisted his body to peer down the alley we'd just passed.

"No, not down there." Since that day with my dogs, I didn't even *glance* into alleys anymore. "Back at Pearl's. When she showed me that riff." My hands lifted into guitar position, fingers fluttering. The moves were in me now, too late to save me from humiliation.

"Oh, the one you had trouble with? What about it?"

"Did you see how Pearl just *did* it?"

He frowned, his own fingers tracing the pattern. "That's how it's supposed to be played."

I groaned. "No, Moz, not *how* she played it. *That* she played it, when it was driving me nuts!"

"Oh," he said, then waited as a garbage truck steamed past, squeaking and groaning. For some reason, there were six guys hanging onto the back, instead of the usual two or three. They watched us warily as the truck rumbled away. "Yeah, she's pretty good. You didn't know that?"

"Hell, no. When did that happen?"

"A long time before we met her." He laughed. "You never noticed how her hand moves when she calls out chords?" His left hand twitched in the air. "And I told you how she spotted the Strat, same as me."

"But—"

"And that stuff in her room: the flute, the harmonicas, the hand drums. She plays it all, Zahler."

I frowned. It was true, there were a lot of instruments lying around at Pearl's. And sometimes she'd pull one down and play something on it, just for a joke. "I never noticed any guitars, though."

He shrugged. "She keeps them under the bed. I thought you knew."

I looked down and swung my boot at the fire hydrant squatting on the curb, catching it hard in one of its little spouty things. It clanked and I hopped back, remembering I didn't mess with hydrants anymore. "That doesn't bug you?"

"Bug me? I don't care if she keeps them in the attic, as long as I get to play the Strat."

"Not that. Doesn't it bug you that *I'm* supposed to be our guitarist, and I don't even play guitar as well as our *keyboard player*?"

"So? She's a musical genius."

I groaned. Sometimes the Mosquito could be spectacularly retarded. "Well, doesn't that sort of imply that the 'musical genius' should be our second guitarist, and not me?"

He stopped, turned to face me. "But Zahler, that won't help. You don't play keyboards at all."

"Ahhh! That's not what I mean!"

Moz sighed, put his hands up. "Look, Zahler, I know she plays guitar better than you. And she understands the Big Riff better than I do, just like she does most music. She probably drums better than a lot of drummers—maybe not Alana Ray, though. But like I said, she's a musical genius. Don't worry. She and I were talking about you, and Pearl's already got a plan."

"Talking about me? A *plan*?"

"Of course. Pearl's always got a plan—that's why she's the boss." He smiled. "I got over it, why can't you?"

"Why can't I *get over it*?" I stood there, breathing hard, hands flexing, looking to grab something by the throat and choke it. "You weren't over *jack* until a couple of weeks ago! And that's only because you think that weird junkie friend of hers is hot!"

He stared at me, eyes wide, and I glared back at him. It was one of those things I hadn't known until I'd blurted it out. But now I could see that it was totally true. The only reason Moz had been so fool lately was that Minerva had clicked the reset button on his brain.

I'd already told Moz what I thought of her. She was a junkie, or an ex-junkie, or a soon-to-be junkie, and was bad news. Even before she'd freaked out at Alana Ray during that first rehearsal, the whole dark glasses and trippy singing had been totally paranormal.

I'm not saying she wasn't a good singer, just that I like my songs with *words*. And I like my skinny, pale chicks with veiny arms as far away as possible.

"Min's not a junkie," he said.

"Oh, yeah? How do you know?"

He spread his hands. "Well, how do you know she *is*?"

"Listen, I don't know *what* she is." I slitted my eyes. "All I know is that it's something that they only let out for two hours a week! That's why we rehearse early Sunday morning, right? And why those two run back to Brooklyn? Because visiting hours are over?"

Moz frowned. "Yeah, I don't really know what that's about." He turned away and started walking again, like I hadn't just been yelling at him. "I think Pearl likes to keep Minerva to herself. They've been friends since they were little kids, and Min's kind of . . . fragile."

I snorted. Junkies might be easy to knock down, but they're never fragile. They have souls like old leather shoes studded with steel, and they're about as much good as friends.

From the fish store across the street, a big Asian guy was eyeing us, a baseball bat in one hand. When I waved and smiled, he nodded and went back to tossing out bucketfuls of used ice, spreading them across the asphalt to let them melt. The icy splinters glittered in the streetlights, and I walked over to crush some under my feet.

Stupid Pearl. Stupid Moz. Stupid guitar.

Against the street, the ice looked black. People said that if you got black water into the freezer fast enough, it would freeze up instead of evaporating, and you'd have black ice. Of course, they never said why you'd *want* anything like that in your fridge. When I went over to Moz's, I still crossed the street so I didn't get too close to that hydrant, even though it had one of those special caps on it now to keep kids out.

"There's something I should tell you about, though." Moz's boots crunched through the ice behind me. "But you can't tell anyone else."

"Great," I murmured, smashing more ice. "Just what this band needs, more secrets." Moz still hadn't told Pearl he was paying Alana Ray, or me where he was getting the money from. And apparently Pearl and Moz had their own secret plans for me. . . .

"Min gave me her phone number."

I spun toward him. He was smiling. "Dude! You *do* think she's hot!"

He laughed, kicking a glittering spray of hail toward me. "Zahler, let me explain something to you. Minerva isn't *hot*. She's way past hot. She's a fifty-thousand-volt plasma rifle. She's a jet engine."

I closed my eyes and groaned. When Moz started talking this way about a girl, it was all over. His obsessions were like an epic guitar solo playing in his brain, endless skittering riffs without any particular logic.

"She's luminous. A rock star. So of course she's a little strange." He sighed. "But, yeah, you're right. It might be weird with Pearl. . . ."

When he said those last words, that's when I probably should have tried to talk him out of it, but at that moment, I was all tangled up about the guitar thing—deeply pissed with Moz and Pearl. They could have at least *told* me I was a worthless doofus instead of thinking it behind my back and making plans.

I opened my eyes. "So, you're plasma-rifle serious? Jet-engine serious?"

"Yeah, man. She's hot."

I shrugged. It wasn't my fault if Moz decided to screw everything up. "When did she give you her number?"

"Sunday before last?"

"Ten days ago?" I rolled my eyes, wanting to make him feel stupid. "Don't you think you should maybe *do* something about it?"

He swallowed, rocking on his feet a little. "It was kind of funny, though. She handed me her number so Pearl couldn't see, and she told me to call at one in the morning. Exactly. She even set my watch to hers."

"So she's weird. We knew that, right?"

"I guess. Yeah, I should call her." He started walking again, kind of twitchy, like Alana Ray before rehearsals.

I sighed, even more miserable now. Here I'd pushed Moz into going after a weird junkie chick, and it hadn't even made me feel any better. I stopped next to a row of mini-Dumpsters outside a restaurant kitchen door and jumped up onto the edge of one, sitting there and pounding my boot heels against its metal side.

"Anyway," Moz said. "What does that have to do with Pearl playing guitar?"

"Can't remember. All I know is that this sucks. I mean, what good is it being the third-best guitarist in a band? Or does Minerva play guitar too?"

He laughed, jumping up beside me. "Listen, Zahler. You're important to the band. You give us energy."

"What, like a puppy?"

"Don't you remember that first day? If you hadn't been there, me and Pearl wouldn't have lasted ten minutes."

"So what? You two are past all that stuff. You don't need me anymore." I looked at him, frowning. "So what's this plan of Pearl's?"

"Well, she figures it's not really New Sound, having more than one guitar."

"Oh." My throat closed up, and my feet stopped swinging, freezing in midair.

I was toast. Gone.

"Pearl was going to tell you this, but I guess I have to now. Um, the thing is . . . we want you to play bass."

"What?"

"We need a bassist. And with this band, anytime we add somebody, everything goes haywire." He shook his head. "I mean, I don't want to have to explain Alana Ray to someone new." His voice dropped. "Or Min, for that matter."

One of my heels hit metal. A soft *boom*. "But Moz, I've spent the last six years playing guitar."

"Zahler, you've spent the last six years playing guitar *like a bass*." He moved his fingers all spastically. "You never noticed that every part I've ever written for you is on the bottom four strings, with hardly any chords? You could switch over in about five minutes. I would've told you to change years ago, except you and me *didn't have a bass*."

"But Moz," I said, my world crumbling. "We still don't have a bass."

"Yeah, we do. Pearl's got one under her bed."

I yelled, pounding both heels against booming metal. "But doesn't that mean she *plays*? Better than me, probably, seeing as how I never even touched one except one time in a music store?"

"Don't you worry about her." He smiled and half-turned, held out his palm toward me. "Come on."

I stared at his hand. "Come on what?"

"Put your hand up to mine."

I frowned, then did it. My fingers stuck out almost an inch longer than Moz's. Big, fat, clumsy fingers.

"Whoa," he said. "That is fawesome. You should try this with Pearl sometime. She's got really tiny hands."

"She does?" I remembered playing the bass that time in the store, slapping at strings thick as steel worms. The frets were miles apart.

"Yeah. She can hardly get her left hand around the neck."

I looked down at my big, fat, fawesome fingers and laughed.

"Can't even hold a bass, huh? Some musical genius."

15. THE NEED

-MOZ-

It felt weird, waiting for one A.M. exactly.

I've always hated clocks and schedules, but this felt different—more like the sensation I'd gotten just before the TV had shattered on the street in front of me. My magic powers were screaming that something was about to happen.

As if I didn't know that already.

I sat there in the kitchen with no lights on, the window wide open and trying to suck in some late September coolness. My parents' apartment is on the sixth floor, and all night long leftover heat filters up from the rest of the building, like we live in the top of a steam cooker. The ancient refrigerator was humming, rattling mightily as it tried to keep beer cold and milk from going sour. An occasional whoop of siren leaped up from the street, along with the staticky pops of police radios.

The darkness was buzzing around me, my skin tingling, fingers drifting over my unplugged Stratocaster's strings, pulling small noises from them. I imagined the notes amplified and her voice singing over the lines I played.

The whole one o'clock thing didn't make sense. Minerva had said something about not waking her parents up, but if they were the problem, why call in the middle of the night?

I wondered if her mom and dad were some kind of religious freaks, the kind who didn't let her talk to boys on the phone. Was that why she only went out on Sunday mornings? Did they think Pearl was taking her to church?

Wouldn't that be perfect? If rehearsal was our church, Minerva was the high priestess.

I skidded one fingernail down my lowest string, making the sound of a tiny jet plane crashing to the ground. I was always edgy calling a girl the first time, even a normal girl with normal parents. Even one who'd never screamed holy sacraments while I played guitar.

Minerva had handed me her number when no one else was looking, had whispered her instructions. She knew this was a bad idea, and I knew too—the sort of thing that broke up bands. The badness of it was all over me in the darkness, hovering an inch from my skin, like a cloud of mosquitoes getting ready to bite.

And one A.M., which had seemed, like, *forever* away fifteen minutes ago, was almost here. . . .

I placed the Strat on the kitchen table, took the phone from the wall, and pulled out the number she'd given me. Her handwriting was sloppy, almost as bad as Zahler's, the paper crumpled from ten days in my pocket, crammed against keys and coins and guitar picks.

I dialed slowly, telling myself it didn't really count until I pressed the last digit. After all, I'd gone this far a few other nights, only to choke.

But this time, five seconds before the hour, I finished the spell.

She picked up before it even rang.

"Ooh, no dial tone," she said softly, which didn't make any sense at first.

"Minerva?"

"You finally did it, Mozzy," she whispered.

I licked my lips, which felt as dry and rough as burnt toast. "Yeah, I did."

"I've been sitting here waiting, ten nights in a row."

"Oh. Sorry it took so long." I found myself whispering back at her, even though my parents' room was at the other end of the apartment.

"I've been really good every night, picking up exactly at one." She sighed. "And every time . . . *buzzzz*."

"Oh, a dial tone." I cleared my throat, not sure what to say.

"A dial tone instead of you," she said, her voice slipping out of its whisper. Minerva talked like she sang, low and growly, a tone that penetrated the rumble of the fridge and the whir of cars down on the street.

I reached over to the Strat and plucked an open string. "Doesn't your phone have a ringer?"

"Yes, it has a ringer." I heard a distant clank on her end, like she'd kicked something. "But it rings in my parents' room and downstairs too. Only Pearl and Luz are sup-posed to know this number."

"That sucks." I wondered who Luz was. Another friend?

"And the worst thing is, Luz took all my numbers away."

"Took your numbers? You mean she stole your address book?"

Minerva giggled. "No, silly Moz. The little buttons with numbers. There's no way for me to dial out."

"Crap. Really?" What was the *deal* with her parents? Or Luz, whoever she was?

"Smelly phone." Another soft *clank.* "So I've been sitting here waiting every night, hoping you would call. Wanting you to, but all nervous in case a little ring squirted out. Picking up exactly at one, and all I get is *buzzzz* . . . like some horrible bee."

"Sorry about that." I shifted my weight on the kitchen chair, remembering staring at my own phone at one o'clock, wishing I'd had the guts to call. "Well, I'm talking to you now."

"Mmm. It's yummy too. We finally get to talk with no one else around."

"Yeah, it's cool." My throat was dry, and the badness was clinging to my skin now, like an itch all over me. It reminded me of hiding in the closet when I was little, excited but scared that someone would open the door. "So, can I ask you something, Min?"

"Sure. You get to ask me anything, now that no one's listening."

"Um, yeah." The fridge turned itself off, leaving me in sudden silence. My voice dropped as I asked, "So, when you and Pearl leave early? You're not really going to Spanish lessons, are you?"

She giggled softly. "No. We have to get back before Luz knows I'm gone."

"Oh. Luz again." I noticed that my right hand was all twisted up in the phone cord, my fingers strangled white and bloodless. I started to unwind it. "But that's, like, a Spanish name, right?"

"It means *light*. 'Let there be Luz.'"

"So she's your Spanish teacher." Or whatever.

"*Sí. Y un problema grande.*"

Even I could figure out that bit of Spanish. Luz was a big problem. But what *was* she? A nanny? Some sort of religious homeschooling tutor? A shrink?

"What are you thinking?"

I shifted around on my chair, skin itching again. "I'm wondering about you."

"Mmm," she purred. "If I'm crazy? If I'm *bad*?"

I swallowed. "No. But I don't really know you, outside of practice."

"I think you do know me, Mozzy. That's why I wanted you to call. Because you know things."

"Um, I do?"

"Sure. Just close your eyes."

I did, and she started humming, the sound barely carrying over the wires. I imagined her singing in the practice room, drawing me into her slipstream as we played. Fragments of her songs echoed in my head. It felt like I was being pulled somewhere.

She stopped humming, but her breathing still reached my ears.

"Where do you get those words, Min? For our songs?"

She laughed softly. "From underneath."

"Like, from underneath your conscious mind or something?"

"No, silly," she whispered. "Underneath my *house*."

"Uh, really?" With my eyes closed, she seemed so close, like she was whispering in my ear. "You write in your basement?"

"I did at first, back when they let me go down there. I had fevers and could feel something under the house. Something rumbling."

"Yeah." I nodded. "I know what you mean. I can feel something kind of . . . underneath us when you sing."

"Something in the ground." She was breathing harder now. "You *do* know things."

"Sometimes I feel like my music's just buzzing around in the air. But you pull it down, tie it to something that's real."

"Mmm. It's realer than you think." She breathed slowly for a while, and I just listened until she said, "Do you want more, Moz?"

I swallowed. "How do you mean?"

"Do . . . you . . . want . . . more? I can give you the rest of it. You're only tasting a little tiny fraction."

I opened my eyes. The darkness in the kitchen was suddenly sharp. "A fraction of what?"

"Of what I have. Come over, and I'll show you."

The table seemed to tremble: my heart beating in my fingertips. "Come over . . . now?"

"Yes, Mozzy. Come rescue me and Zombie."

"Um . . . Zombie?"

"He's my undead slave."

I swallowed. "Yeah?"

She let out a giggle, just above a whisper. "And his breath smells like cat food."

"Oh." I let out a slow breath. "Zombie has whiskers too, doesn't he?"

"Yeah, and he also knows things. But . . . Moz?"

"What?"

"I'm *hungry*."

I laughed. She was so skinny, I never thought of Minerva getting hungry. She ate a lot of beef jerky at rehearsal, but I figured that was for her voice or something.

"You want to go and get something? I'll wait." I wanted to sit there in silence for a minute or two, just to recover. Just to scratch myself all over.

"Can't."

"Why not?"

"See, here's the thing. The door of my room has this smelly lock. On the outside."

"Really?" I blinked. "Like, your parents keep you locked in at night?"

"Daytime too. Because I was sick before."

I closed my eyes again. A new layer of hovering badness sprang up all around me, filling the room with a buzzing sound.

"That's why you have to come rescue me," she said. "Come let me out and I'll show you everything."

I bit my lip. "But you live in . . . Brooklyn, right?"

She groaned. "Don't be lame. Just take the F train. Half an hour."

Just half an hour. Plus however long it took the train to come, maybe an hour total. Not forever; I wasn't afraid of the subways yet.

And if I didn't go see her, how long would it take to fall asleep in my room all alone? A thousand hours, at least.

Every time I'd watched her sing, her songs moving through my hands as I played, I'd gone to bed that night with her cries still echoing in my brain. Every time, I'd imagined a thousand ways of following her back to Brooklyn, and now she was inviting me.

If I said no, this itch would never leave my skin.

"Everyone's asleep here," she was saying. "And I can show you where my music comes from."

"Okay, Min. I'll come." I stood up, like I was heading out the door right then, but my head started to spin. I sat back down. "But how are you going to get out?"

"You're going to rescue me. It's easy. Pearl does it all the time."

"Um, am I supposed to climb up to your window or something?"

"No, silly. Just walk up the stairs." She giggled. "But first, you have to find the magic key. . . ."

16. LOVE BITES

-MINERVA-

Mozzy was taking for*ever*.

I was dressed up so pretty, it was killing me just sitting here at my desk, staring at myself in the mirror. Zombie was pacing, knowing from the tinkle of my earrings that we were going out.

"Not long now," I said softly. My stomach rumbled.

The thought of Moz coming over had changed the balance inside me—the hungry thing had woken up, stirred from the sleep Luz had forced upon it. I'd already chewed through all my emergency beef jerky, trying not to think of the way he smelled. So yummy and intense.

I took a bite of pork rind, letting its unctuous texture coat my mouth. Zombie wandered over and *mur-row*ed, so I gave him my fingers to lick.

"You can go play with your little friends soon."

I looked at the clock: after two. Smelly Moz. What if he'd chickened out? I wanted to get closer to the earth. Singing felt wonderful, but I needed to feel the dirt under my fingernails, to smell and taste the things down there.

I needed to learn more, to put flesh on the words in my notebooks.

My stomach rumbled again, and I felt funny in a way I hadn't for a while. Like before Luz came along—kind of . . . inhuman. That wasn't good.

Mustn't eat Mozzy, I thought, and peeled a clove of garlic. It was fresh, the way Luz said was best, the papery skin still flecked with purple. The clove split between my teeth, sharp and hot as fresh chicken blood. My next breath sucked the flavor into my lungs, and my nerves steadied.

"That'll teach you," I whispered to the hungry thing inside me, then took a swig from the little bottle of tequila Pearl had smuggled in, swishing it around my mouth. Didn't want to taste funny for Moz.

In the clarity of my garlic buzz, I took off my dark glasses and stared into the mirror, wondering in which direction I was headed tonight.

Some things, like Luz's teas and tinctures, made me better, more boring and sensible. Others, like singing with Pearl's band, brought out the magnificent beast inside me and summoned the big things underground. It was the same old balancing act—how far to go with boys, with booze, with dangerous places—but magnified until the whole earth shook.

I wasn't sure yet which way Moz was going to take me. I knew that both halves of me wanted badly to take him under the ground, but I was pretty certain they had different ideas about what to *do* with him down there.

I gnashed another clove of garlic, swilled another shot of tequila, just in case.

The stairs creaked. . . . *Moz.*

I stood up, crossed to the door, and pressed my ear against it. He was down at the very bottom, making his slow way up. My thirsty hearing swept through the house: Max's heart beating in the room next door, Daddy snoring low and even, no pages turning from my mother reading late in bed. Silence, except for the slow, cautious feet creeping up the stairs, the occasional crinkle of the house cooling down.

Zombie did figure eights around my feet.

"No purring," I hissed. "Mommy's listening."

I slid my cheek along the door, put my nose up to the crack. Sniffed.

Moz was still too far downstairs to smell. I counted my own heartbeats to a thousand, spread my palms out on the door, pressed my anxious weight against it, groaning. Even shiny Pearl didn't climb the stairs this slowly.

Finally he reached the top floor and I caught his scent, nervous and unsure.

And *hungry*. I smiled.

He turned the hasp free, the faint vibrations traveling through wood and into my thirsty skin. The metal bolt slid across.

I took a step back, dizzy. Being rescued was *much* better when it was Mozzy doing it.

The door opened the tiniest crack.

"Min?" On a little puff of air, smelling of yummy Moz breath.

I didn't answer, just stood there behind the door, Zombie warm against my ankle. Everything was tingling.

The door pushed open another nervous inch. "Minerva?"

"Mozzzz," I buzzed.

"Jesus." His face peeked through, shiny in the candle-light, expressions squirming across it.

I put my hand out to stroke his cheek. Brought it back and licked my fingers. Nervous-tasting, but Mozzy.

He pushed through into my room, leaned back to softly shut the door. Closed his eyes. "Jesus, Min. Those are some creaky-ass stairs."

I giggled, slipping a hand through the unzipped top of his jacket, pressing my palm against his chest. His heart was pounding deliciously. If he hadn't been breathing so hard, I could have heard the warm blood rushing through his veins.

Don't think naughty thoughts, I scolded myself.

"You made it, though."

His eyes opened, a relieved grin making his face shimmer. "Yeah."

I pulled my hand back from the hothouse of his jacket, pressed fingers against the door. "No one heard you. Relax."

Mozzy nodded but didn't relax at all. His expression was so naked, tension transforming into excitement, his own hunger rumbling. His eyes rolled across my tight black dress and boots, growing wider, about to burst.

"You're all dressed up."

I smiled. "Well, we're going somewhere special, you know."

"Oh." He glanced down at himself: T-shirt under leather jacket, jeans. "I didn't think . . . I mean, it's two in the morning."

"Shush, Moz. You look delicious." I bent down and swept up Zombie. "Come on. Time for the creaky-ass stairs again."

"Okay . . ." He frowned. "The cat's coming?"

I sighed. Why was everyone always giving Zombie funny looks? He never stuck his nose into *their* business. Zombie had things to do, places to be. Zombie needed rescuing too. And he knew things.

If he could talk, Zombie would've told us what was coming.

But all I said was, "He's got a date with a tree."

"Oh, sure." Moz smiled and softly opened the door.

With no smelly sun wrecking everything, outside was much better.

In beautiful soft starlight, I could see the dead leaves scattered on the ground, the spiderwebs sparkling in the grass, captured insects making them dance. The unburnt air was moist, thick with scents and sounds.

I put Zombie down, watched him slip in among the glistening piles of plastic bags. Those garbage mountains were alive in the darkness, the steady breeze carrying messages from deep inside.

I put my hand against one, felt its cool slickness. It had a scent like my room, my bedclothes, like something that Zombie and I shared. Little tremblings were rampant in the pile's depths, answering my presence.

"Family," I murmured, rustles of understanding moving through me.

"Um, yeah. Your family," Moz whispered, glancing nervously back at my house, as if the porch light was about to pop on, Daddy emerging with a shotgun. "Where're we going anyway?"

His anxious smell made hunger bubble up inside me again, and I wished I'd brought more garlic. I turned and took his hand, pulling him down the street. "This way. I'm taking you where I can show you things."

"Oh, okay." He followed in a silent trance, obedient in my grasp. As we neared the first intersection, though, my steps slowed. Everything was muddled.

I'd grown up on this street, but somehow things had changed. A new world had descended on my old neighborhood—a terrain of smells, skittering sounds, and territorial boundaries. The old maps inside my head had crumbled over the last two months, turning the street signs into gibberish.

"Which way's the F stop, Moz?"

"We're going somewhere by *subway*? It's, like, two-thirty, Min!"

I frowned. "We're not getting on a train. Just need to remember." I squeezed his hand, looking up into his bulging, thirsty eyes. "I've been locked up for a while, you know."

"Oh, right." His throat rippled with a swallow. "Sure. It's back this way."

I followed him, familiar landmarks seething with the new reality—the vacant lot one block over, alive now with shivering forms; my old preschool, playground swings creaking in the breeze; the best Lebanese restaurant in Brooklyn, its garbage smelling of rancid honey and chickpeas, trembling with movement.

Luz has been robbing me of all this, I thought. She wanted to cure me of my new senses, to lock me away from this sumptuous half-lit world. Every step I took, I was finding out more. . . . I still had enough crazy left to understand.

Moz took me to the F station down the block, and I pulled him to the lip of the stairs, breathed in the subterranean hum for a dizzy and exultant moment, like when *la musica* traveled through me. The beast rumbled, twisting happily in my guts.

"But I thought we weren't—"

"We're not taking the train," I said. "This is just a shortcut."

"A shortcut?" he said, not quite believing.

"You can only get what you want underground, Mozzy. But believe me, you'll love the way it tastes."

He blinked, then nodded. I smiled, covering my eyes as I pulled him down into the fluorescent lights, his pulse fluttering under my fingers.

Every step we took, the pull was getting stronger. Moz could sense it too, as if its influence traveled through my skin and into his, an electric current of desire. Or maybe he could smell it on me—here underground I felt myself glowing with it, the beast inside me doing back flips, screaming that it was almost loose. Whatever was down here had freed it from Luz's restraints. My tongue ran across my teeth uneasily.

Must . . . not . . . eat . . . Mozzy.

But I couldn't stop moving forward either.

Behind me Moz was panting, eyes glittering like wet glass. When I jumped down from the platform onto the empty subway tracks, he didn't say a word, just paused for a moment before following. His lips were full of blood, and I could see his heart racing in his throat. It was all I could do not to take him right there, but I knew it would only get better the farther down we went. I pulled him into the darkness of the tunnel.

Gravel crunched under our feet, and the skitters and smells of tiny things were all around us. My friends, my family.

Then a shiver traveled up into my toes . . . *danger.*

Moz pulled me to a stop. He'd felt it too. "Crap! Is that a train?"

I knelt, put one hand on a rail.

"Watch out! That's—"

"Don't be scared, Moz." I pointed with my free hand. "*That's* the electric one. This one's just for listening. . . ." The smooth, cold metal under my palm was trembling, but not with the approach of a train. Everything around us shivered: gravel, iron beams, the work lights hanging from their cords. The earth was shuddering in fear.

Calling me to the struggle—*la lucha*. Calling Moz too.

And suddenly I knew something that Luz's cures had hidden from me, something I'd only glimpsed in my songs. The thing underground, the thing that made the earth rumble, was our *enemy*.

The beast inside me had been created to fight it.

"We have to be careful. It's close."

He sucked in deep breaths through his nose. "I've heard this, Min, at practice. It's in your music."

"Clever Mozzy."

He shook his head. "But how come it has a . . . *smell*?"

I shrugged. "Because it has a body. It's real and dangerous. And I don't think we want to meet it just yet, so shush." I dragged him farther into the tunnel, toward the trail that the old enemy had left behind—the perfect place to quicken the beast inside me.

As we grew nearer, I felt the rest of Luz's restraints stripped away, the lures and tangles and spores of the beast spilling through my system. Finally I understood how it worked. Down here, the beast inside me didn't want to eat Mozzy, it wanted to spread itself.

The old enemy somehow made it . . . *horny*.

Here was the hole, chewed and broken earth, like a wound in the side of the man-made tunnel, stained with the black stuff the enemy used to melt the earth. The ancient enemy was huge, I realized now, big enough to make its own tunnels, though it loved the subway's free ride.

I dragged Moz into the gashed stone of its trail, pushed him against the crumbling edge, easily holding his shoulders in a grip he couldn't break.

His pupils were as big as starless skies. "Min . . ."

"Shhh." I put one ear against the tunnel wall and listened. . . . The enemy was drifting away, my bad hunger growing as its influence faded. My teeth wanted to pull Moz to pieces, to sate my hunger in a way no chicken blood could touch. . . .

"I need to give it to you *now*," I said.

"But what—"

"Mozzy . . ." I put my hand over his mouth. "Here's the thing: if we stand here talking, I think I'll eat you."

His eyes wide, he nodded.

Pulling away my hand, I leaned forward, my mouth covering his, and the beast exploded. It struggled to filter through my skin, trying to wring itself out every pore, squeezing itself into my sweat and spit and blood, saturating every drop of me.

Infecting Moz, injecting him.

The kiss took long seconds, and when it was over I was dripping.

I pushed myself back from Moz and stared into his glittering eyes. He was panting, beautiful, infected. Relief swept through me, and I kissed him softer this time, finally certain that he was safe. Just this once, sane had beaten crazy.

After that first kiss, the hungry beast inside me didn't want to consume this new warrior in the struggle. It was satisfied.

But me . . . I was only getting started.

17. FOREIGN OBJECTS

-PEARL-

I'd bought a new dress just for this, and nine kinds of makeup. My hair had been redone that afternoon, cut and blown and sculpted with goo. I was dripping borrowed bling and staring at my bathroom mirror, a contact lens balanced on the tip of my finger.

Color my mother ecstatic.

"You can do it, Pearl." She was hovering behind me, similarly glammed.

"That's not the question." I stared at the contact lens, which shimmered like a tiny bowl of light. A dreadful, painful glow. "The question is whether I *want* to."

"Don't be silly, darling. You said you wanted to look your best tonight."

"Mmm." Foolish words that had sent Mom into a spending rampage.

Back a million years ago when she was seventeen, she'd actually had a coming-out party, like a real old-fashioned debutante. She still had the pictures. And we'd stayed in

New York City no matter how high the garbage got, no matter how dangerous the streets—because this was where the parties were. So she probably hoped this was the beginning of a new era of Pretty Pearl, no more blue jeans or glasses or bands.

"I could just go there blind."

"Nonsense. To be truly lovely, one must make eye contact. And I don't want you stumbling all over the art."

"She's a photographer, Mom. Photos are traditionally hung on the wall; you can't stumble on them." Typical. It was my mother who always got invited to these things, but she never bothered to Google the artist. Which was lucky, I guess. A glance would have revealed who else was on the guest list tonight, giving away the real reason I wanted to go.

"Quit stalling, Pearl. I know you can do this."

"And how do you know that, Mom?"

"Because I wear contact lenses and so did your father. You've got the genes for it!"

"Great," I said. "Thanks for passing on those sticking-a-finger-in-your-eye genes to me. Not to mention the crappy-eyesight genes." I stared at the little lens gradually drying to razor-sharpness on my fingertip, imagining all my totally lateral caveman ancestors jamming rocks and sticks into their eyeballs, none of them realizing the whole thing would pay off a thousand generations later when I had to look good at an art gallery opening.

"Okay, guys, this is for you," I said, taking a breath and prying my left eye open wide. As my finger approached, the little transparent disk grew until it blotted out everything, dissolving into a fit of blinking.

"Is it in?" my mother asked.

"How the hell should I know?" I opened one eye, then the other, squinting at myself in the mirror.

Blurry Pearl, clear Pearl, blurry Pearl, clear Pearl . . .

"Hey, I think it's in."

"See?" my mother said. "That was easy as pie."

"Pi squared, maybe. Let's get going." I scooped new makeup into my brand-new handbag, its silver chain glittering softly in my blurry eye.

My mother frowned. "What about the other one?"

I alternated eyes again—blurry mother, clear mother—and shrugged. "Sorry, Mom. I don't think I've got the genes for it."

As long as I could recognize faces, the demimonde was good enough for me.

Out on the street, Elvis made a big deal about my new look, acting like he didn't recognize me, trying to get me to blush. The older I got, the more he thought his job was to make me feel ten years old. Lately, he was tragically good at it.

The weird thing was, though, by the time we arrived at the gallery, I felt twenty-five. There weren't any cameras popping as Elvis swung the limousine door open for me, but there was a guy with a clipboard and headset, other blinged-up art lovers sweeping into the entrance, their bodyguards piling up out in the street, the clink and chatter coming from the crowd inside. . . . It was almost like going onstage.

Even with everything going on, New York still had *gallery openings*. Civilization was still kicking ass, and here I was, in costume and in character. Ready to charm.

Once inside the gallery, the first trick was extricating myself from Mom. She kept showing me off to friends, all of them dutifully not recognizing me and dropping their jaws, reading from the same script as Elvis. Soon Mom was striking up conversations with strangers, dropping "my daughter" comments and clearly craving "Not your sister?" in response.

And she wonders why I don't dress up more.

Finally, though, I weaseled out of her orbit with the lame excuse of wanting to look at, you know, the *art*. Her fingers trailed on my shoulder as I slipped away, reminding everyone one more time that I was her daughter.

I made my way straight to a table full of champagne, rows and columns of it bubbling furiously, and smiled. The open bar: where else would a record company rep hang out at an art opening?

I snagged a glass and hovered near the table, keeping an eagle eye (just one) out for the face I'd downloaded that morning. My trap was finally set—I was ready. All my lines were memorized; I was dressed ravishingly and standing in the perfect spot. There was nothing more I could do but wait.

So I waited. . . .

Twenty minutes later, my enthusiasm had faded.

No record company talent scout had materialized, the glass was empty, and my feet were unhappy in their new shoes. The party buzzed around me, ignoring my little black dress and borrowed bling, like I was some kind of nonentity. Bubbles rattled unpleasantly in my head.

All my life I'd wondered how my mother's sole life

purpose could be going to parties, even while the world was crumbling around her. Finally Google had shown me the answer: her reason for existence was to get *me* into *this* party. Astor Michaels, Red Rat Records' most fawesome talent scout, was also the biggest collector of this photographer's work. He'd discovered the New Sound, signing both Zombie Phoenix and Morgan's Army—not huge, commercial bands, but gutsy bands like us.

It was a perfect match, like when Moz and I had been brought together. Surely this was fate playing with my mother's social calendar.

But as I picked up my second glass and wandered through the crowd, squinting at two hundred half-blurry faces and recognizing none of them, I started to consider an awful possibility: could fate be *messing with me*?

What if Astor Michaels was out of town? Or busy scouting bands at some undiscovered club instead of here? What if Google had lied to me? All my efforts tonight would be wasted—in fact, my mother's whole *life* would be wasted. . . .

I stood there, dizzy on my feet, staring at a half-empty glass and realizing something equally dismaying: the champagne gene was another one my mom hadn't passed on. Maybe it was my half-blurry vision or the buzz of the uncaring crowd around me, but I felt like reality was in a blender.

I had to get control.

I took a deep breath and pulled myself out of the crowd, wandering to the party's edge to look at the pictures. They were gigantic photos of the sanitation crisis: glimmering mountains of plastic bags, garbage guys on strike, lots of rats. All were dramatic and weirdly beautiful, almost life-size, as if you could walk straight into them. Which begged the question: Why would you want this stuff on your wall when it was all happening right outside?

The crowd seemed to agree. People were crowded into the middle of the room, shrinking from the images of decomposition. Only a few of us hovered at the fringes of the party, sullen and extraneous, like sophomore guys at the senior prom.

Poor art lovers, I thought, and then, in a fit of champagne-stoked genius, I realized where Astor Michaels had been hiding.

He wasn't here for the prom; he was here for the art. He was one of the sophomores.

I started to circle the room, ignoring the crowd in the middle this time, the ones who looked well connected and happy and cool. I looked for the lonely guys, the losers.

Halfway around, I spotted him out of the corner of my eye—my good eye, luckily. He was ogling a vast photo of a shrine built by sanitation workers out in the Bronx: praying hands and crosses and skulls (*again!*) all jumbled up to provide protection on their route.

I took a deep drink of champagne to steady myself, my lines beginning to tumble through my head.

"What am I listening to? Oh, just this lateral new band."

My fingers fumbled with the sticky clasp of my new handbag, scrambling around inside until they found my music player at the very bottom. Its earphones were non-helpfully tangled with makeup and hair goo and a million other things I never normally carried. After long seconds of unwinding, I managed to drag the player out and get the phones into my ears. But where was my neck strap? I peered down into the bottomless handbag in horror, realizing I hadn't brought it.

I flashed back to my hours spent at the Apple store looking for just the right strap: sleek black leather with a shiny steel USB connector. I could see it in my mind's eye, still in its packaging, sitting on my bed with all the other *crap*.

And of course this stupid cocktail dress, like all stupid cocktail dresses, had no pockets. It would look way too obvious just carrying the music player in my hand, and a pair of earphones snaking out from my handbag wasn't going to make me look like the hip young trendsetter I was supposed to be. The kind who says things like . . .

"No, they're not signed. Everyone just knows *about them."*

I squeezed my eyes shut, trying to think.

There was only one place to put it.

I took a gulp of champagne, switched the music player on, and dropped it down my cleavage. It fit perfectly and was kind of warm down there. *Really* warm—I looked down and realized that while scrabbling in my handbag I'd locked the screen backlight on.

Framed by the black velvet of my dress, my breasts glowed softly blue.

In my champagne haze, it was kind of cool looking. Carrying your music this way might not be the Taj Mahal of class, but it was definitely going to get the guy's attention.

I moved closer.

"What language is she singing in? I don't think it is one, really."

The player was set to shuffle our four best songs—

long, intense rants of Minerva's peppered with Moz's cleanest, simplest lines, Alana Ray shattering it all into a thousand glittering shapes, Zahler finally playing a proper bass underneath. As I drew nearer, the music began to synchronize with the bubbles in my bloodstream, my footsteps falling with the beat. I was cool and connected, seventeen and covered with bling, a record company's dream demographic in the flesh.

The world began to shift around me, just like when we played, my fingers twitching with the keyboard parts. Huge photographs rolled past my shoulder, a galaxy of rats' and cats' eyes flickering on my blurry side.

"What's their name? I don't think they have a name yet, actually. . . ."

By the time I walked up beside Astor Michaels, swirling one last smidgen of champagne in the bottom of my glass, I was cool and predatory and confident, the embodiment of our music.

He turned and looked at me, his eyes following the white cords from my ears down into my glowing cleavage. His gaze flashed a little, reflecting the soft blue light.

Then Astor Michaels smiled at me, and his teeth were pointy, a hundred times sharper than Minerva's. . . .

All my lines flew from my head, and I pulled my earphones out, pushing them toward him with quivering hands.

"You've got to listen, man," I said. "This shit is paranormal."

PART IV

THE DEAL

About seven hundred years ago, the disease that fin-ished the Roman Empire returned.

Humanity was already in a bad way. China had just suf-fered a brutal civil war, Europe had endured a destructive famine, and the Little Ice Age was descending. Across the world, temperatures dropped, crops failed, and whole countries fell into poverty. Wars were sparked by what little wealth remained.

Then a relentless and deadly plague appeared in Asia. In some parts of China, nineteen out of every twenty people perished. The disease was carried to Europe and the Middle East, where it killed a third of the population. The most intense part of the outbreak lasted only five years, but worldwide it left 100 million dead.

Historians once assumed that the Black Death was bubonic plague, a bacterium spread by rats. But that never quite added up: too many people died too quickly. According to some, it might have been a new form of anthrax transmitted from animals to humans. Others believe that an Ebola-like virus suddenly evolved to become airborne, spreading across the world via handshakes and coughs, then disappeared.

But what was the Black Death really, and how did it come and go so quickly?

Keep your ears open, and you'll find out.

NIGHT MAYOR TAPES:

313–314

18. ANONYMOUS 4

-ZAHLER-

The offices of Red Rat Records were fawesome.

Maybe they weren't the biggest label in the world—Red Rat was only an independent—but they had an old town house in the East Twenties all to themselves. Astor Michaels took us inside, saying that the richest family in New York City had once lived there. The ground floor was still fitted out like a money-counting room: antique brass bars guarding the receptionist's desk, the doors solid oak, thick as dictionaries.

There were a bunch of kids waiting in line to deliver CDs and press packets by hand, most of them in full stage dress: black eyeliner and fingernails, ripped clothes and Mohawks. All of them were trying to look fool, but they stared wide-eyed as the five of us were ushered past the brass bars and inside. I got a weird jolt, thinking, *We're rock stars, and they're not.*

I'd always known Pearl would take us

places, but I hadn't thought it would be this fast. I didn't feel ready for it, especially since I'd only been playing my new instrument a week.

But Pearl was unstoppable. She'd even managed some kind of deal with Minerva's parents, getting her into Manhattan on a workday. The two of them were supposedly out buying Minerva new clothes, something about her birthday coming up.

We tromped downstairs to the basement, where Astor Michaels's personal office occupied the steel cube of an old walk-in safe, lit only by the flickering glow of a computer screen. It was as big as a one-car garage, the walls lined with rows of safe-deposit boxes. The foot-thick metal door looked too heavy to move—I hoped it was anyway. If anyone shut it, I would've started screaming.

Huge photographs hung from the walls, artsy pictures of garbage-strewn alleys, gushing black water, and rats.

Yes: rats. And that wasn't the weirdest thing about Astor Michaels.

Our new rep licked his lips a lot, and when he smiled, his teeth never showed. He kept his sunglasses on until we got down into the darkness, and once he took them off, I wished he'd put them back on again. His eyes were way too wide and spent a lot of time lingering on the three girls, especially Minerva.

It was creepy, but I guess when you're a record company rep, you get to ogle all the girls you want. And anyway, it didn't matter whether I liked the guy or not. We were *signed*.

Well, almost. Pearl said her lawyer was still going over

the contract. That's right—she said "my lawyer," the way she'd say "my gardener" or "my driver" or "my house in Connecticut." Like a lawyer was something you kept in a drawer along with the double-A batteries and spare apartment keys.

"In a few minutes, we'll all go upstairs," Astor Michaels said. "Marketing is dying to meet you. They love the music, of course, but they want to make sure you really have it."

What's "it"? I almost asked. But I figured that if you did have it, you probably didn't need to ask what it was, which meant I didn't, so I should just shut up.

"Should we have dressed up for this?" Pearl asked, which didn't make any sense because she looked fexcellent in her tight black dress, a thin choker of diamonds around her neck. The only bad thing was that her glasses were missing, which made her look less smart and in charge.

Still, she looked amazing.

Astor Michaels waved a hand. "Just be yourselves."

What if myself happens to be a big sweaty ball of nerves today? I wanted to ask, but that also didn't sound like a very "it" thing to say.

We went upstairs, where a bunch of people with six-hundred-dollar haircuts sat around a conference table shaped like a long, curvy swimming pool. Pearl took charge, of course. She talked about our "influences," naming a bunch of bands I'd never heard of except for seeing their CDs on Pearl's bed.

Minerva sat at the head of the table, shimmering,

sucking up all the compliments that came her way. She obviously had it—even I could see that now, reflected in the marketing people's gazes. Ever since Minerva and Moz had secretly hooked up, her junkie vibe was slowly changing into something else—whether less creepy or more, I couldn't tell.

But the haircuts ate it up.

Moz also seemed to make an impression on them, like he had it too. As if Minerva had given it to him. He was much more intense these days, his eyes radiating confidence and a new kind of hungriness that I couldn't understand.

That was the weird thing: as Minerva got less junkie-like, she seemed to push Moz in the opposite direction, so we were really only breaking even.

Me and Alana Ray stayed quiet, like a rhythm section should. I was a bass player now, after all, and we don't say too much.

After a while we headed back down to the safe, leaving the haircuts upstairs to talk about us. Astor Michaels said we'd done a good job, then gave us some fexcellent news.

"We want you to play a showcase. Four Red Rat bands in a little club we're renting." He licked his lips. "In two weeks . . . I hope that's not too soon."

"Soon is good," Pearl said, which was probably the smart thing to say, but a wave of panic was rolling through me. Two more Sunday rehearsals with my new instrument didn't seem like enough. I practiced hours every day, of course, but that was nothing like playing with the whole band. Those big bass strings still felt clumsy under my fingers, like playing with gloves on.

"There's one issue, though," Astor Michaels was saying. "We're printing the posters tomorrow. Taking out ads as well."

"Oh, crap." Pearl cleared her throat. "And we don't have a name yet."

"We've been meaning to come up with one," I blurted. "But there hasn't been time."

"Can't agree on anything," Moz growled.

Pearl shifted uncomfortably next to me on Astor Michaels's big leather couch. "Can't we just be 'Special Guests' or something?"

He shook his head, lips parting, a little glimpse of teeth slipping into view. "Posters and ads cost money, Pearl. That money's wasted if your name is missing."

"Yeah, I guess so." She looked around at us.

"Here's what we'll do," Astor Michaels said. "I'll leave you five to discuss this while I go and have lunch. When I come back in an hour, you give me a name you all agree on. Not a list, not suggestions or ideas: one name. Either it'll be perfect or it won't be."

Pearl swallowed. "So what if it's not?"

He shrugged. "Then the deal's off."

"What?" Pearl said, eyes widening. "No showcase?"

"No nothing." Astor Michaels stood and headed out. "If you five can't agree on a name, then how are you supposed to tour together? How are you supposed to make records? How can Red Rat commit to you for five years if you can't commit to one simple name?" He stood in the doorway, slipping sunglasses over his laughing, too-wide eyes. "So unless you agree on something perfect, the whole deal's off."

"But . . . not really," Pearl said. "Really?"

"Really. You have an hour." Astor Michaels looked at his watch. "How's that for motivation?"

We sat there in silence for a moment, the blown-up photos of rats staring down at us. The room was full of guilt, like we'd all committed some terrible crime together.

"Was that meant ironically?" Alana Ray asked.

"Um . . . I don't think so," Pearl said.

"Crap," Moz said. "What are we going to do?"

Pearl turned to me and Moz, suddenly angry. "I *knew* we should have figured this out when it was just us three, in that first rehearsal. Now it's all *complicated*!"

"Hey, man," I said, holding up my hands. "That's the day I said we should call ourselves the B-Sections. Why don't we go with that?"

Moz and Pearl just stared at me.

"What?" I said. "Don't you remember? B-Sections?"

Pearl glanced at Moz, then turned to me. "Yeah, I remember. But I didn't want to be the one to explain that band names based on musical terms—the F-Sharps, the Overtones, the Tapeloops—are in fact the lamest. Thing. Ever."

Moz shrugged. "I just thought you were kidding, Zahler. I mean, for one thing, being plural is stupid."

I frowned. "Being what?"

"Plural. With an *s* at the end. Makes us sound like some fifties band, like the Rockettes or something."

Minerva let out a giggle. "The Rockettes are dancers, Moz. They have long, tasty legs."

Okay, maybe she wasn't totally normal yet.

"Whatever," Moz said. "I don't want to be a plural band. Because if we're the B-Sections, then what's one of us? *A B-Section*? 'Hello, I am a B-Section. Together, me and my friends are many B-Sections.'"

Minerva giggled again, and I said, "You know, Moz, anything sounds retarded if you say it a bunch of times in a row. So what's your great idea?"

"I don't know. A 'The' in front is cool, as long as the next word isn't plural." He kicked Astor Michaels's desk in front of him. "Like, the Desk."

"*The Desk*?" I groaned. "Now that's just a genius band name, Moz. That's much better than the B-Sections. Let's go upstairs and tell them we want to be the Desk."

Moz rolled his eyes. "It was just an example, Zahler."

I sank back into the big leather couch. I could see how this was going to go. It was that old classic, the Moz Veto. Like whenever we're trying to figure out what movie to see, Moz never suggests anything, so I have to keep coming up with suggestions while he goes, "No," "Not interested," "That sucks," "Seen it," "Subtitles are lame. . . ."

Pearl leaned forward. "Okay, guys, we don't have to panic about this."

"Panic!" I said. "We could be the Panic!"

"I'd rather be the Desk," Moz said quietly.

"Hang *on*!" Pearl said. "One idea at a time. A couple of weeks ago, I thought of something."

Moz swung his veto gaze toward her. "What?"

"How about Crazy Versus Sane?"

"Pearl, darling," Minerva said. "Don't you think that's kind of . . . pointed?" She looked at Alana Ray, not noticing that everyone else was looking at her.

"It's not about *us*," Pearl said. "It's about all the weird stuff going on. Like the black water, the sanitation crisis, the crime wave. Like that crazy woman who dropped the Stratocaster on me and Moz . . . That's how this band got started."

"I don't know," Moz said. "Crazy Versus Sane. Sounds kind of artsy-fartsy to me."

Score another one for the Moz Veto.

I tried to think, random words and phrases spilling through my head, but Pearl had been right. Band names only got harder the longer you waited to pick one. The deeper the music got into your brain, the more impossible it became to describe it in two or three words.

The silence was broken by the shriek of some metal band's demo tape echoing out of another scout's office. The steel walls of the safe seemed to be closing in, the air growing stale. I imagined Astor Michaels shutting the door, giving us until we ran out of oxygen to come up with a name.

I thought of the growling, thumping rehearsal building on Sixteenth Street and wondered if all the bands in there had names. How many bands were there in the whole world? Thousands? Millions?

Looking up at the ranks of safe-deposit boxes surrounding us, I wondered if we should all just get numbers.

"Why don't we just pick something simple?" I said. "Like . . . Eleven?"

"Eleven?" Moz said. "That's great, Zahler. But it's no 'the Desk.'"

Minerva sighed. "That's the problem with Crazy Versus Sane: it's false advertising, seeing as how we're kind of short on sane."

"What's not sane is making us choose a name this way," Pearl said, glaring up at the rat photos.

"Is this sort of ultimatum normal for record companies?" Alana Ray asked.

"No. It's totally *para*normal," I said.

Pearl's eyes lit up. "Hey, Zahler, maybe that's it. We should call ourselves the Paranormals!"

"Plural," Moz said. "Do you guys not *get* the plural thing?"

"Whatever," Pearl said. "Paranormal? *The* Paranormal, if you want to be all *the* about everything."

"*Paranormal* can mean two things," Alana Ray said.

We all looked at her. Those rare times Alana Ray actually said something, everybody else listened.

"*Para* can mean *beside*," she continued. "Like paralegals and paramedics, who work beside lawyers and doctors. But it can also mean *against*. Like a parasol is against the sun and a paradox against the normal way of thinking."

I blinked. That was just about the most words Alana Ray had said in a row since that first rehearsal. And like everything she said, it was very weird and kind of smart.

Maybe Paranormal *was* the right name for us.

Pearl frowned. "So what's a parachute against?"

Alana Ray's eyebrows twitched. "The chute of gravity."

"Gravity sucks," I said softly.

"So if we go with Paranormal," Alana Ray said, "we should figure out whether we are *beside* normal or *against* it. Names are important. That's why I ask you all to call me by my whole first name."

"Hey, I just thought Ray was your last name," Moz said, then frowned. "What *is* your last name anyway?"

I held my breath. With Alana Ray, asking her last name was practically a personal question. But after a few seconds, she said, "I don't have a real last name." She didn't continue right away, her hands flickering nervously.

"How do you mean?" Pearl asked.

"At my school, they gave us new last names, ones that anyone could spell. That way, when we told our names to people, no one would ever ask us to spell them. It was to save us from embarrassment."

"You have trouble spelling?" Pearl asked. "Like, dyslexia?"

"Dyslexia," Alana Ray answered. "D-y-s-l-e-x-i-a. Dyslexia."

"Dude," I said. "I couldn't spell that."

She smiled at me. "Only some of us had trouble spelling. But they renamed us all."

"Maybe it doesn't matter," Minerva said softly, and everyone turned toward her. "As long as the music's good, people will think the name's brilliant too. Even if it's just some random word."

Moz nodded. "Yeah, the Beatles had a pretty stupid name, if you think about it. Didn't hurt them much."

"Dude!" My jaw dropped open. "They did *not* have a stupid name! It's a classic!"

"It's lame," Minerva said. "*Beatles*, like the insect, except spelled like *beat*, because it's music?"

Pearl cleared her throat. "Had to do with Buddy Holly and the Crickets, actually."

"Whatever," Minerva said. "It's a really pathetic pun. *And* it's plural." She smiled at Moz.

"Whoa . . . really?" I blinked. But they were right: *beetle* didn't have an *a* in it. They'd spelled it wrong.

Moz and Minerva were laughing at me, and he said, "You never noticed that?"

I shrugged. "I just figured they spelled it that way in England. I mean, I read this English book once, and all kinds of stuff was spelled wrong."

Now *everyone* was laughing at me, but I was thinking maybe Minerva was right. Maybe it didn't matter what we called ourselves: the Paranormals, the F-Sharps, or even the Desk. Maybe the music would grow around the name, whatever it was.

But we kept arguing, of course.

When Astor Michaels came back expecting an answer, Pearl pulled out her phone. "It's only been forty minutes! You said an hour."

He snorted. "I've got work to do. So what do we call this band?"

We all froze. We'd come up with about ten thousand ideas, but nobody could agree on a single one. Suddenly I couldn't remember any of them.

"Come on!" Astor Michaels snapped his fingers. "It's do-or-die time. Are we in business or not?"

Naturally, everyone looked at Pearl.

"Um . . ." The silence stretched out. "The, uh, Panics?"

"The Panic," Moz corrected. "Singular."

Astor Michaels considered this for a moment, then burst out laughing. "You'd be amazed how many people come up with that."

"With what?" Pearl said.

"Panic. Whenever I give bands the Name Ultimatum, they always wind up calling themselves something like the Panic, the Freakout, or even How the Hell Should We Know?" He laughed again, his teeth flashing in the semi-darkness.

"So . . . you don't like it?" Pearl asked softly.

"It's crap," he chuckled. "Sound like a bunch of eighties wannabes."

No one else was asking, so I did: "Does this mean we're dumped?"

He snorted. "Don't be silly. Just trying to motivate you and have a little fun. Lighten up, guys."

Minerva was giggling, but the rest of us were ready to kill him.

Astor Michaels sat down behind his desk, his smile finally showing all his teeth, a row of white razors in the darkness. "Special Guests it is!"

19. THE IMPRESSIONS

-ALANA RAY-

When the doorman heard our names, he didn't bother to check the list or use his headset. He didn't even meet our eyes, just waved us in.

Pearl and I walked straight past the line of people waiting to have their IDs checked, to be patted down and metal-detected, to pay forty dollars (a thousand dollars for every twenty-five people) to get in. It had all happened just as Astor Michaels had promised. We were underdressed, unpaying, and in Pearl's case underage, but we were getting in to see Morgan's Army.

"Our names," I said. "They worked."

"Why shouldn't they?" Pearl grinned as we followed the long, half-lit entry hall toward the lights and noise of the dance floor. "We're Red Rat talent."

"Almost Red Rat talent," I said. The "almost" part was making me twitchy. Pearl's lawyer was still arguing about details in the recording contract. She said that we would thank her for this diligence in a few years, when we were famous. I knew that details were important in legal documents, but right now the delay made the world tremble, like going out the door without a bottle of pills in my pocket.

"Whatever," Pearl said. "Our band is nine kinds of real now, Alana Ray—and real musicians don't pay to see one another play."

"We were already real," I said as we crossed the dance floor, the warm-up DJ's music making my fingers want to drum. "But you're right. Things do feel different now."

I looked at one twitching hand in front of me, mottled with the pulsing lights of the dance floor. Flashing lights usually made me feel disassociated from my own body, but tonight everything seemed very solid, very real.

Was it because I'd (almost) signed a record deal? My teachers at school always said that money, recognition, success—all the things normal people had that we didn't—weren't so important, that no one should ever use them to make us feel less than real. But it wasn't exactly true. Getting my own apartment had made me feel more real, and making money did too. The night I'd gotten my first business cards, I'd taken them out of the box one by one, reading my name again and again, even though they were all exactly the same. . . .

And now my name had gotten me to the front of a long line of people with more-expensive clothes and better haircuts, people who hadn't gone to special-needs schools. People with real last names.

I couldn't help but feel that was important.

Pearl was beaming in the dance-floor lights, as if she was feeling more real too. It was illegal for her to be here, and I'd expected the doorman to know she was only seventeen, even if Astor Michaels had said it wouldn't be a problem.

That thought made me nervous for a moment. At my school they'd taught us to obey the law. Our lives would be complicated enough without criminal records, they liked to point out. Of course, saying that people like us couldn't afford to break the law suggested that other people could. Maybe Pearl and I were more like those other people now.

My fingers started to itch and pulse, but not because of the flashing lights: I wanted to sign that record deal soon. I wanted to grab this realness and put it on paper.

As we waited for the first band to start, I looked around for Astor Michaels. He made me shiver sometimes, even though he seemed to like me, always asking my opinions about music. He also asked about my visions, which didn't upset him the way they did Minerva. Of course, I never saw Astor Michaels upset by anything. He didn't care that his smile made people nervous, and he only laughed when I told him that he moved like an insect.

I found him easier to talk to than most people, just not to look at.

"Too bad Moz couldn't make it," Pearl said. "What did he say he was doing tonight?"

"He didn't," I answered, though I had guesses in my head.

Moz was different now. In the last month he'd started borrowing things from the rest of us—Astor Michaels's smile, my twitchiness, Minerva's dark glasses—as if he wanted to start over.

He and Minerva whispered when Pearl wasn't looking, and the two sent messages to each other while we played. When my visions were strong enough, I could see their connection: luminous filaments reaching up from Minerva's song to Moz's fluttering notes, pulling them down toward the seething shapes beneath the floor.

I tried not to watch. Moz still paid me and said he would keep paying until Red Rat Records had actually given us money. He had never broken his promises to me, so I didn't want to tell my guesses to Pearl.

And I didn't want to make her sad tonight, because it was nice of her to have asked me along to see her favorite band.

The opening act had just been signed by Astor Michaels—like us, except for our "almost." But they already had a name. *Toxoplasma* was stenciled on their amps.

"What does that word mean?" I asked Pearl.

"Don't know." She shrugged. "Don't quite get it."

Neither did I, but I also didn't understand why Zahler never used his first name, or why Moz had started saying "Min" instead of "Minerva," or why no one ever called Astor Michaels anything but "Astor Michaels." Names could be tricky.

After his little joke, Astor Michaels had said it didn't matter what we called ourselves, that our real audience would find us by smell, but that sounded unlikely to me. I hoped we would come up with our own name soon. I didn't want one tacked onto us, like "Jones" had been to me.

"How did Morgan's Army get their name?" I asked. "Did Astor Michaels give it to them?"

"No." Pearl shrugged. "They're named after somebody called Morgan."

"Their singer?"

She shook her head. "No. Her name's Abril Johnson. There are a lot of rumors about who Morgan is, but nobody knows for sure."

I sighed. Maybe Zahler was right, and bands should just have numbers.

Toxoplasma was four brothers covered with tattoos. I liked the singer's voice—velvet and lazy, smoothing the words out like a hand across a bedspread. But the other three were brutally efficient, like people cooking on TV, chopping things apart in a hurry. They wore dark glasses and scattered the music into little pieces. I wondered how one brother could be so different from the others.

When their first song was done, I felt myself shiver—Astor Michaels was hovering behind us in the crowd. Pearl saw me glance back at him and turned and smiled. He handed her a glass of champagne.

That was illegal, but I didn't worry. Here in the flashing lights, the law felt less real.

"So what do you think of Toxoplasma?" he asked.

"Too thrashy for me," Pearl said.

I nodded. "I think three insects is too many for one band."

Astor Michaels laughed and his hand touched my shoulder. "Or maybe too few."

I pulled away a little as the second song began; I don't like people touching me. That makes it hard to go to clubs sometimes, but it's always important to see what new music people are inventing.

"Just think," he said. "In a week you'll be playing in front of a crowd as big as this one. Bigger."

Pearl's smile widened, and I could tell she was feeling realer by the minute. I turned to watch the audience. It wasn't like when I played in Times Square, where people could come and go as they pleased, some watching intently, some throwing money, others just passing by. Everyone here was focused on the band, judging them, waiting to be impressed, demanding to be energized. These weren't a bunch of tourists already wide-eyed just from being in New York.

Toxoplasma was making an impression. Rivulets of people were streaming forward, pressing toward the stage, dancing with the same chopping fervor as the three insect brothers. They hadn't looked much different from the rest of the crowd until now, but suddenly they all moved like skinheads, a wiry strength playing over the surface of their bodies.

They were insects too, and my heart started beating faster, my fingers drumming. I'd never seen so many together before.

I already understood that there were different kinds of insects—Astor Michaels was very different from Minerva, after all, and I had seen many other kinds back when I'd played down in the subway—but the ones in front of the stage made me nervous in a new way.

They seemed dangerous, ready to explode.

My vision was starting to shimmer, which almost never happened with music I didn't like. But the air was rippling around Toxoplasma, like heat rising from a subway grate in winter. In front of the band they'd started moshing, which is why I always stay away from the stage. Shock waves seemed to travel from their slamming bodies outward through the crowd, their twitches spreading like a fever across the club.

"Mmm. Smell that," Astor Michaels said, tipping back his head with closed eyes. "I should have called *these* guys the Panic." He giggled, still amused by his little joke on us.

I shivered, blinked my eyes three times. "I don't like this band. They're *against* normal, not beside it."

"They won't last long anyway," he said. "Maybe a couple of weeks. But they serve their purpose."

"Which is what?" Pearl asked.

He smiled, wide enough to show the Minerva-like sharpness of his teeth. "They shake things up."

I could see what he meant. The tremors spreading from the insectoid moshers were changing things inside the club, making everyone edgy. It felt like when news of some strange new attack broke once while I was playing Times Square, and the crowd seemed to turn all at once to read the words crawling by on the giant news tickers. Most of the audience didn't like Toxoplasma's music any more than Pearl and I, but it tuned their nervous systems to a higher setting. I could see it in their eyes and in the quick, anxious motions of their heads.

And I realized that Astor Michaels was good at manipulating crowds. Maybe that was what made *him* feel more real.

"The audience expects something big to happen now," I said.

"Morgan's Army," Astor Michaels answered, letting his teeth slip out again.

It worked: Morgan's Army shook things up more.

Abril Johnson held an old-fashioned microphone, clutching it in two hands like a lounge singer from long ago. Her silver evening dress glittered in the three spotlights that followed her, covering the walls and ceiling of the club with swirling pinpricks. As the band slid into their first song, she didn't make a sound. She waited for a solid minute, barely moving, like a praying mantis creeping closer in slow motion before it pounces.

Bass rumbled through us from the big Marshall stacks, setting the floor trembling. Glasses hanging over the bar began to shudder against one another—my vision already shimmering, the sound looked like snow in the air.

Then Abril Johnson started singing, low and slow. The words were barely recognizable; she was stretching and mangling them in her mouth, as if trying to twist them into something inscrutable. I closed my eyes and listened hard, trying to pick out the half-familiar, half-alien words entwined in the song.

After a moment I realized where I'd heard them before: the strange words were shaped from the same nonsense syllables that Minerva always sang. But Abril Johnson had hidden them in her drawl, interweaving them with plain English.

I shook my head. I'd always thought that Minerva's lyrics were random, made-up, just leftover ravings from her crazy days. But if she shared them with someone else . . . were they another language?

My eyes opened, and I forced myself to look at the floor. Minerva's beast was moving underneath us. Its Loch Ness loops rose and fell among the feet of the unseeing crowd—but much, much bigger than in our little practice room, as thick as the giant cables of the Brooklyn Bridge. It had been made huge by the stacks of amps and the focus of the spellbound throng, and I could see details in the creature now. There were segments along its length, like a sinuous earthworm testing the air.

"How's that for intense?" Pearl murmured, her empty champagne glass clutched tightly in both hands, echoing the singer's grip on the microphone.

"Very." Astor Michaels cocked his head. "But not as intense as you'll be, my dears. Not as authentic."

I shuddered a little, knowing what he meant. Minerva's songs were purer, unadulterated by English. Our spell would be stronger.

The beast coiled faster, and the floor of the nightclub rumbled under my feet, as if some droning bass note had found the resonant frequency of the room. I thought of how wineglasses could shatter from just the right pitch and wondered if a whole building might disintegrate when filled by some low and perfectly chosen note.

Pearl suddenly looked up, her eyes wide. "It's them!"

I followed her gaze and saw a pair of dark figures on the catwalks high above us, climbing gracefully among the rigging of stage lights and exhaust fans.

"*Those* people." Astor Michaels shook his head. "New fad: physical hacking, climbing around on roofs and airshafts and down in the subways. Can't keep them out of the clubs anymore. They especially like the New Sound."

"Angels," Pearl said.

"Assholes," Astor Michaels corrected. "Takes away from the music."

The song moved into its B section, and I dropped my gaze back to the floor, catching the last flicker of the worm disappearing. The hallucinations faded as the music grew faster, the air returning to stillness, the lyrics to ordinary English.

"She lost it," I said.

"Yeah." Pearl frowned. "Kind of blew the momentum there."

Astor Michaels nodded. "The Army never gets that transition right, for some reason. It always feels like something is about to break through." He clicked his tongue against his teeth. "But it never does."

"Are you sure you want it to?" I asked. "What if it's . . . ?" *Dangerous?* I thought of saying. *Monstrous?*

"Not commercial?" Astor Michaels laughed. "Don't worry. I've got a feeling that whatever it is, it's going to be the Next Big Thing. That's why I signed you guys."

Pearl looked annoyed. "Because we sound like Morgan's Army?"

He shook his head, pulling her empty champagne glass

from her hands. "No, you sound like yourselves. But someone has to take the New Sound to the next level. And I'm pretty sure it will be you."

He turned toward the bar to get her more champagne, and the band slowed into the A section again, as if trying to call back my visions. But they'd lost their grasp on the beast, and Abril Johnson's lyrics were just normal words now. I saw that she wasn't an insect at all; she was just imitating them, mimicking the madness she'd seen on the subway and in the streets.

I realized that Minerva was more real than her.

And I wondered: what if one day the beast under the floor turned real?

20. GRIEVOUS ANGELS

-MOZ-

The noise in my body never stopped. All night I lay awake, tissues struggling against one another, blood simmering. I could feel the beast fighting against everything I'd been, trying to remake me into something else, trying to replace me. Even my sweat raged, squeezing angrily from my pores, like a bar fight spilling out onto the street.

When I looked in the mirror, I didn't see my face. It wasn't just that I was thinner, cheekbones twisting at new angles, eyes widening—it was something deeper, pushing up from beneath my skin, remote and con-temptuous of me.

As if someone else's bones were trying to emerge.

The crazy thing was, part of me was dying to know what I was changing into. Sometimes I just wanted to get it over with, to let go and slip across the edge. I'd almost said yes tonight when Pearl had asked me to the

Morgan's Army gig, wondering what hundreds of bodies pressed in close would do to my hunger, already halfway to uncontrollable. I imagined their scents filling the air, the crowd noise mingling with the roar inside me. . . .

But not yet—not without Min. In her arms, I still felt like myself. Besides, I had plenty more to learn down here, playing for quarters underground.

A woman was watching me, listening carefully, clutching her purse with both hands. She wasn't sure yet whether to open it and reach in, risking that extra tendril of connection with the strange boy playing guitar in the subway. But she couldn't pull herself away.

Union Square Station was almost empty at this hour, my music echoing around us. The red velvet of my guitar case was spattered with silver, and more coins lay on the concrete floor. All night, people had thrown their quarters from a distance and moved on. Even through dark glasses they could see the intensity leaking out of my eyes. They could smell my hunger.

But this woman stood there, spellbound.

I'd always wondered if charisma was something in your genes, like brown eyes or big feet. Or if you learned it from the sound of applause or cameras snapping. Or if famous people glowed because I'd seen so many airbrushed pictures of them, their beauty slammed into my brain, like advertising jingles with faces.

But it had turned out that charisma was a *disease*, an infection you got from kissing the right person, a beast that lived in your blood. Connecting with this woman, drawing her closer, I could feel how I'd been magnetized.

She took a step forward, fingers tensing on the purse clasp. It popped open.

I didn't dare stare back into her spellbound eyes. There were no police down here anymore, not late at night. No one to stop me if I lost it.

Her fingers fumbled inside the purse, eyes never leaving me. She stepped closer, and a five-dollar bill fluttered down to lie among the coins. A glance at her pleading expression told me that she was paying for escape.

I stopped playing, reaching into a pocket for my plastic bag of garlic. The spell broken, the woman turned and headed for the stairs, the last strains of the Strat echoing into silence. She didn't look back, her steps growing hurried as she climbed away.

Something twisted inside me, angry at me for letting her go. I could feel it wrapped around my spine, growing stronger every day. Its tendrils stretched into my mouth, changing the way things tasted, making my teeth itch. The urge to follow the woman was so strong. . . .

I put the plastic bag to my face and breathed in the scent of fresh garlic, burning away the noises in my head, smoothing the rushing of my blood.

Min had given me the bag for emergencies, but I used it all the time now. I'd even tried to make Luz's disgusting mandrake tea, which Mom said stank up the apartment. Nothing soothed the beast like meat, though, and nothing—not even Min—tasted as good. Raw steak was best, but there was a shortage these days, the price climbing higher all the time, and plain hamburger ripped out of the plastic still fridge-cold was almost as wonderful.

I stood there inhaling garlic, listening.

Min was right—you could learn things down here. Secrets were hidden in New York's rhythms, its shifts of mood, the blood flow of its water mains. Its hissing steam pipes and the stirrings of rats and wild felines all rattled with infection, like a huge version of the illness inside my body.

My hearing could bend around corners now, sharper every day, filling my head with echoes. I could hear our music so much better, could almost *see* the beast that Minerva called to when she sang.

And I knew it was down here, somewhere . . . ready to teach me things.

A little after eleven-thirty, its scent came and found me.

The smell was drifting up from below, carried on the stale, soft breeze of passing trains. I remembered it from that first night I'd gone out to Brooklyn, when Minerva had led me down the tracks and pushed me into that broken section of tunnel; the scent made me angry and horny and hungry, all at once.

Then I heard something, a low and shuddering note, more subtle than any subway passing underfoot. Like when Minerva made the floor rumble beneath us as we played.

I scooped up the glittering change and stuffed it into my pockets, shut the Stratocaster safely into its case, snatched up the little battery-powered amplifier. By then the smell had faded, pulled away by the random winds of the subway, and I stood there uncertainly for a moment. Union Square sprawled around me, a warren of turnstiles and token booths and stairways down to half the subway lines in the city.

I half closed my eyes and walked slowly through the station, catching whiffs of perfume and piss, the bright metal tang of disinfectant, the blood-scent of rust everywhere. Finally, another dizzying gust welled up from the stairs leading down to the F train. Of course.

F *for* fool, I thought. *Or* feculent.

Downstairs the platform was empty, silent except for the skitter of rats on the tracks. The push-pull wind of distant trains stirred loose bits of paper and kept the scent swirling around me, the way the world spins when you've had too much beer.

I pulled off my dark glasses and stared into the tunnel depths.

Nothing but blackness.

But from the uptown direction came the faintest sound.

Walking toward that end of the platform, a cluster of new smells hit me: antiperspirant and freshly opened cigarettes, foot powder and the chemical sting of dry-cleaned clothing . . .

Someone was hiding behind the last steel column on the platform, breathing nervously, aware of me. Just another late-night traveler scared to be down here.

But from the tunnel beyond, the other scent was calling.

I took another step, letting the man see me. He wore a

subway worker's uniform, his eyes wide, one hand white-knuckled around a flashlight. Had he heard the beast too?

"Sorry," I said. "I'm just . . ." I shrugged tiredly, adjusting the weight of my guitar and amp. "Trying to get home."

His eyes stayed locked on mine, full of glassy terror. "You're one of them."

I realized I'd taken my sunglasses off; he could see straight through to the thing inside me. "Uh, I didn't mean to . . ."

He raised one hand to cross himself, drawing my eyes to the silver crucifix at his throat. He looked like he wanted to run, but my infection held him in place—the way I moved, the radiance of my eyes.

An itch traveled across my skin, like the feeling I got climbing the stairs to Minerva's room. I was salivating.

The fear in the man's sweat was like the scent of sizzling bacon crawling under your bedroom door in the morning—irresistible.

"Stay away from me," he pleaded softly.

"I'm *trying*." I put down the amp and guitar and fumbled in my jacket for the plastic bag of garlic. Pulling out a clove, I scrabbled to peel it, fingernails gouging the papery skin. The pearly white flesh poked through at last, smooth and oily in my fingers. I shoved it in my mouth half-peeled and bit down hard.

It split— sharp and hot—juices running down my throat like straight Tabasco. I sucked in its vapors and felt the thing inside me weaken a little.

I breathed a garlicky sigh of relief.

The man's eyes narrowed. No longer transfixed, he shook his head at my torn T-shirt and grubby jeans. I was just a seventeen-year-old again, tattered and weighted down with musical equipment. Nothing dangerous.

"You shouldn't litter," he snorted, glaring at the garlic skin I'd dropped. "Someone's got to clean that up, you know."

Then he turned to walk briskly away, the scent of fear fading in his wake.

I breathed garlic deep into my lungs.

Mustn't eat the nice people, Minerva's voice chided in my head.

I was going to try that mandrake tea again. Even if it did taste like lawn-mower clippings, that was probably better than the taste of—

Down the tunnel the darkness shifted restlessly, something huge rolling over in its sleep, and I forgot all about my hunger.

It was down there, the thing that rumbled beneath us when we played.

I grabbed my Strat—leaving the amp behind—and jumped down onto the tracks. The smell carried me forward into the darkness, the tunnel walls echoing with the crunch of gravel, like Alana Ray's drumbeats scattering from my footsteps. The scent grew overpowering, as mind-bending as pressing my nose against Minerva's neck, drawing me closer.

The ground began to swirl, the blackness suddenly liquid underfoot. As my eyes adjusted, I realized it was a horde of rats flowing like eddies of water around my tennis shoes, thousands of them filling the tracks.

But the sight didn't make me flinch—the rats smelled familiar and safe, like Zombie sleeping warm on my chest.

The scent led me to a jagged, gaping hole in the tunnel wall, big enough to walk into, just like the cavity where Minerva and I had first kissed. It led away into pitch-blackness, its sides glistening. The rats swirled around me.

I could smell danger now, but I didn't want to run. My blood was pulsing, my whole body readying for a fight. I listened for a moment and knew instinctively that the hole was empty, though something had passed this way.

I reached out to touch the broken granite, and a dark gunk as thick as honey came off on my fingers. Like the black water, it shimmered for a moment on my skin, then faded into the air.

But its scent left behind a word in my mind . . . *enemy*. Just like Min always said: *I call the enemy when I sing.*

The ground rumbled underfoot, and the rats began to squeak.

I started running down the subway tunnel, feet crunching on gravel, the rats following, anger rippling across my skin. My tongue ran along my teeth, feeling every point. My whole body was crying out to fight this thing.

Then all at once I heard it, smelled it, saw it coming toward me. . . .

A form moved against the darkness, shapeless except for the tendrils whipping out to grasp the tunnel's support columns. It dragged itself toward me—without legs, with way too many arms.

I staggered to a halt, a nervous garlic burp clearing

my head for a few seconds. I realized how big it was—like a whole subway car rolling loose—and how *unarmed* I was. . . .

But then the thing inside me tightened its grip on my spine, flooding me with anger. I pulled the Stratocaster from its case and held its neck with both hands, bringing it over one shoulder like an ax. Steel strings and golden pickups flashed in the darkness, and suddenly the beautiful instrument was nothing but a weapon, a hunk of wood for smashing things.

The rats flowed around me, scrambling up the walls and columns.

The thing refused to take any shape in the darkness, but it was heading toward me faster now, its body spitting out gravel to both sides. It lashed at the dangling subway work lights, popping them one by one as it grew closer, like a rolling cloud of smoke bringing darkness.

Then something glimmered wetly at its center, an open maw ringed with teeth like long knives—and me with an electric guitar. Some small, rational part of my mind knew that I was very, *very* screwed. . . .

It was only twenty yards away. I swung the Stratocaster across myself; its weight made my feet stumble.

Ten yards . . .

Suddenly human figures shot past me out of the darkness, meeting the creature head on. Bright metal weapons flashed, and the monster's screech echoed down the tunnel. Someone knocked me to one side and pinned me against the wall, holding me there as the beast streamed past. Cylinders of flesh sprouted from its length, grasping the steel columns around us, ending in sharp-toothed mouths that gnashed wetly. Human screams and flying gravel and the shriek of rats filled the air around us.

And then it was gone, sucking the air behind it like a passing subway train.

The woman who'd shoved me against the wall let go, and I stumbled back onto the tracks. The monstrous white bulk was receding into the darkness, leaving a trail of glistening black water. The dark figures and a stream of rats pursued it. Weapons flickered like subway sparks.

I stood there, panting and clutching the Strat like I was going to hit something with it. Then the creature slipped out of sight, disappearing into the hole I'd found, like a long, pale tongue flickering into a mouth.

The hunters followed, and the tunnel was suddenly empty, except for me, a few hundred crushed rats, and the woman.

I blinked at her. She was a little older than me, with a jet-black fringe of bangs over brown eyes, a scuffed leather jacket and cargo pants with stuffed-full pockets.

She eyed the guitar in my hands. "Can you talk?"

"Talk?" I stood there for another moment, stunned and shaking.

"As in *converse*, dude. Or are you crazy already?"

"Um . . ." I lowered the Strat. "I don't think so."

She snorted. "Yeah, right. So, like, dude, are you *trying* to get yourself killed?"

She led me to an abandoned subway stop farther up the tracks, a darkened ghost station. The stairways were boarded over, the token booth trashed, but the graffiti-covered platform was abuzz with hunters regrouping after the chase. They slipped up from the tracks, as graceful as the dark figures climbing down the fire escape that night I'd met Pearl.

Angels was what Luz called the people in the struggle. But I'd never figured on angels carrying backpacks and walkie-talkies.

"Easy with that thing," the woman who'd saved me said. "We're all friends here."

"What? . . . Oh, sorry." I was still clutching the Stratocaster like a weapon. The shoulder strap dangled from one end, so I slung the guitar over my back.

Confusion was finally setting in. Had I really just seen a giant monster? And wanted to *fight* it?

I looked at her. "Um . . . who *are* you?"

"I'm Lace, short for Lacey. You?"

"Moz."

"You can say your own name? Not bad."

"I can do what?"

Instead of answering, she pulled a tiny flashlight from a pocket and shone it in my eyes. The light was blinding.

"Ouch! What are you *doing*?"

She leaned closer, sniffing at my breath. "Garlic? Clever boy."

A guy's voice came from behind me. "Positive? Or just some wack-job?"

"Definitely a peep, Cal. But a self-medicator, by the looks of it."

"Another one?" Cal said. His accent sounded southern. "That's the third this week."

Tracers from the flashlight still streaked my vision, but I could see Lace's silhouette shrug. "Well, garlic *is* in all the folklore. Who told you to eat that stuff, Moz?"

I blinked. "Um, this woman called Luz."

"A doctor? A faith healer?"

"She's, uh . . ." What was Min's word? "An esoterica?"

"What the hell's that?" Cal said. My vision returning, I noticed he was wearing a Britney Spears T-shirt under his leather jacket, which seemed weirdly out of place.

"Probably something esoteric," Lace said.

I shook my head. I'd never met Luz face-to-face. "She's a healer. Some kind of Catholic, I guess. She uses tea and stuff."

"Amateur hour," Lace said in a singsong voice. "So, Moz, how long have you had an appetite for rare meat?"

I thought of Min's kiss. "Three weeks and four days."

Cal raised an eyebrow. "That's pretty precise."

"Well, that's when I first . . ." My voice faded. It didn't seem like a good idea, telling them about Min. "Who *are* you guys anyway?"

Lace snorted. "Dude. We're the guys who saved your butt. You almost got flattened by that worm, remember?"

I swallowed, watching as two angels lifted a third onto the platform. He was bleeding from a huge gash on one leg, black water dripping from the wound. He didn't cry out, but his face was knitted in pain, his teeth clenched.

And I'd been about to fight that thing *alone*?

"Uh, thanks."

"Uh, you're welcome." Her eyes narrowed. "Have you got any girlfriends? Any roommates? Cats?"

"Cats?" I thought of Zombie's strange gaze. "Listen, I don't know what you're talking about. Or what that thing was! What's going on here?"

"He doesn't know anything, Lace," Cal said. "Just bag him and let's get moving. That beastie's only wounded; it might swing back around."

The woman stared at me for another moment, then nodded. "Okay. So here's the thing, Moz. Old-fashioned folk remedies aren't going to keep your head together for much longer. Very soon, you're going to do unpleasant things to your friends and neighbors. So we're taking you for a little trip to New Jersey."

"*New Jersey?*"

"Yeah, Montana's full." Lace smiled, pulling a small, thin object from her cargo pants. A needle glistened in the darkness at its tip. "This won't hurt a bit, and you shouldn't be there more than a week or two, thanks to your esoterica friend. Got to admit, she kept you in pretty good shape."

"Hey, wait a second." I backed away, holding up my hands. "I'm not going anywhere. I've got a gig next week."

"A gig?" Lace glanced at the guitar on my back and shrugged. "Cool. But I'm afraid you're going to miss it. We need to train you."

"Train me for *what*?"

"Saving the world," Cal said.

I swallowed. "You mean Luz is right? There really is a struggle?"

"She told you about the . . . ?" Lace's voice faded, and she closed her eyes, sniffing the air. "Hey, Cal—did you feel that?"

I had. My magic powers were spinning. I took a step away.

"Not so fast, Moz!" Lace grabbed my arm, thrusting the needle closer.

As I pulled free from her grip, the ground broke open beneath us. . . .

Columns of flesh tore themselves up from the concrete of the platform, rings of teeth flashing in the darkness. One whipped past me, leaving my jacket sleeve in ribbons. I was already running, dodging through the flailing tendrils, stumbling over broken concrete.

The angels fought back, swords whistling through the air around me, as deadly as the gnashing teeth.

I jumped from the platform, then glanced back. Lace was spinning in place, her long sword slicing low through the air, cutting through columns of flesh as they thrust up from the ground. Black water spewed from the ragged stumps.

My hands reached for the neck of my Strat again, itching to pull it off my back. I was dying to run back and rejoin the fight, but I shut my eyes, yanked out the garlic, and bit straight into an unpeeled clove.

The burning sharpness cleared my head: I didn't want to be part of any struggle. I didn't want to go to some camp in New Jersey. All I wanted was to stay here, be in my band, play gigs, and get famous!

I turned away from the battle and dashed down the tracks, running back toward Union Square Station. As I passed the gash in the tunnel, a storm of rats spilled out, headed back toward the fight. I danced like a barefoot kid on hot asphalt as they swept past.

Finally the lights of the station glimmered in front of me. I leaped up onto the platform and kept running, climbing stairs and slanting tunnels until I'd dashed into the open air.

My pockets were heavy, jingling with enough change to catch a taxi out to Brooklyn. I had to tell Min what I'd seen. The enemy was just like she'd said: something monstrous. There really were angels, and they were recruiting, taking infected people away to . . . *New Jersey*?

Whatever. The struggle was real.

I hailed a cab and gave the driver Minerva's street name. When he said he didn't go to that part of Brooklyn anymore, I leaned forward and bared my teeth, asking him to reconsider. He turned, met my demented rock-star gaze, and changed his mind.

Once the cab was speeding up the Williamsburg Bridge, climbing away from the earth, my nerves began to calm. I was headed toward Minerva, to safety. I'd escaped the angels, and as long as I stayed out of the subways, they'd never find me again. . . .

Then I remembered that my guitar case and amp were back there, underground. I sank down into the vinyl seat, eyes squeezing shut.

The amp didn't matter—I didn't need it anymore—but the *case*. If the angels came looking for me, they'd find it on the tracks. Inside was a polite note, asking anyone who found this guitar to please call Moz at this number. Big Reward!

And, of course, the note gave my address as well.

21. THE RUNAWAYS

-MINERVA-

I pulled out Astor Michaels's birthday present right before midnight, just like he'd told me to.

It was wrapped in silver foil, my own face gazing back at me in the candlelight, blurry and twisted. Zombie jumped up onto the bed and sniffed the package, then looked up at me, his little face worried.

Astor Michaels wasn't family to me and Zombie—and now Moz. He was more like a distant relative, part of the clan who spelled their last names differently. It made him smell funny.

"It's okay, Zombie. Astor's going to make Mommy a rock star."

When I pulled on the red ribbon, its knot only tightened, so I lifted the box to my mouth. The ribbon tensed for a moment as my teeth closed, then relaxed, like a chicken when Luz broke its neck.

Teeth were useful for all sorts of things these days. Mozzy could open beer bottles with his.

I slid the box out from its wrapping, checking the clock. Ten seconds.

I counted down, hoping the present wasn't something heart-shaped. *Eww.* Astor Michaels knew I was with Mozzy. He'd spotted it faster than anyone else, except maybe smelly Alana Ray—and Zahler, of course, who Moz had told before he'd even called me. (Okay, really it was only Pearl who didn't know. Poor little Pearl.)

My fingernails slit the box open, and I smiled.

It was a cell phone, shiny and microscopic. Lifting it up, hefting the insubstantial weight, I felt its shape fitting into my palm. What a very excellent idea . . .

Zombie, who'd been batting at the red ribbon, came over for another sniff, and at that moment the phone buzzed silently against my palm, like a housefly trapped in my fist. Zombie looked up at me and meowed.

"Must be for me," I said.

I kept Astor Michaels waiting for three vibrations before I pushed the big green button.

"Aren't you clever?"

"It's my job to keep the talent happy."

"Mmm." I was already wondering when Mozzy would be home from playing down in the subway. He was supposed to call me exactly at one; I could phone him right before and give him a little surprise. . . . I giggled.

"Sounds like I've succeeded," Astor Michaels said.

"Very much so." Then I frowned. "Why didn't Pearl ever give me one of these?"

"Maybe she thought you'd get yourself into trouble."

"Hmph." Pearl probably liked being the only one with

my number. Showed what she knew. "It's about time. Luz stole my buttons, you know."

"So you said. You needed a real phone, Min. In fact, it's about time you had a real life."

Zombie stared up at me, as if listening.

"What do you mean by that, Astor Michaels?"

"Why don't you move out, Min?"

"Move . . . out?" My eyes swept the candlelit darkness around me.

"Red Rat has a few apartments set aside for our special artists, for when they come to town to record. Nicely furnished and in Manhattan. You could move in anytime."

I swallowed, reaching out to stroke Zombie. His fur had the shivers. "But what about—"

"Your parents?" He made a disappointed noise. "You're eighteen in two weeks, Min. You can disappear for that long, can't you? Do you think the police will spend much time looking for a runaway who's about to turn legal?"

I didn't answer. I didn't care about the police, or my parents much either. But I wasn't sure how long I could go without Luz. She could be a total pain, but she'd cured me, more or less.

And Mozzy needed her even more than I did. I was splitting Luz's medicines with him, making sure he got through the first stages of the illness. So far, he was keeping it together just fine, but I didn't want him to turn all bitey.

"Min?"

I covered up the microphone. "What do you think, Zombie?"

His eyes opened wide, glistening, nervous but . . . excited.

Mozzy needed to get well, but *we* needed things too—to breathe the air outside at night, sucking in the smells and the moonlight. To go down in the subway, like Mozzy got to *every night*.

I wanted to learn more . . . to make my songs stronger.

In a couple of weeks I could call up Luz and have her come to my new place. She could make birthday mandrake tea for both of us. Once I was eighteen, it wouldn't matter if she told my parents where I was.

Me and Moz could make it for that long, couldn't we? We knew to eat lots of garlic. Probably all those other smelly herbs were just for show.

Zombie meowed, still staring at me with gleaming eyes. In our own place, he could go play with his little friends whenever he wanted.

Astor Michaels was talking again. "Once you're out of that room, the band can rehearse every day. Think what that would do for you, especially with your first gig coming up."

I bit my lip. Pearl had been complaining about having only one more Sunday to rehearse. Zombie stared at me, tail twitching, anxious.

"Okay. I'll move."

"I thought you might say that," Astor Michaels said, and I could hear his smile. It slid through the airwaves like a needle. "Go pack."

"What, right now? But it's midnight."

"Best time to run away, don't you think? I'm on the road as we speak, coming over to collect you."

"Um, but Moz said he was going to call later."

He filled my ear with a little sigh. "You can call *him* instead, Min. Remember my little present? The one we're talking on?"

"Oh, right." I giggled. "Clever Astor Michaels."

"I'll see you in twenty minutes. Pack light."

Pack light? Puh.

I needed lots of dresses—all my black ones, for wearing onstage. All my necklaces and rings too, even though my old jewelry box was pink and tattered. Only a few pairs of shoes, because I really had to buy all new ones; none of mine were very rock star. I packed every bit of the underwear me and Pearl had bought the day we'd gone to Red Rat Records, but no pajamas, because I was so bored of lying around all day. Bored of sleeping.

Never again, I thought as I stuffed my two suitcases full. I could save up all my sleeping for the grave.

I packed my notebooks, of course. I'd memorized most of the songs in them, but they smelled good, and I liked to stare at my old handwriting. It was sweet how only I could read the songs, all of them in my own special language.

Zombie trilled from the top of the dresser, reminding me to bring cat food and a place for him to pee. I grabbed his bag of dry food and promised to get him a litter box. And big piles of bones—Moz and I were going to need lots of meat, especially without Luz's tinctures and teas to help us.

I wondered if he would come and stay with me. . . .

The thought made me shiver a little, and I looked around my room again, the place I'd lived for almost eighteen years. It was time to grow up, after all.

The illness had emptied this room of meaning. Luz had cleared all my old possessions out, back when they'd made me scream. She was reintroducing familiar things one by one, but none of them held any significance now. Everything from before the disease smelled like old toys from childhood, sugary with memories, a little embarrassing.

Better to let my parents keep it all.

Mommy and Daddy would be upset, but I could call them from my new phone and tell them how happy I was.

I snapped the suitcases shut, then crossed to the door, closing my eyes to listen. Maxwell was sleeping loudly down the hall. He'd started snoring lately, puberty making him prickly and restless. He'd be much happier without a crazy big sister sucking up everyone's attention.

I listened harder, trying to hear through Max's snuffling. The slightest creak of settling sounded below . . . was it Astor Michaels on the stairs? But he didn't know about the secret key.

The phone vibrated again, like a tiny, nervous animal in my hand.

"I'm ready," I whispered.

"Excellent. We're just pulling up now. Heavens, this neighborhood's seen better days."

"It's not our fault. The mean garbagemen won't come here anymore."

"Well, I'm glad I'm taking you away."

I frowned. Suddenly I wished it wasn't Astor Michaels helping me escape. Maybe this wasn't such a great idea, rushing off with him. Mozzy could help me instead. . . .

But I couldn't imagine unpacking my bags, putting everything back into closets and drawers and under the bed, defeated.

One more day, even one more hour, was too long to stay here.

"Okay," I whispered. "First you have to get the key. Then you sneak to the top of the stairs without making any noise—"

He laughed. "Just a moment, darling Min. I don't *do* sneaking."

"But . . . there's a lock on my door."

"Yes. And you can break it."

"The lock?"

"The *door*. You've had the condition for five months, Minerva. You can feel your strength, right? I've broken doors down *by accident*. Just hit it with the palm of your hand. Hard."

I touched the door softly, thinking of all the nights I'd tried to stare holes in it. But knock it down?

"It'll make noise," I whispered. "Wake them all up."

"You'll be down and out the front door while they're still wondering what's going on. Don't be shy. Just hit it, Min."

I remembered how I'd lifted Pearl's mixing board with one hand last Sunday, making her eyes as round as buttons.

But bash down my own door?

"Do you want to stay in your room forever?" he said.

I hissed at the phone. Astor Michaels and his little tests. Were we mature enough to stay together? Tough enough to face a nasty audience? Strong enough to . . . bash things down?

Fine.

I hung up, scooped Zombie from the floor, and placed one palm against the wood. Drew my arm back . . .

And smashed it into smithereens.

Moz stood just outside, his jaw open.

"Mozzy!" I cried.

His smell rushed into the room, and Zombie struggled to jump down and say hi.

I stared at my stinging palm. "I'd have heard you coming up except for smelly Astor Michaels distracting me."

"Um, I . . ."

"Poor Mozzy. You look frazzled."

"Something happened to me. Something weird." He looked down at the bits of wood around him. "Why did you do that?"

I bent to pick up a suitcase. "I'll tell you on the way."

"What way? The way where?"

"My new place," I said. "Quit squirming! Not you, Mozzy. Grab that, would you?"

He blinked a few times, then saw my other suitcase and gripped its handle.

I paused for a moment, listening. Maxwell was definitely awake, his snores shattered into little pieces, just like my door. I could hear him twisting on his bed, snuffling with confusion.

Downstairs in my parents' room, the floor was creaking with footsteps.

"Come on," I hissed.

We didn't bother sneaking. The stairs complained, but it felt so good not to be worrying over every squeak of the cranky old steps. We were past my parents' room, almost at the front door, when Daddy flicked on the lights above us.

"Minerva?" he called softly. "Max?"

I pulled open the front door. The outside smells rushed in: the garbage mountains, the rotting leaves of fall, Zombie's little friends skittering in the dark.

"Bye, Daddy," I called up, trying to sound a little sad at leaving. "Don't worry, please. I'll call you soon."

"What are you doing? Who *is* that?"

Moz looked very embarrassed to be stared at. But it was Daddy in his pajamas who looked silly.

"Tell Max and Mommy goodbye and that I'll see you all on my birthday, okay?"

"Minerva! You can't just leave. . . . You're not well! Where are you—?"

"I said I'd call you!" Daddy never *listens*. I stomped out the door.

"How are we going to get anywhere?" Moz sputtered, running after me. "Won't they call the cops? I sent my cab away, and we can't take the subway! There's this thing down—"

"It's okay, Moz. Look, there he is!"

Astor Michaels was half a block away, standing next to his limo, looking surprised to see Mozzy. His driver hovered close to him, scanning the piles of garbage nervously, one hand in his pocket like he was getting ready to shoot some of Zombie's little friends.

We ran up, and I handed Astor Michaels my suitcase. "Take this; Zombie has his claws in my dress."

"You're bringing your cat," he said flatly, staring at Moz.

"And Mozzy too!" I said.

"Yes, I see that." Astor Michaels sighed tiredly. "Hello, Moz."

"What's going on here?" Moz said, sounding all manly and jealous, which made me giggle.

But then Daddy yelled something, and we all got in the limo, dragging the suitcases in behind us instead of opening the trunk. The driver put the car into gear and whisked us away.

I waved to Daddy out the back window.

"We're going to our new place, Moz," I explained. "You should come stay there with me."

"Um . . ." Astor Michaels said.

"I can't go home," Mozzy said, staring out at midnight Brooklyn rushing past. "I saw this thing down in the subway, and the angels caught me. They almost took me away, like Luz always says."

"Angels?" I asked. For the first time, I noticed how shaky Moz was. He was pale with shock, twitching and sweating like he'd seen something much worse than my door exploding.

"It's real, Min," he said softly. "The struggle's real."

I wrapped my arms around him. "Don't worry, Mozzy. We'll take you someplace safe."

"By all means," Astor Michaels said. "Must keep the talent happy."

-PEARL-

The morning after the Morgan's Army gig, my phone rang—Astor Michaels calling.

"You gave me a hangover," I answered, still feeling all the glasses of champagne he'd brought me. Mom gave me a stern look across the breakfast table, but I ignored her. Stupid champagne genes.

Astor Michaels laughed at me from the other end. "Well, at least we have something to celebrate. They're finally ready."

I squinted in the sunlight streaming into the dining room. "The contracts?"

"In my hand."

"Your lawyer works on Saturday morning?"

"They were ready yesterday."

Mom was pretending not to listen, but I tried not to swear too loud. Everyone had been nine kinds of bugging me to get the negotiations over with, like the delay was all my fault. "And you didn't mention this last night *why*?"

"I had a very busy evening in front of me."

"Oh. Your mysterious errand." He'd left me and Alana Ray at the club before the gig had ended, smiling like he had a dirty secret.

"And after that, things got even busier." Astor Michaels sighed tiredly. "If you meet me downtown in two hours, I'll explain everything."

"Explain whatever you want," I said. "Just bring the contracts."

"Contracts?" my mother said the moment I hung up. "Does this mean you're really going through with all this?"

I looked down at my hands, which were quivering a little—half hangover, half excitement. "Yeah, I really am."

She looked out the window. "Why we wasted all that money on school, I don't know, if you were just going to do something like this."

"Juilliard wasn't a waste, Mom. Not hardly. But it's . . . over."

She looked at me, trying to muster up a look of disbelief, but she knew I was right. Fewer students showed up for classes every day, and those that were still around were all planning some kind of escape from the city. Ellen Bromowitz had called it exactly right: one week ago, the senior orchestra had been officially put on hold for the rest of the year. The infrastructure was already failing.

"Plus," I said, "this *is* my lifelong dream and everything."

"Lifelong? You're only seventeen, darling."

I looked up at her, about to reply with some snark, but her eyes had turned shiny in the sunlight. Suddenly I saw something I'd never even imagined before: my indestructible mother looking fragile, as if she really was worried about the future.

I wondered if her friends were all doing the same as mine—heading to Switzerland, leaving the city behind. What if no one bothered anymore to raise money for museums and dance companies and orchestras? What if all the parties she lived for had no more reason to exist and simply stopped happening, leaving all her diamonds and black cocktail dresses useless?

Mom needed her infrastructure too, I suddenly realized, and she was watching it crumble away.

So all I said was, "Seventeen years is a long time, Mom. I just hope this isn't too late."

I called Moz's house right away to tell him to come along. The two of us had started the band, after all. This was *our* moment of success.

His mother hadn't seen him that morning. She wasn't sure if he'd come home the night before and didn't sound very happy about it. Maybe sometimes in the past Moz hadn't made it home on Friday nights, she kept saying, but the way things were these days, he really should know better. . . .

I hung up a little worried, hoping Moz wasn't going to go all lateral on me. Except for Alana Ray and almost-eighteen Min, all our parents had to countersign the Red Rat contracts. With our first gig only six days away, now was not the time to pick a fight.

I called Zahler's house next, but there was no answer, and my brain started to spin with every imaginable reason the two of them might have gone missing. The police were investigating a lot of disappearances lately, especially underground; there was talk of shutting the trains down altogether. But Moz and Zahler wouldn't be stupid enough to go down into the *subway*, would they?

Not now, when we were this close . . .

Astor Michaels had given me the address of a huge block of apartments on Thirteenth Street. I got there right on time and found him waiting in the lobby, an alligator-skin briefcase clutched under one arm.

"Shall we go on up?" he said.

"You live here?" I frowned. The lobby carpet was a bit threadbare in spots, and two security guards sat in reclining chairs behind the doorman, eyeing us carefully, shotguns across their laps.

"Heavens, no. Red Rat owns a few apartments here. I thought you might want to see one."

I didn't know what he meant by that, but I looked at his briefcase. "Whatever."

The elevators were the old-fashioned kind, zoo cages on cables. An ancient guy in uniform slid the door closed after we stepped in, then wrenched a huge lever to one side. The machine began to rise, the floors passing just through the bars. My hangover started to grumble about the three cups of coffee I'd had.

Astor Michaels turned to me, clutching his briefcase a little tighter. "Pearl, I've been doing this since the New Sound was really new."

"That's why I tracked you down."

"And I've signed fifteen bands in that time. But yours has something special. You know that, right?"

As I watched the floors slide past, I let myself smile, remembering how thrilled I'd been to find Moz and Zahler. "We've got heart, I guess."

"That heart is Minerva, Pearl. *She* is what makes you special."

We came to a stomach-jerking halt. I swallowed, my heart beating harder, wondering where Astor Michaels was going with this. Did he not want to sign the rest of us? Was he trying to make me jealous of Min?

The elevator man was nudging his lever one way and then the other, bouncing us up and down to align our feet with the red-carpeted floor on the other side of the bars. I tried to remember how many glasses of champagne Astor Michaels had bought me last night.

"I know Minerva is special," I said carefully. "I grew up with her."

"Indeed."

Finally the elevator lurched and bumped its way to a halt, and we stepped off into a long hallway. The cage rattled shut and slipped away.

Astor Michaels just stood there. "Of my fifteen bands, Pearl, eleven have self-destructed so far."

I nodded. That was pretty famous, how Red Rat bands tended to explode. "All part of the New Sound, I guess."

"And why do you suppose that is?"

"Uh, I don't know. Drugs?"

He shook his head. "That's what we usually tell the press. But it's rarely true."

I narrowed my eyes. "You mean, you cover up the truth by saying it was *drugs*? Isn't it supposed to be the other way around?"

"Generally. But certain things are worse than drugs." He shivered. "Late last night, Toxoplasma had something of a meltdown. Right after their very first gig too. Those boys never really got along, you know."

I saw a line of sweat roll down his forehead. It was the first time I'd ever seen Astor Michaels looking discomposed.

"What happened?"

"Who knows, exactly? It was all very stressful. And expensive to clean up." He looked down at his free hand, picking under the fingernails with his thumb. "And messy."

"They broke up?"

"Not exactly." He didn't smile. "As you say, that's *always* been the problem with the New Sound. Toxoplasma had heart, but they only lasted a single gig. *One gig!*" He let out a long sigh. "Morgan's Army may last forever, but of course they're not the real thing."

"Hey, maybe they weren't perfect last night, but I thought they played a great set. What do you mean, 'not real'?"

Astor Michaels glanced up and down the empty hall. "I'll tell you inside."

He turned and walked away, and as I followed, my stomach started to roil again. My knees felt shaky, as if someone was adjusting the exact height of the floor beneath me. What were we *doing* here?

Reaching an apartment door, he rapped on it twice

sharply, then waited a moment. "Don't want to disturb the tenants, but I think they're out."

"Whose place *is* this?"

He pulled out a key, opened the door.

Zombie was waiting just inside.

"I could always see them," Astor Michaels began. "Even before it happened to me."

I was staring at the couch, where half of Min's clothes were draped: black dresses and shawls and stockings strewn across the room. Two open suitcases lay on the floor.

My stomach twisted again. Minerva lived here now. Astor Michaels had installed her here, his special girl.

"They were coming to the clubs, leaking sex out of their eyeballs, only a few of them at first. But once they got onstage . . ." He shook his head. "They're natural stars, charismatic as hell. Except for that one little problem."

"They're bug-ass crazy?" I said harshly, looking at the dresser—the old pink jewelry box I'd bought Min when she was twelve was splayed open, full of shiny things.

"Crazy? I work for a record company, Pearl. Crazy I could deal with." He leaned forward. "But they're bloody cannibals."

I looked up into his eyes. Had he just said *cannibals*?

But then I remembered how Min had hospitalized one of her doctors in the days before Luz. I thought of all the raw meat she ate, the way her teeth grew sharper every day.

Almost as sharp as Astor Michaels's.

There in the darkened apartment, something cold

crawled down my spine. "Why did you bring me here?"

He looked puzzled for a moment, then let out a snort. "Please, I never even *tried* it, not once. I'm different than the rest of them." His eyes twitched; he still looked nervous. "Sane. And I wouldn't hurt you for the world, my dear little Pearl. You've done me such a huge favor."

"A favor?"

"For the last two years, I've been looking for someone like me—someone who's infected but immune to the hunger. A singer who can get onstage and take the New Sound to the world without . . ." He looked down at his fingernails again, then shrugged. "Quite so much cannibalism."

I wondered again what exactly had happened with Toxoplasma the night before. Probably nothing a rehab clinic could fix.

"That's why I was so thrilled when you brought me Minerva," Astor Michaels said. "She's *real*, don't you see? Not a mimic, like Abril Johnson. But not like those lost boys in Toxoplasma either." Zombie jumped onto his lap, and he stroked the cat's head. "She's immune to the hunger."

"I wouldn't go that far," I said, looking at the clothes strewn around the room. "She had it pretty bad there for a while."

"Then somehow you've kept her together, Pearl."

"But it wasn't me. Her parents hired this . . . esoterica. Someone who knew what to do for her." I looked around the apartment, wondering how Min was going to get what she needed now. How long would she last without Luz's medicines?

"Well, if someone's figured out how to cure this thing, we really do need to move fast. Won't be long before they bottle it and *everyone's* a rock star." He shivered. "What a disaster."

I looked at his hands, with their long, sharp, manicured nails. "And it never made you . . ."

"Crazy? A cannibal?" He shook his head. "Just hungry for raw meat sometimes. And horny, always."

"Horny?" My skin was crawling now.

"Of course." He giggled. "That's how it spreads, you know. It's nothing but a disease, Pearl. Just some new bug in the water. And as far as I can tell, it's sexually transmitted. It makes you *want* to spread it."

I closed my eyes. So Luz had been right about boys. What else was she right about? I wondered where her angels were, now that I needed them. . . .

Then I remembered that Mark had cracked up too. Had he given it to her? Or vice versa? One of them had to have been cheating. . . .

Zombie jumped up onto my lap, and I opened my eyes.

Astor Michaels was still talking. "I've been shagging wannabe singers for two years now, trying to find someone who could keep it together after the charisma set in, and every single one went nuts. *Fifteen bands*, Pearl. And finally you bring me a rock star already made!" He leaned back, rubbing his palms across Min's dresses and sighing. "After all my labors."

I sat there, stroking Zombie, trying not to scream as what he'd just said sank in. Astor Michaels had intentionally spread this disease; he'd been making more casualties like Minerva, broken people stuck in attics by their families, or lying huddled on the street, on subway platforms. . . .

We were in business with a monster. The New Sound was the music of monsters.

I took a deep breath, reminding myself about the contracts. This didn't have to change anything. Artists had been bat-shit crazy before; it was what you did with your insanity that mattered. We were still a good band, a *great* band even, even if our whole style of music was based on . . . a disease.

As long as we were the Taj Mahal of cannibal bands, maybe it wasn't so bad.

"Okay," I said.

It wasn't really, but sometimes saying that word helps.

Astor Michaels smiled. "So we're in this together, right, Pearl? We have to keep Min healthy, so that all our hard work—yours and mine—finally pays off. Even if she does something that makes you really, really angry. Okay?"

I looked at him through narrowed eyes. "Like what?"

"You know, something she's not necessarily . . . in control of." He shrugged. "The disease makes people crazy, violent, and especially horny. Sometimes even I can't control myself."

"Doesn't sound like you've been trying that hard."

He smiled, revealing his razor teeth to the gums. "A small price to pay for art."

Zombie's ear perked up, and he jumped from my lap and ran to the door. A second later came the jingling of keys outside.

"Ah. They're home," Astor Michaels said, eyes twitching. "Just remember, we all want this band to be a success. So don't get mad at poor Min. I've seen the change happen with my own eyes, and she's been through more than you can imagine. So be nice, all right?"

I nodded, but my head was spinning again.

They're home, he'd said.

They.

The door opened, and Minerva breezed in. Moz followed behind, carrying a threadbare duffel bag.

"Mozzy! Look who's here!" Min cried, beaming all the wattage of her fawesome beauty at me, her cannibal-rock-star charisma. Moz just stood there staring, looking a little surprised, a lot guilty.

With a twist in my stomach, I remembered his mother's anxious voice on the phone that morning.

He took a slow breath, then shrugged the duffel bag from his shoulder. It thumped to the floor like a dead body—stuffed full.

He was moving in.

"Hey, Pearl. How's it going?"

I tried to answer, but my gut was writhing now, squeezing the taste of stomach-ripe champagne up into the back of my throat. Minerva moved a step closer to Moz, five pale fingers wrapping protectively around his arm.

He was hers now. Completely.

With the three of them here together, I could finally see the changes in Moz, all the clues I'd managed to blind myself to: the luster of his skin, the beautiful, inhuman angles of his face. Just like Min back in spring—when the hunger was first welling up—he'd grown a heart-twisting shade more fetching.

Even slitted against the dim candlelight, his eyes glowed, full of pity for me. He must have known what I'd wanted.

But *she'd* taken it instead.

Suddenly the desolate feeling in my stomach was swept away by fury: Minerva had done it *again*, hooked up with someone in the band—in *my* band. Even after what had happened with Mark and the System, after everything Luz had told her, Min had done this to me *again*. I clenched my fists. Of course she would throw it in my face now, when we were *this* close, the contracts near enough to touch, ready to be signed.

I felt Astor Michaels's gaze, willing me to keep it together. For the good of the band. For the good of the New Sound . . . the music of monsters.

He snapped open the locks on his briefcase, pulled out his pen.

I swallowed my screams whole. They went down my throat as sharp-cornered and cold as ice cubes.

"Hi, guys," I said. "Nice place."

PART V

THE GIG

Study the Black Death, and you'll understand one truth: when things start to go wrong, human beings always *find ways to make them worse.*

The year the Death came to Europe, a city called Caffa on the doorstep of Asia was under siege. When the attackers found themselves coming down with a strange new disease, they wisely decided to run. But first they cata-pulted plague-ridden corpses over the walls of the city—so both *sides would get the disease. Brilliant move.*

When the Black Death was at its worst, the church decided to look for someone to blame and began to perse-cute heretics, Muslims, and Jews. As people fled these attacks, the disease fled with them. Nice work.

England and France had gone to war one year before the Black Death struck, but instead of making peace while the pandemic raged, they kept on fighting. In fact, they kept on fighting for 116 years, keeping their people poor, malnourished, susceptible to disease. Now that's commit-ment.

The Black Death was helped along by war, by panic, even by the weather, but it had no greater ally than human stupidity. Sometimes, you wonder how our species has made it this far.

Not without a lot of help, I assure you.

NIGHT MAYOR TAPES:

411–421

23. MORAL HAZARD

-ALANA RAY-

I still hadn't made a decision, but my hands were steady.

I'd been here at the nightclub more than three hours and hadn't needed to drum my fingers or touch my forehead even once. Like being suspended in that moment before playing, the cadence of the universe around me needed no adjustments.

The club was at one end of a long alleyway in the meatpacking district, one free of garbage, the walls painted with giant murals and tagged with graffiti. I'd come in through a huge loading dock, trucks full of equipment rumbling in a tight line, waiting to disgorge.

Inside, the space was more than three hundred feet from stage to back wall, the echoes returning lazily, almost a whole second late—two beats at 120 beats per minute. Useless for playing, but that was fine with me. I liked my fake echoes with this band, just to be in control of *something*. My visions, my emotions, even the patterns I played all seemed to spring unbidden from the air, but at least my echo boxes obeyed me.

Astor Michaels had asked me to come early for sound check, so that the engineers could get used to my paint buckets. I'd brought thirty-six to arrange in eight stacks (8! = 36), along with my special buckets: unusual sizes and thicknesses, even the broken ones that gave off the buzz of cracked plastic.

Unlike Pearl, the engineers here thanked me when I ran only two channels from my board to theirs. They had four bands to worry about tonight—each with its own array of treble, bass, effects, and volume settings—and wanted things as simple as possible. They let me hang out for the whole sound check, watching as they plastered the club's huge mixing board with notes scribbled on masking tape. Its backside sprouted a tangle of cables, four bands' worth of musical specificities sculpted in color-coded spaghetti.

I was still watching them work when I felt Astor Michaels behind me.

"Miss Jones," he said, a sheaf of papers in his hand.

"I prefer Alana Ray."

He smiled. "Sorry to be formal, but we have business to conduct." The papers rustled, making the air ripple. "You're the only one who hasn't signed yet. Not embarrassed about your penmanship, are you?"

"Top of my class," I said, then shrugged. "The competition was less than average."

"Ah. Didn't mean it that way." He pulled out a thick

fountain pen. "I'm sure your signature's more legible than Zahler's—or his mother's, for that matter."

The drummer on stage started a long fill, rolling across his whole set, the sound phasing and twisting as engineers played with their settings. For a few moments, we couldn't speak.

When the drumroll stuttered to a halt, Astor Michaels spread the contracts out on the mixing board. "Shall we?"

I stared down at them, all those carefully chosen, hair-splitting words. When I'd read the contract, it had made a tangle in my mind, the numbered and cross-referenced paragraphs twisted around one another like the theme of a fugue.

"What's wrong?"

"I'm concerned about . . . the ethics of signing."

"Ethics?" He laughed. "Good God, Alana Ray. This band has four minors, two of whom are bat-shit crazy. Minerva had to forward-date her contract to next week. We've got a simpleton and a control freak as well. The ethics of *you* signing? You're practically the only one of sound mind!"

I didn't like how he was talking about the others, but first I had to explain: "I'm not concerned about my own competence. I am worried about tonight."

"Stage fright?" His voice softened. "Is it tough with your condition?"

I shook my head. "This is not about me. What if signing this contract risks harm to others? In the law, that is called a moral hazard."

"I don't follow you."

I looked up from the mass of words spread out across

the mixing board, finally meeting Astor Michaels's eyes. "I think that something dangerous may happen here tonight, because of us. Because of what Minerva is."

"Oh." He blinked. "So you've . . . seen something?"

"Only what I always see when she sings."

"Your little Loch Ness hallucination?" He smiled.

"I also saw it at the Morgan's Army gig, but stronger." The drummer hit his snare, its echo bouncing across the vast club. There would be a thousand people here tonight. Huge stacks of amplifiers waited on either side of the stage, buzzing in the silence, crinkling the air. "More people makes the beast bigger; more sound makes it bigger."

"I hope so, Alana Ray, but that doesn't make it real." Astor Michaels frowned. "You know that, don't you?"

"Do I?"

He stared at me for a moment, genuinely puzzled. Then he shook his head. "We've both seen strange things in our lives, I'll grant you that. We've both had . . . *conditions* to deal with. But both of us made something from them. That's why we're sitting here across this contract, you and me."

I looked at his teeth, remembering what Pearl had told me on the phone last night. How Astor Michaels had made a career out of making more insects.

He stabbed at the papers with one long fingernail. "What you have right here is real, and your visions aren't. You know that."

I was suddenly angry. "How can you be certain? This is in *my* head, not yours. No one else can see the things I do."

His stare held me coolly. "But you're the most logical person I've ever met, Alana Ray. And you wouldn't have come here for a sound check if you weren't going to play tonight, and you wouldn't play tonight if you weren't going to sign. So you don't really believe in monsters, do you?"

I swallowed, looking down at my hands—perfectly still, ready to play. I had dreamed of drumming all last night, of being under the spotlights. "But you say Minerva is going to change things. What if she makes the beast real?"

"I've watch this epidemic roll across New York City for two years, and I've never seen anything like what you describe."

I stared at him, wanting to believe. Astor Michaels had discovered the New Sound, after all. Maybe he knew what he was talking about.

"Don't you trust me?" he said, the pen flickering in his hand. "Don't you think I'll do right by you?"

"I think it was right, what you did for Minerva."

He let out a snort. "Finally somebody thanks me."

"Yes. Thank you," I said. Minerva's freedom had frightened Pearl, but I'd watched too many schoolmates graduate into mental institutions, into group homes and jails, and I knew that locking people up was paranormal—*against* normal, not beside it. Locks didn't cure; they strangled.

"Well, then." He held out the pen, eyes glinting. "I don't think you're afraid of me or afraid of monsters. I think you're just afraid of your own success."

I shook my head. Astor Michaels was very wrong about that. That morning, I'd thrown my change bucket away. Moral hazard or not, I wanted to be more real than someone begging on the streets.

So I signed, as he'd always known I would.

24. 10,000 MANIACS

-ZAHLER-

The crowd was filling the main room now—a thousand people, Astor Michaels said, but it sounded like millions. Here in the backstage dressing room the noise was smoothed to a hum, like a hive of bees just waiting for someone to poke it with a stick.

The more I listened, the more they sounded like they were ready to boo somebody off the stage. Especially some lame bassist who'd only been playing for about four weeks . . .

I swallowed. *Nobody* had ever been this nervous before.

This was real. This was actual. This was happening *right now*.

Under the dressing room fluorescent lights was the worst place to practice, but I sat there in my chair slapping at the strings. Maybe I would get a little bit better, maybe just enough to save myself from humiliation.

Sometimes, playing my new instrument,

my fingers moved more gracefully than they ever had across a guitar. Lately I'd been dreaming of the whole world expanding from guitar-size to bass-size, everything suddenly scaled just right for me and my big, fat, clumsy hands. But right now, the strings of Pearl's bass felt an inch thick, dragging at my fingers like quicksand in a nightmare.

Moz didn't look much happier. He was standing in one corner of the dressing room, wearing dark glasses and trembling. A sheen of sweat covered his face and bare arms.

"You look like you got the flu, Moz," I said.

He shook his head. "Just need my cup of tea."

"Almost ready, Mozzy." A teapot was plugged into the wall next to where Minerva sat doing her makeup. She had some weird herbs waiting to be brewed.

"Your *cup of tea*?" I shook my head. Living with a girl had turned Moz totally lame. And it was all my fault, because I'd told him to call Minerva, because I'd been so mad at him for wanting me to switch instruments. . . .

It was all the stupid bass's fault!

Alana Ray stood right in the center of the room, staring at her own outstretched hands. Their rock-steadiness made her look incomplete, as if Moz had stolen all her twitchiness.

She'd traded her usual army jacket for this fawesome Japanese kimono over jeans. No one had told *me* we were supposed to dress up. I looked down at my same old unfool T-shirt. Would the crowd boo me for wearing it? They sounded really impatient now. The whole thing was starting an hour late, which Astor Michaels kept saying would make everything really intense. . . .

But what if it just pissed them off?

Pearl was in the opposite corner from Moz, in the same dress she'd worn to Red Rat Records. She looked fawesome, I could tell, even if my brain was melting.

But she didn't look happy. She kept swearing under her breath: "Special Guests? More like Special Retards. I can't *believe* we're going out as 'Special Guests.' Why don't we just call ourselves Special Education?"

"The band going on first is called Plasmodium," Moz said. "How much does that name suck?"

Pearl looked at him, gave Minerva a two-second glare, then said quietly, "Sounds a lot like Toxoplasma."

"We should pick a real name soon," Minerva said, staring at her reflection in the mirror, applying makeup with steady hands. She was wearing a long evening gown, lots of jewelry, and didn't look nervous at all. She didn't notice the looks Pearl had been giving her. "If we let Astor Michaels choose one, it'll have the word *plasma* in it."

"What does *plasma* even mean?" Moz asked.

"It can mean two things," Alana Ray said. "Electrified gas or blood."

"Gee," Pearl muttered. "Which one do you think he was going for?"

The teakettle suddenly spit out a crooked screech, the sound fading into a moan as Minerva unplugged it. She poured the boiling water into her cup of herbs, and the smell of compost heap filled the room. "Here you go, Mozzy."

An explosion of sound came from the walls, a thudding from the floor beneath us.

"Crap!" I hissed. "It's the first band. We're the second band. That means we're next!"

"That is correct," Alana Ray said.

My stomach started roiling like that time when I was little and I swallowed part of my chemistry set. We were going to face a possibly homicidal crowd in . . . *"Half an hour."*

"Plus changeover time," Alana Ray said.

I shut my eyes and listened. The crowd wasn't booing yet. Maybe they weren't such a nasty bunch after all. But Plasmodium sounded tight, not like they'd been forced to switch instruments, say, in the last month or so. . . .

"Listen to that," I said. "Their bass player is way faster than me. Everyone's going to think I suck."

"You don't suck, Zahler," Moz said. "And he sounds *too* fast to me."

"Be dead by tomorrow at that speed," Pearl said, staring down at her fingernails.

"Dead?" I said. "What do you mean?" Did people ever *die* on stage? I wondered. Like from heart attacks? Or the audience killing them because they sucked?

"Relax, Zahler." Moz was sipping his tea now, still trembling, Minerva mopping at the sheen of sweat across his face with a towel. "You've got half an hour to get yourself together."

Great. I was being told to chill out by a guy who looked like he was dying of Ebola fever. Maybe Moz was about to collapse, and then we could do this whole Special Guest thing *after* he recovered—and I got some more practice in.

Alana Ray was still staring at her hands. She'd hardly moved the whole time, like some kind of kung-fu Zen master contemplating destiny. I was thinking how maybe I should have worn something Japanese—then I'd at least *look* fool. Well, actually, I already looked fool. In the usual sense of the word.

"Time is a strange thing, Zahler," Alana Ray said. "If you focus your mind, thirty minutes can seem like five hours."

But it didn't. It seemed like five seconds.

Then Astor Michaels came in and said that it was showtime.

A thousand of them waited out there, all just looking at us.

Random shouts filtered up from the audience—they weren't heckling us exactly, just bored and ready for another band to start. We didn't have any fans yet—the few friends Moz and I had invited were too young to get in. The sight of the unfriendly crowd made me realize one big thing missing from my rock-star dreams:

In all my fantasies about being famous, I was *already* famous, so I never had to *get* famous. I never had to walk out in front of a crowd for the first time, unknown and defenseless. In my dreams, this awful night had already happened.

I looked over at Moz, but he was staring down at his feet and still trembling, like he was having a seizure. Behind her paint buckets, Alana Ray's eyes were shut, and

Pearl was peering down at her keyboards, flicking switches as fast as she could, like she was about to take off in a spaceship. Nobody looked back at me, like they were all suddenly embarrassed to be in the same band.

It's not my fault! I wanted to shout. *I never wanted to play the bass!*

Minerva was the only one who looked happy to be onstage. She was already leaning over her mike stand, talking to a bunch of tattooed guys down in front, flirting with them, flicking at their grasping hands with spike-heeled black boots. Even through her dark glasses you could see that her eyes were scary-wide and glowing, sucking energy from the crowd before she'd sung a single note.

Pearl gave me a low E, and I took a deep breath and tuned up. The sound boomed out from my bass like a foghorn, rumbling through the club. A few howls from the audience answered the noise, as if I'd interrupted someone's conversation and they were pissed.

The guys flirting with Minerva had big muscles and tattoos on their shaved heads. I'd read the night before about a big riot in Europe, a whole crowd at some soccer game going crazy all at once, attacking one another. Hundreds had died, and nobody knew why.

What if that happened here, right now? The whole crowd turning into deadly maniacs? I knew exactly who everyone would choose to kill first.

The half-assed bass player in the lame T-shirt. That's who.

When we were all tuned up, the stage lights lowered.

Total darkness, like I'd suddenly gone blind from freaking out. More impatient shouts filtered up from the crowd, and someone yelled, "You suck!" which people laughed at, because we hadn't even started yet.

We were so dead.

I swallowed, waiting to begin. . . .

"Zahler!" Pearl hissed.

Oh, right. We were doing the Big Riff first. *I* was supposed to start.

My fingers groped for the strings, and I heard the amps squeak with the sweat on my fingers. I tried to remember what to play.

And I couldn't.

No, this wasn't happening. . . .

I'd been playing this riff for six years, and yet it had somehow disappeared from my brain, from my fingers, from my whole body.

I stood there in silence, waiting to die.

Zahler had frozen up.

Perfect.

My head was burning, sweat running into my eyes, heart pounding like something in a cage. But it wasn't stage fright; it was the beast gone wild in me. I'd been anxious all day, too nervous to eat, and now the hunger had caught up with me all at once.

Garlic and mandrake tea wasn't cutting it. I needed flesh and blood.

"Play, Zahler!" I heard Pearl hiss, trying to get him going.

The crowd was growing impatient, a restless hum building before us, but at least the delay gave me a few more seconds of darkness. My vision had been doing weird things all day: I hadn't been able to look at Min, as if her face were made of sharp angles that cut into my eyes. Even the smell of her clothes and perfume was making my head spin, as if living together had somehow given me an overdose of her.

But here in the darkness I felt alone, almost under control.

Zahler still wasn't starting the Big Riff, though, which left only me. I could play his old guitar part and wait for him to come in. But once the music began, the lights would pop back on, so bright, so sharp. . . .

And then the hunger would take control again.

I could run offstage right now, slip out of the club and into some all-night store, wolf down a slab of raw meat. Probably a better idea than taking a chunk out of someone right here in front of a thousand witnesses.

But even with the beast ravenous inside me, I had to stay. I couldn't let Zahler live forever with the shame of having blown it tonight.

I took a deep breath, and just as my fingers moved . . . Zahler finally began to play.

Six years of practice took over: the Big Riff grabbed me, coiled around my spine and out my fingers, my nervous system responding as automatically as breathing. Pearl followed, then Alana Ray came in, the echoes of her paint buckets making the space huge around us.

The lights came up, and the crowd was suddenly cheering.

Good move, Zahler, I thought. *Making them wait for it.*

Minerva kept them waiting too, left the Big Riff grinding for a solid minute before she brought the microphone anywhere near her lips. But you could tell she hadn't frozen up—her whole body moved with the beat, drawing every eye in the crowd, gulping in their energy.

She played with them, drawing the microphone close,

then pushing it away, grinning behind dark glasses. The Big Riff could hypnotize you, I knew all too well—Zahler and I sometimes played it for hours at a stretch. When Minerva let it flow through her body, she was as spellbinding as a swaying cobra.

Then she pulled off her glasses, braving the spotlights to peer into the audience, to fix them with her gaze. I saw their faces ignite with the light reflected from her, as if somehow she'd made eye contact with everyone.

That was when she started to sing, and when I started to feel *really* funny.

The words that Minerva had scrawled down in her basement tumbled out of her, as lunatic as the first time she'd played with us—incomprehensible, ancient, and wild. They dredged up weird pictures in my mind, the skulls and centipedes carved into the iron lock on her bedroom door.

The ground began to rumble.

Maybe it was just my stomach, the gnawing hunger changing into something sharper. It felt as if all the raw hamburger I'd consumed over the last few weeks had gotten to me at last, my iron gut finally succumbing to food poisoning.

The sight of Minerva with her glasses off made my head spin, the spotlights flashing from her face like crystal. I felt the garlic leaving my body in a hot sweat, as if giant hands were squeezing me, wringing out every protection I had against the beast inside.

Disgust was leaking into me, a loathing for everything that had put me on this stage: Minerva, this band, the

Stratocaster in my hands. The whole insane idea of fame and adulation and even *music itself* . . .

I wanted to throw it all away, to run from all these pointless complications and let the beast inside take over. To hide in some distant, shadowy place and gnaw on nothing but flesh and bones—perfectly sated, an animal.

But my fingers kept playing. The music held me there, balanced between love and hatred.

I stared down at the stage, not looking at Minerva, but I couldn't keep her song out of my ears. It kept pouring from the amplifiers, echoing back and forth across the club, building like feedback in my head.

The cables at my feet were moving, shivering like dizzying snakes across the floor. I tore my eyes from them, glaring out into the darkness of the nightclub.

I saw it start out there.

A shape moved through the crowd, a swell of hands thrown up into the air, like a stadium wave carrying itself along, traveling toward us from the back of the club. It broke against the stage, shattering into wild cries of surprise.

The ground rumbled under my feet.

Then the swell appeared again, moving from right to left this time, carrying screams along with it. That's when I realized this wasn't something innocent, like upraised arms at a baseball game. . . . Reality was bending before my eyes.

The floor itself was surging up, the bulge moving like a rat scurrying under a rug. More violent this time—the people in its path were thrown into the air, tossed up to fall into the outstretched arms of the crowd, like stage-jumpers.

My sharp ears caught a thin scream behind me, and I glanced back to see Alana Ray crying out, "No, no, no . . . ," unheard in the booming beat of the Big Riff. But she kept playing: the music had also captured her, locking her hands into their fluttering patterns.

The moving surge of floor turned again, growing stronger. As I watched, the ground began to split, the earth opening like a huge zipper, vomiting up black water and cracked pieces of concrete. A choking smell filled my nostrils.

It was headed toward the stage, but none of us stopped playing.

A few people began to scramble away from its path, trying to run through the crowd, but most were staring raptly up at us, too mesmerized by Minerva to move.

It was the enemy, of course, the same beast I'd seen down in the subway. She had finally called it up.

The Stratocaster burned my fingers, my whole body rejecting the music we were making, but still I couldn't stop.

Screams filled the nightclub now. More of the crowd fought to scramble over one another for safety, trying to avoid the snapping maws of the beast. It grew closer and closer to us.

And then angels starting falling.

They dropped from the ceiling on thin filaments, cables that sparkled in the spotlights, descending toward the creature and onto the stage. One angel swung to the top of each set of amplifiers, swords flashing in their hands. They rappelled down the stacks, stabbing each speaker right in its center, every thrust bringing forth a high-pitched shriek from the equipment—a squealing counter-point to the Big Riff.

Dozens of them dropped onto the beast and into the crowd, pushing people away. They brought the creature to a halt, hacking with swords and stabbing with long, tele-scoping spears. Its cries of pain joined the squawking of the amplifiers, until the music finally began to stumble. . . .

Minerva's voice faltered, and the spell was shattered.

I broke free, pulling the Stratocaster's strap from my shoulder and grabbing the guitar by its neck, despising it with every fiber of my being. I raised it over my head and swung it down against the stage, smashing it again and again, its strings snapping, its broken neck twisting like a dying chicken's. The guitar buzzed and squeaked out a last few tuneless notes, its death cries leaking from the sur-viving amps.

Around me, the others had ground to a halt. In tears, Alana Ray threw her sticks aside, kicking wildly at her paint buckets. Zahler just stood there openmouthed, staring at the battle on the nightclub floor. I couldn't look at Minerva anymore.

Stepping back from the broken guitar, my hands bent into claws, I started to stomp at it with my boots. It peeped and squawked.

Then an angel landed on the stage in front of me, dressed in commando black, trailing a thin cable from her waist. She held a small object in one hand.

I recognized her: Lace.

I turned to run, to escape her and everything else: this band, this music, the monstrous thing we'd called up. But after a few steps, before I'd even reached the edge of the stage, she'd caught up with me, grabbing my arm and spinning me around, her needle flashing in the spotlights.

I felt a pinprick at my neck, then her arms supporting me.

"Say good night, Moz," Lace said.

The sound of my own name almost made me vomit, and then nausea and pain melted into darkness.

THE TOUR

PART VI

THE TOUR

There has never been a better time for a pandemic.

Airplanes can carry people across the globe in a single day, and half a billion people fly every year. Cities are far larger and more crowded than at any point in history.

The last great disease was Spanish flu, which appeared at the end of World War I. (Pandemics love wars.) It spread across the planet faster than any previous disease. Within one year, one billion people were infected, a third of the world's population. Its spread was so frighteningly quick that one U.S. town outlawed shaking hands.

And all this was before airplanes could fly across oceans, before most people owned a car. These days, any pandemic would travel much, much faster. We've got it all these days: dense cities, instant transportation, and all the wars you could want. For the worms, that's motive, means, and opportunity.

When the last days come, they will come quickly.

NIGHT MAYOR TAPES
END HERE.

-MINERVA-

The smelly angels took us all away.

I tried to explain to them that I was fine—had been for weeks—and that Zahler, Pearl, and Alana Ray weren't even infected. But one look at sweaty, frothing, guitar-smashing Mozzy convinced them we were all insane.

That was the angels' big problem: they thought they knew *everything*.

I could have run. I was as fast and strong as them now—I could shatter bedroom doors with a single blow, after all. With the angels busy protecting a thousand bystanders and catching Astor Michaels and killing the giant worm that I'd called up (okay . . . *oops*), disappearing would have been a cinch.

But that would have meant leaving Moz and the others behind, and we really were a band now; I couldn't let them be kidnapped without me. So I let the angels stick me with their stupid needles. . . .

And woke up all the way across the river in

New Jersey. They'd put me in a locked room, a cross between a cheap hotel and a mental hospital. Nothing to do but watch the world fall apart on TV.

Smelly angels.

"We're very interested in you, Minerva."

"Really, Cal?" I batted my eyelashes. He was kind of handsome—in a boring, clean-cut way—and had a cute southern accent. Not as yummy as Mozzy, of course, but I liked how Cal turned pink when you flirted with him. "Then why don't you let me out of here? It's not like I'm *dangerous*, after all."

His eyes narrowed. Cal never wore sunglasses, like the other angels did. They were all infected, of course, and only sane because they took their meds. The angels had a big pill factory out here. No skulls or crucifixes on the walls, though—they were *very* scientific.

But Cal was different. He didn't need pills and smelled a little bit like Astor Michaels. Fellow freaks of nature.

"We can't let you go because we don't know what you *are*," Cal's girlfriend said.

I glared at her. Her name was Lace-short-for-Lacey, and she'd stuck Mozzy with her needle.

"But I'm *cured*. You can see that." They'd tried to give me their smelly angel medicine, but I was refusing it. Fresh garlic was enough for me now.

Cal scratched his head. "Yeah, you told us about your esoterica already. We're checking her out."

"You be nice to Luz," I warned. "She knows things."

"We know things too," he said.

242

Lace got all bossy then, hands on hips and voice too loud. "We've been around for centuries, cured a lot more peeps than Luz ever will. Your friend might know a few folk remedies, but the Watch has this stuff down to a science."

"Science, huh?" I ran one finger down the side of my neck, making Cal all squirmy. "So what *am* I, then?"

Lace frowned. "What you are is freaky."

"We've been watching Astor Michaels for a while now," Cal said. "We knew he was spreading the parasite, but this whole *singing* thing . . . It kind of caught us by surprise."

I didn't say how the worm had caught me by surprise too. I'd always felt it rumbling when we played, but I'd never thought it would come *visit*.

Even humming made me nervous now. Smelly underground monsters.

I shrugged. "Why don't you ask Astor Michaels about it, then?"

"He doesn't know any more than we do," Lace said. "He's just some record producer, trying to find the Next Big Thing. He's immune to the parasite's worst effects, but that's more common than you'd think."

"I'm a carrier myself." Cal smiled, all proud of himself. He'd already come by my room to explain how he was naturally immune and how he'd been a badass vampire-hunter even before the crisis. Now he worked for something called the Night Watch, which was run by someone called the Night Mayor. Oooh! Spooky.

I batted my eyes again. "Did you get up to tricks like Astor Michaels did, Cal? Were you *bad*?"

"No." He swallowed, then Lace gave him a look. "Well, not on that scale. And never on purpose . . ."

"Did you infect *her*?" I asked, pointing at Lace-short-for-Lacey. I'd seen them being all kissy through the bars of my window.

"No," he said in a tiny voice. "My cat did."

"Your cat?" I blinked. "Kitties can do that?"

"Felines are the major vector," Cal said. "The parasite hid in the deep-dwelling rat population for centuries, until the worms drove them up to the surface. . . ."

As Cal went on with his parasite-geek lecture, which he *loved* to do, I remembered back to before I got sick. As the sanitation crisis had settled over our street, Zombie started spending a lot of time outside. And every night he'd come home and sleep on my chest, breathing his cat-food breath into my face.

That was how I'd gotten sick? From *Zombie*?

That meant that Mark wasn't such a dirty dog after all. He hadn't given the nasty to me; I'd given it to him. . . .

"Oops," I said softly.

I wondered where Zombie was now. I always left the apartment window open so he could visit his little friends, but Manhattan looked pretty bad on TV. The whole island had been sealed off by Homeland Security, like *that* was going to keep the parasite from spreading.

Cal had explained to me how clever the parasite was: it turned infected people horny, hungry, bitey—anything to pass on its spores—and made them despise everything they'd loved before. That's why I'd thrown away Mark and my dolls and my music, why Moz had smashed his

Stratocaster to bits. The anathema, as Cal called it, pushed infected people to run away from home and head to the next town over, and the next town after that. . . .

It wouldn't be long before the whole world had it.

There were full-scale riots in most big cities now, blood-thirsty maniacs running around doing vile things—and not all of them were infected, you could totally tell. Schools were shutting down, the roads were choked with refugees, and the president kept making speeches telling everyone to pray.

No shit.

But the news never mentioned cat food supplies, not that I ever saw. So what was Zombie eating now? He didn't *mind* birds and mousies, but he always puked them up.

"Anyway," Lace said, noticing I wasn't listening. "We don't really care how you got the disease or how your voodoo friend cured you. This is about your songs."

I smiled. "They make the ground rumble. Want me to sing one for you?"

"Um, not really," Cal said, then he frowned. "That worm was probably just a coincidence anyway. But certain people around here are interested. They've been listening to recordings from that night, and they want to know where you got those lyrics."

"You need my help? But I thought you had this stuff down to a science."

Lace took a slow breath. "Maybe what happened that night wasn't strictly science."

Cal turned to her. "What do you mean by that?"

"Dude! You saw what happened! That shit was . . ." Her voice faded.

"Paranormal?" I looked down at my fingernails, which needed a manicure. They were still growing faster every day, even though I was cured. "Okay. I'll tell you everything I know . . . *if* you let me see Mozzy and the others. I want us to be together. We're a band, you know."

"But the other three tested parasite-negative," Cal said.

"I told you they would."

He frowned. "Yeah, I guess you did. But if we let you see them, you can't do anything that would compromise their health."

"Eww! I wouldn't kiss any of *them*."

"Kissing's not the only vector."

I tried not to roll my eyes. Anything to get out of this smelly room. "Okay, I promise not to share my ice cream."

"Cal," Lace said. "If she really wanted to infect them, she could have already." She turned to me. "But Moz is still dangerous."

"I can handle Mozzy. He just needs his tea."

"He's getting better stuff than tea," she said. "But he's still in bad shape. It's not pretty."

I snorted. "I've been tied to a bed in a nuthouse, screaming and trying to bite my doctors' fingers off. And then locked in my room for three months, hating myself and eating dead chickens raw. Don't talk to *me* about pretty, Miss Lace-short-for-Lacey."

The two of them looked at each other all seriously, then argued for a while longer, but I knew that eventually I'd get my way. They wanted to know about my songs real bad.

And like Astor Michaels always said, you had to keep the talent happy.

27. FAITHLESS

-PEARL-

The Night Watch stuck me, Zahler, and Alana Ray in one of their "guest rooms," a little cluster of cabins at the forested edge of the compound. We were free to go where we wanted in the compound, except the hospital where Moz was, but outside our door a tall fence stretched in both directions. Razor wire coiled down its length, reminding us that we were prisoners; not because they wouldn't let us out, but because outside was too deadly for us now. Special Guests all over again.

There wasn't much to do except watch the world end on TV.

Thanks to jet planes, overcrowded schools, and the sheer six billion of us all crammed together, the disease was spinning out of control. It hit critical mass in New York City in that first week we were out in Jersey, spreading faster than anyone could contain, conceal, or comprehend what was happening.

The talking heads all went lateral, of course, blaming terrorists or avian flu or the government or God. All non-sense, though at least they'd stopped pretending this was just a sanitation problem. But none of them seemed to get that the world was ending.

Sometimes they'd interview people in small towns, where everything was weirdly normal, the disease invisible so far. They were all smirking at New York, like we'd had it coming. But the boondocks wouldn't be fun for very long. Credit cards, phones, and the Internet were already starting to fail. Hardly anyone was making contact lenses, movies, medicines, or refined gasoline anymore. Even in the smallest towns, they'd miss all that infrastructure when it was gone.

Ellen Bromowitz had been right: there weren't going to be any symphony orchestras for a while. No celebrity interviews in magazines, no album cover photo shoots or music videos. And the biggest hit on local radio these days was "Where's the National Guard Camp Nearest You?"

No way to get famous.

Of course, now that I knew the scale of what was happening, becoming a rock star seemed less important. In fact, it seemed just plain stupid, unbelievably self-centered, and nine kinds of deluded.

I'd seen this coming. Even back when all I'd had to go on was Min's craziness and Luz's strange tales, I'd understood somehow that the world was about to break. So what had I done? Tried to escape reality by becoming *famous*. As if the world couldn't touch me then, as if bad things didn't happen to people with record deals. As if I could just leave all the nonfamous people behind.

What a joke. A sad, demented joke.

So that was me now: depressed and deflated in New Jersey, shell-shocked that our first gig had turned into a bloodbath, that the world was crumbling, and that my life-long dream had turned out to be the Taj Mahal of shallow.

I never wanted to go onstage again, never wanted to play another instrument . . . and just when I'd finally thought of a really fexcellent band name.

How's that for annoying?

Every morning the Night Watch brought in truckloads of peeps—parasite positives—they'd captured the night before. They treated as many as would fit in their hospital, an empty elementary school they'd taken over. Hundreds of them, reborn as angels, trained on the assembly field every day. Their swords glittered like a host of flashbulbs popping in unison.

An army was building here.

Cal said that in all of human history, this was the fastest the infection had ever spread—those jet planes again. And what nobody but the Watch realized yet was that the worst part was yet to come. The creature that Min had summoned, the worm, was one of thousands rising up to attack humanity. Just like Luz had said, the sickness was merely a sign that a great struggle was about to begin.

When Cal visited to give us his geeky lectures, he'd offer the scientific version. It was all a chain reaction: the rising worms upset deep-dwelling rats, who carried the parasite to the surface; they infected felines, who gave it to their humans, who turned into peeps and spread it to still more humans. The disease made people stronger and faster, vicious and fearless—the perfect soldiers to fight the worms.

Through most of history, vampires were rare; but every few centuries, humanity needed tons of them. This epidemic was our species' immune system gearing up, peeps like killer T-cells multiplying in our blood, getting ready to repel an invader. Of course, as Cal liked to point out, immune systems are dangerous things: lupus, arthritis, and even asthma are all caused by our own defenses. Fevers have to be controlled.

That's where the Watch came in, to organize the peeps and keep them from doing too much damage. Like your mom bringing you aspirin and cold compresses and chicken soup—but with ninja uniforms.

Early one morning a week after we'd arrived, they finally let us see the others.

Moz was in a hospital bed, looking worse than I'd expected. His arms and legs were restrained, and long IV tubes snaked into both arms, dripping yellowish liquids into his bloodstream. Electronic monitors were taped all over his bare, pale chest. A plastic shunt jutted from his throat, so they could inject things without opening up a vein.

Moz's eyes looked bruised, his skin stretched taut across his cheekbones. The room was dark and smelled vaguely like garlic and disinfectant.

Minerva sat silent beside him. The sight of her sent a tremor of rage through me: *she'd* done this to him, infected him with her kiss.

Cal said she'd been partly under the parasite's control. Always trying to spread itself, it made its hosts horny, greedy, irrational. But I was still pissed off. Parasite-positive or not, you should never, *ever* hook up with anyone in your band.

Not twice in a row.

"Hey," I said. They'd warned us not to say his name, because of the anathema. He'd only just recovered enough to look at our faces.

"Hey, man," Zahler said. "How's it going, Minerva?"

Minerva pointed to her own mouth, then made a key-turning gesture. *My lips are sealed.*

Of course . . . Moz had been in love with Min. Her sultry, beautiful voice would burn his ears. I noticed that he looked at Zahler and Alana Ray and me, but kept his gaze averted from Min.

Not that I could look at her myself.

"Hey," Moz said hoarsely.

"You look like crap!" Zahler said.

"Feel like crap too."

"At least you aren't smashing things," Alana Ray said. She tried to smile, but her head jerked to one side instead. Since the gig, she was twitchier than I'd ever seen her.

Moz winced, as if remembering the wreckage he'd left of the Strat. He must have loved the guitar more than Minerva, I realized, half smiling. He hadn't smashed *her* to pieces, after all.

Small favors.

"Pretty intense gig, though, huh?" Moz said.

I nodded. "Yeah, fawesome. For most of one song anyway."

"That crowd thought we were totally fool." Zahler sighed. "Too bad about the, uh . . . giant worm, though."

"Yeah. That part sucked," Moz said.

We were all quiet for a while. The Watch hadn't told us anything about that night, and the news had much bigger things to talk about, but we all were pretty sure that people had been killed. Of course, so had the beast we'd raised—one less underground monster.

That was why the New Watch was interested in us.

They knew the secret history of how worms and peeps had always appeared together and had a grip on modern science as well. Cal said they'd known before anyone else that this apocalypse was coming. They had cures and treatments for turning maniacs into soldiers to fight the enemy. They had cool worm-killing swords.

But we could do something they couldn't.

We could sing the worms up. We could bring them out of hiding and to the surface, which made them a lot easier to destroy. . . .

After we'd been talking for a while, Min handed me a note. Her handwriting was still a mess, but I could understand it. More or less.

"So, Moz, we have to leave for a while," I said. "Just for a day or so. We'll be back before you're out of bed."

"Where?" he croaked.

My fingers folded the note up small. "Manhattan."

"Are you kidding?" Zahler said. "It's dangerous back there! And I promised my mom I'd stay right here!"

I nodded. Local phones were mostly still working, so we knew that my mom was safe in the Hamptons, Elvis at her side, and that Zahler's parents were at a Guard camp in Connecticut. Minerva's family had been scooped up by the New Watch, who'd wanted to check and see if they also carried her weird monster-calling strain of the disease. But Moz's parents, like most New Yorkers, were holding out in their building. And they'd said things looked ugly down on the street.

"Sorry, Zahler. But there's someone the New Watch wants us to meet."

"Can't this someone come out to Jersey?" he asked.

I crumpled the note and shrugged. "Apparently not."

"Well, screw that!" Zahler said. "New York is one big Maniac City! They can't *make* us go, can they?"

"Pearl," Alana Ray said. "Does it say what they want to talk about?"

"Only that maybe we can help. What happened that night—we might be able to use it to save people." I turned to each of them as I spoke, pushing my glasses up my nose, like this was a rehearsal and I wanted to get them to stop tuning up and playing riffs and listen to me. "These New Watch guys are the only people in the world who aren't clueless about what's going on. When that thing turned up at our gig, they were the ones who stopped it from killing everybody, remember? It won't hurt us to listen to them."

"It's not the listening that I'm—"

"I am sorry to interrupt, Zahler," Alana Ray said, tapping her forehead twice, a shiver moving across her. "But I agree with Pearl. We called that creature up; we were responsible."

"We didn't know it was going to happen!" Zahler cried.

"Whether that is true or not . . ." Alana Ray's eyes dropped to the floor, as if she saw something there. "It would be unethical not to help if we can."

I looked at the others. Minerva nodded silently, trying to catch my eye. Moz crooked one thumb into the air, and Zahler let out a defeated sigh.

-ZAHLER-

There was a checkpoint at the Jersey end of the Holland Tunnel, swarming with New York cops and Guardsmen and guys in khaki toting machine guns. It didn't look to me like they were letting anyone through.

I figured this was the end of the trip—too bad, we'd tried—and that was fine by me. But then Lace zipped down her window, flashed a badge, and said, "Homeland Security."

The unshaven Guardsman stared at the badge, his eyes red. He looked like he'd been awake for days, like he'd seen some scary shit, and like he thought we were crazy.

But he waved us through.

"Homeland Security?" I asked. "Are you guys, like, *really* Homeland Security? Some sort of paranormal branch?"

"Please." Lace snorted. "Those guys can't even handle *natural* disasters."

Our convoy slid into the tunnel. We were in two big military-looking vehicles, a bunch of angels riding on the outside. I wondered what the cops thought of them. But I guessed everyone had seen much weirder stuff than black ninja suits and swords lately.

The tunnel was completely dark. Lace flicked on the headlights and drove straight down the middle, ignoring the lane dividers. As I watched the entrance disappear behind us through the back window, blackness swallowed everything except the red tinge of our taillights. It felt like sinking to the core of the earth.

"Aren't there worms down here?" I asked.

"They'd never attack us here," Lace said. "The whole Hudson River's balanced over our heads. They breach this tunnel, and a million tons of water gush down on us *and* them."

"Oh. Fawesome," I said, reminding myself to shut up forever, as of now.

"Are they that smart?" Alana Ray asked.

Lace shrugged. "It's all instinct. They evolved underground."

I swallowed, thinking about how much earth there was below us. Room for all kinds of weird stuff to be brewing, and I'd never even thought about it.

"Okay, let's get a few things straight about Dr. Prolix," Cal said. "There's a red line painted on the floor of her office. Whatever you do, don't step across it."

"A line on the floor?" Pearl said. "Doesn't she like musicians?"

"She's a carrier, like me," he explained. "A really old one, so she's got a few diseases that aren't around much anymore. Typhus and stuff. Bubonic plague. If you get too close to her, we sort of have to . . . burn your clothes."

I looked at the others, wondering if I'd really heard him say that. These angels or New Watch guys or whatever were always saying stuff that was just messed up. Talking to Cal was like watching some psycho version of the History Channel that only showed the nasty parts—epidemics, massacres, and inquisitions, twenty-four/seven.

"Burn our clothes?" Minerva said. "But this is my last nice dress! Shouldn't you put *her* in a glass bubble or something?"

Cal shook his head. "The whole house is set up for negative air-pressure prophylaxis, so the germs around Dr. Prolix can't get to where you'll be standing. Just don't cross the line."

"Bubonic plague?" Alana Ray repeated. A shudder traveled through her body, and she pressed her hands together. "Exactly how old is this woman?"

"Old," he said.

In Manhattan, the streets were still alive.

Rats moved among leaking piles of garbage, stray cats sliding under smashed and motionless cars. You could see long ripples in the asphalt where the worms had passed, leaving gleaming stains of black water in the high sun. A few gaping holes showed where they'd burst through the surface. I wondered if anyone had been standing right there when they had. . . .

According to Cal, it was all natural: they were hunters and we were their prey.

Nature can blow me.

"There are no bodies," Alana Ray said.

"The peeps are cannibals," Lace said. "And the worms are human-eaters."

"Much neater than your usual epidemic," Cal said.

A flash of disbelief went through me; this wasn't *really* the Manhattan I'd grown up in. For a moment, it was all a big movie set—a giant, evil version of Disney World. There weren't really any monsters under our feet, or crazy people hiding in the darkened buildings, and all our parents were actually back in the real Manhattan, wondering where we were.

But then we passed an empty school yard, the concrete ripped and torn from one end to the other. An ice-cream truck waited beside it—split almost in half, ripped open from underneath. It was bleeding white goo into the street, and the breeze carried a smell like spoiled milk and burnt sugar through the open windows.

A basketball sat abandoned in the middle of the playground. It stirred in the wind, and the realness of everything settled over me again.

Our convoy weaved slowly downtown, avoiding the worst streets and any people we spotted. Small groups were scurrying from place to place, carrying water and food and other stuff they must have looted from the stores. Smashed and gaping windows were everywhere.

"Are all these people infected?" Pearl asked.

"If they are, they're not symptomatic yet," Cal said. "Peeps can't stand direct sunlight."

I looked out the back window, twisting my neck to see up. It was almost noon, the sun reaching down into the narrow canyons of downtown. The angels all wore dark glasses, except for Cal.

The problem was, this close to winter the sun went down early in New York. An hour from now the shadows of the empty skyscrapers would begin to lengthen.

I hoped this wasn't going to be a long conversation.

We made our way down to the Stock Exchange. It was the worst part of the city we'd seen, the streets empty and broken. Papers and trash blew in little cyclones around us, and Lace honked her horn to scatter a big posse of rats. I guessed the stock market wasn't going to open back up anytime soon.

Lace turned the vehicle's engine off, rolling the last dozen yards to a silent halt. The angels climbed carefully down, drawing their swords and forming a circle around us. The asphalt was pitted and gouged, as if worms popped through all the time around here.

"Everybody out," Lace said. "Step lightly, though. The worms can hear our footsteps." I opened my door and stared down at the street. It was stained with black water, with old gum, and with something viscous and red.

Crap, I thought. All my life I'd been at the top of the food chain and had never really appreciated it. Peeps were bad enough, even worse than junkies, I figured. But the worms—something about the ground opening up and swallowing people was just *wrong*.

I lowered one foot softly to the street, then the other, a shiver of nerves traveling through my body. The asphalt felt fragile, like the ice on the Central Park Reservoir does when you sneak onto it in early spring. As I took my first step, my foot resisted, and I almost screamed, imagining a hungry mouth bursting through to grab my leg.

But it was just the old wad of gum, softened to stickiness by the sun. It tugged at my sole with every step, making a sucking sound.

The angels led us into a long, crooked alley. The old-fashioned cobblestones were broken and bulging, with a few gaping holes that seethed with rats. I shivered at the sight of all those furry bodies. Cal and Lace talked about rats like they were on our side, something about them storing the parasite and bubbling up to spread it when the worms began to rise. But how that was a good thing, I had *no* idea. . . .

We crept slowly down the alley, keeping clear of the wormholes. At the end was an old town house, its stoop covered with silent, watchful cats.

Their red eyes followed us as we went in.

There really was a red line on the floor.

A breeze pushed me toward it, like a gentle hand pressing against my back. Cal had explained that all the air in the house moved toward Dr. Prolix, sucking her ancient germs away from us and down into a big, germ-killing furnace. She was immune to all her own diseases, being infected like the rest of the angels, but we'd be dead meat if we got too close. Even Cal and Lace kept away from the line. Didn't want their fexcellent ninja suits burned, I guess.

I stayed against the back wall, as far away as I could get. Not just to stay away from the Plague Lady but to be farther from the weird old dolls that lined the shelves of her office. Real-looking hair sprouted from their crumbling heads, and all their faces were painted with smiles.

Kids in the old days must have loved nightmares or something.

"You're the one who sings," Dr. Prolix said, her gaze dismissing the rest of us and locking onto Minerva. Her voice was dry and raspy, like two sheets of paper rubbing together. Her unwrinkled face didn't look that old, except for the thinness of her skin and the stiffness of her smile. She looked like one of her own dolls, decorated with glowing human eyes.

"Yeah, that's me," Minerva said in a small voice.

"And where did you learn these songs, young woman?"

"When I first got sick, I felt something down in my basement calling me, making me sort of . . ." She let out a giggle.

"Sexually aroused?" Dr. Prolix asked.

"Yeah, I guess. When I went there in my fevers, I could hear whispering from the cracks." Minerva shrugged. "So I started writing down what they said."

I swallowed. I'd never really thought about where her lyrics had come from, but then, Minerva had never mentioned that they'd bubbled up from underground. That seemed like the kind of thing you might *mention*.

"Perhaps I might hear a few words?" Dr. Prolix said.

"Um, is that a good idea?" Pearl asked softly.

"Don't sing, dear," the old woman said. "Just speak them."

Minerva paused a moment, then cleared her throat.

A few syllables came from her mouth, at first halting and tangled, like someone trying to imitate the sound of a sink gurgling. But then she started speaking in rhythm, and the weird sounds smoothed into words.

Then Minerva fell into the verses and choruses Pearl had built around the nonsense syllables, pitching her voice in a singsong way. I recognized a few phrases from Piece Two, and my fingers moved half-consciously, playing the bass line in the air, so I didn't notice when she started singing.

Maybe the floor trembled a little.

"Stop that!" Dr. Prolix snapped.

Minerva came to a halt, shaking her head as though she were snapping out of a daydream. Then she shrugged. "Sorry."

"I always wondered how that worked," Dr. Prolix said softly from behind her desk.

"How what worked?" Cal said. "What *is* that?"

"The last time the enemy came was seven hundred years ago, before I was born. But the Night Mayor was born toward the end of those times."

I blinked. Okay, this woman was talking about centuries—about being alive for *centuries*. I felt my brain trying to switch off, like when a crazy person is ranting on the subway and you totally don't want to hear it, but you can't stop listening.

Dr. Prolix spread her hand on her desk. "Have you ever considered, Cal, how the previous invasions were dealt with? Without seismographs? Without walkie-talkies and cell phones?"

"Um . . . I thought maybe they didn't deal so well?" he said. "Of course, they didn't have Homeland Security in the way, making it hard to move medicine into regions suffering outbreaks, and there weren't any subway tunnels for the enemy to slide around in. But it must have been hard. What did they lose last time? Two hundred million people?"

"And yet humanity survived." She folded her hands. "Legend has it that they didn't have to wait for the worms to come up. Certain peeps, called 'singers,' were able to bring them forth. So the Watch set traps and ambushes and killed the enemy at will."

Cal breathed out a little sigh. "And we believe this?"

Dr. Prolix nodded. "The Night Mayor saw it happen when he was a child. He saw a woman call up a worm." Her glowing eyes swept across the rest of us. "Along with fifteen drummers and bell-ringers and a man with a conch horn, with a great throng watching, waiting for the kill."

Conch horn? I thought. Oh, great. I was going to have to switch instruments *again*.

"Dude," Lace said, punching Cal in the shoulder. "How come you never told me about this?"

"First I've heard of it," he muttered.

"Some of the old ways were lost." Dr. Prolix looked down at her hands. "Many of us burned in the Inquisition."

"Those guys again," Cal said.

"But the knowledge was not completely lost, it seems." Dr. Prolix looked at Minerva. "Where do you live, child?"

"Um, Boerum Hill."

The doctor nodded. "Some of the old families are buried there."

"Buried?" Minerva said. "Eww."

My jaw dropped. "You mean, like, we were doing songs that *dead people* wrote?"

"Excellent point, Zahler," Cal said. "Come on, Dr. Prolix, this is just wishful thinking. Even if the Watch used to know how to call worms back in the old days, the information's lost, burned at the stake. Why would it be sitting around waiting for some kid in a basement, especially here in the New World?"

"I don't know, Cal."

He shook his head. "We only saw it happen once, and that was hardly a controlled experiment. More like a coincidence. The enemy loves to feed in big crowd situations, like that riot the other day in Prague."

Dr. Prolix was silent for a moment, and I dared to relax a little. Maybe they were going to forget this whole Minerva thing and take us back to New Jersey. We'd only been here half an hour; the sun would still be bright outside. . . .

"No," Alana Ray spoke up. "It was not a coincidence."

Everyone looked at her, and she shivered. Then she touched her own chest three times and pointed a quivering finger at Dr. Prolix.

"I can see things. I have a neurological condition that may cause compulsive behavior, loss of motor control, or hallucinations. But sometimes they are *not* hallucinations, I think, but the realness that comes from the patterns of things. I can see how music works, and I often saw something happening as we rehearsed, and when Morgan's Army played. . . ."

"Morgan's Army?" Lace said. "Isn't their guitarist infected?"

"By Morgan herself," Cal said softly.

"But not their singer," Alana Ray said, her head jerking toward Minerva. "That's why *we* made it real, not them."

Great, I thought. Ten thousand bands in New York City and I had to be in the monster-calling one.

"Alana Ray's right." Pearl stepped right up to the red line. "It's not just Minerva. Everyone in the New Sound has stumbled on bits and pieces of this." She turned to Cal. "You're always saying how nature stores things: in our genes, in the diseases we carry, even in our pets. Everything we need to fight the worms is all around us. So maybe music's a part of that."

"Music?" Cal said. "Music isn't biology."

I nodded. "Yeah, Pearl. We're not talking about some force of nature. We're talking about *us*."

She shook her head. "What *I'm* talking about is whenever a thousand people gather in one spot and move together, all focused on the same beat, mouthing the same words, riding the same twists and turns. I'm talking about the Taj Mahal of human rituals: a huge crowd hanging on the edge together, waiting for a single note to be played. It's lateral and magic and irresistible, even if you happen to be a giant worm."

"In other words, music *is* biology." Minerva smiled. "Just ask Astor Michaels about that, Cal."

He rolled his eyes. "And dead people wrote your lyrics?"

"I don't know where Min's words came from, okay?" Pearl said. "Maybe they're passed on through the disease somehow, and Min just imagined them coming out of the walls. Or maybe they're really nonsense, and it's the melodies that count. But they work, don't they?"

Alana Ray nodded. "They make the air shiver."

"They're something I thought we'd lost," Dr. Prolix said softly. "We can't fight what we can't find, after all. But if we could call the worms to a place of our choosing, this war might be much shorter."

"Maybe it's worth a controlled experiment, Cal," Lace said. "A little science, a little art."

Cal looked at them one by one, then sighed. "You're the boss, Doctor. Once their guitarist gets well, I'll set it up."

"Hang on!" I said. "You're not saying that we're actually going to play those songs *again*?"

Minerva let out a giggle. "Let's put on a show!"

29. THE KILLS

-ALANA RAY-

We set up in an old amphitheater in the East River Park.

Surrounded by the crumbling and graffiti-covered concrete, thick grass reaching up through the cracks, it felt as if the world had ended long ago. This place had been abandoned by the city early in the sanitation crisis, but it showed how all of Manhattan would look in a few years: nothing but a ruin in the weeds.

Along one edge of the park the FDR Drive sat empty, the whole city strangely silent behind it. I saw only faint movements in the windows that faced us, the barest pulses of life.

The New Watch angels set to work, bringing us everything we'd asked for, looting equipment and instruments from the music stores in Midtown. They brought me a brand-new set of Ludwig drums and Zildjian cymbals, but Cal wanted a controlled experiment, as few differences as possible from our first gig. So Lace and three other angels and I made our way to an East Village hardware store, hurrying to make it before the sun started to go down.

The windows were all smashed in, and the angels stepped through without hesitation. My sneakers skidded on shattered glass; I was blind in the darkness inside. As my eyes adjusted, I saw that the shelves were almost empty, every tool looted, every can of spray paint gone.

I listened for anyone, or anything, hiding in the wreckage.

As the angels searched, I stood in the broken window, terrified to step in from the sunlight but not wanting to stand out in the street alone. I drummed my fingers against my thighs, watching the way the fragmented glass reflected sunlight on the ceiling.

Finally Lace shouted that she'd found what we needed. Luckily, no one had bothered to steal the paint buckets.

As we emerged, a pair of young boys called to us from a window overhead. They needed food, they said, and more flashlights to drive the peeps away from their doors and windows at night. Their parents had gone out and hadn't come back.

The angels climbed up and gave them the few remaining batteries they'd found in the store. Then other people started yelling at us from other windows, asking for help. My hands opened, as if they were offering something. But we had nothing else to give.

I felt helpless, the world shimmering with guilt. I'd signed Astor Michaels's contract, had written my name into that tangle of words and consequences. And the monster I'd seen had really come; people had died that night, scores of them. Maybe hundreds.

And I was accountable.

The moral hazard was still following me, slithering underfoot like Minerva's beast, half visible in the corner of my eye. It stirred the grass out in New Jersey and rattled in the drain when I took showers. But it was growing bigger here in the city, drinking in the energy of shattered glass and empty streets. It never left my side.

I knew it was just a hallucination, a trick of my mind as I began to ration my last bottle of pills. But standing there, the blank expanse of First Avenue stretching in both directions as far as I could see, my moral hazard felt more real than I did.

Moz wasn't completely recovered yet, but he could hear his own name without wincing and could look at Minerva, even touch her. The two of them waited in the shadow of the amphitheater's shell, Moz limbering his fingers up on a new guitar.

"As good as your Strat?" I asked, knowing the answer.

He winced at the memory and shook his head.

We did a short sound check as the shadows lengthened, pulling electricity from one of the New Watch's military vehicles. It had a powerful engine, enough to run the instruments, the mixing board, and the thirsty stacks of amplifiers.

The angels had constructed a tower for stage lights on either side of the amphitheater. Once night had fallen in darkened Manhattan, our lights would be visible for miles, a beacon of safety. We were hoping to lure a crowd from among the millions of survivors left in the city.

An audience was necessary, I was certain: it focused Minerva's music, made it more human, and that was what the enemy hungered for.

Once the angels were ready, we gathered onstage and waited for the sun to go down. The worms would never rise up in broad daylight, not long enough for us to kill them.

The park began to come alive. Cats moved among the broken concrete, and the scurrying of smaller creatures stirred the weeds. Lace told Pearl, Zahler, and me to sit on top of one of the New Watch vehicles, so that we wouldn't be bitten by an infected rat. That seemed wise. Bands with too many insects, like Toxoplasma, could only play fast and twitchy music.

And I didn't want to become a peep. I didn't want to hate my drums and my friends, my own reflection. Lace said that peeps who'd been devout Christians even feared the sight of the cross. Would I be terrified of my own pills? Of paint buckets? Of the sight of music?

The sky changed from pale pink to black, and I saw human forms moving in the near distance, parasite-positives out hunting, looking for the uninfected. They shied away from the bright band shell for now, but I wondered if a few spotlights and a dozen angels could really protect us from an entire city full of cannibals.

I drummed on my thighs and tried to remember that the worms were the real enemy: incomprehensible, inhuman. They came from some unlit place we'd never even imagined existed.

But peeps were still people.

Moz and Minerva were my friends and were human enough to be in love. The infection had made Moz sweaty and sick and violent at first, but I'd seen normal love do that. He was already playing his guitar again; maybe soon he would become like the angels, powerful and sure.

I remembered Astor Michaels talking happily about all the bands he'd signed. He thought of the peeps as *more* than human, as gods, as rock stars. He'd even tried to give them a new kind of music.

Of course, if Pearl was right, the New Sound wasn't new at all. Despite our keyboards and amps and echo boxes, the songs shimmering nervously through my head might be like the struggle itself: very, very old.

I'd never seen Manhattan pitch-black before. Normally the pink glow of mercury-vapor streetlights filled the sky, the rivers sparkled with lights from the other side, the windows of buildings shone all night. But the grid was failing now, and outside the band shell's radiance, the only light trickled down from the strange profusion of stars.

Lace joined us up on the truck. "I can think of one problem with this whole idea."

"Only one?" Zahler asked.

"Well, one big one." Lace pointed across the highway toward the darkened city. "These people have seen their whole world fall apart, and they've only survived this long by being very careful. So why would they leave their barricaded apartments for something as random as a free concert?"

I looked up at the lightless rows of windows. "Before we had a name, Astor Michaels said that our real audience would find us by smell."

"Smell?" She sniffed the air. "The parasite improves your senses, you know. But aren't we talking about people who *aren't* infected?"

I frowned. Astor Michaels had been ethically broken, a tangled maze of moral hazards, but he knew brilliantly how crowds worked. Even if the people hiding in the city were terrified, they still needed some kind of hope to cling to.

"Don't worry," I said, tapping my forehead. "They'll come."

By ten P.M. the wind had grown stronger, cutting slices of cold salt air from the East River.

The angels had disappeared, hidden among the trees and up in the light towers, perched across the arched top of the amphitheater—watching over us, just like at the nightclub. Ready to descend.

And hopefully to protect us, if this all went horribly wrong.

Pearl switched on her mixing board, and the columns of speakers began to buzz. She gave Zahler a low E and he tuned his bass, the stage rumbling beneath me. Moz and Minerva came out of the shadows to take their places, trembling in the cold.

We waited for a moment, looking at one another. Pearl had finally come up with the perfect name for us, but there was no one to announce it.

So we just started playing.

This time Zahler didn't freeze. He began the Big Riff, the bass notes thundering out across the park, bouncing lazily back from the wall of housing projects along Manhattan's edge. The rest of the lights came up, bright white instead of the colored gels we were used to, as harsh as a movie set. We were blinded now to anything out there in the darkness, terrifyingly exposed. We had only our angels to trust in.

It was Moz who froze this time, his body shuddering for a long moment as he fought the anathema of his own music. But finally his fingers danced into motion on the strings, years of practice beating aside the parasite inside him.

I started drumming, muscles falling into familiar patterns, but the motion of my hands didn't calm me. It wasn't the blank and empty darkness before me, or the thousands of deadly, infected maniacs all around us. It wasn't even the thought of those huge, human-eating creatures we were trying to summon.

What scared me was being drawn again into the engine of our music. I remembered playing, unable to stop, while the worm had rampaged through the crowd, cutting them down while they watched us, mesmerized. My moral hazard still lurked in the corners of my vision, watching me and waiting.

If the world wasn't cured soon, that vision would become too real. I was running out of pills, the last bottle shaking half empty in my pocket, more depleted every day. I wasn't being heroic, risking my life here on the cold edge of Manhattan. I was being logical.

I was one of those people who needed civilization simply to survive.

Minerva began to sing, her voice searching the darkness, keening through the empty and weed-choked park around us. Calling.

The air began to glisten, and soon I could see the music: Moz's notes hovering in the air, Pearl's piercing melody like a thin spotlight moving among them, making them sparkle. Minerva's song wound through it all, stretching out into the darkness, and Zahler and I played with a fierce determination, as tight as fingers locked together, like sentries afraid to turn their heads.

We played the whole piece through, hoping someone would hear.

When we reached the end, no cheers or applause answered us, not even a lonely shout of encouragement. No one had come.

Then the lights faded around us, and I looked out at where the audience should have been.

A galaxy of eyes reflected back at me. Night-seeing eyes.

Peeps.

They stared at us, transfixed, undead. Not like the angels or Minerva or even trembling Moz, not sane or reasonable or human. These had been fully taken by the disease. They wore filthy and tattered clothes, logos ripped from them as the anathema had taken hold. Many were barely covered, shivering in ragged pajamas and sweatpants—the sort of clothes you'd wear to bed when you felt feverish and half-crazy, coming down hard with the flu.

Their fingernails were long and shone black, as if they'd glued the husks of dead beetles to their fingers. A hundred of them stood there. Motionless.

The survivors hadn't gathered to hear us. The vampires had.

Astor Michaels had been all too right. Our real audience had found us by smell.

"Oh, crap," Zahler said next to me.

A stir moved through them, forms shifting in the silence, the spell of the song fading. Glimmers of hunger flashed in their eyes.

"We have to keep playing," I said.

"We have to *run*," Zahler hissed. He started to back away.

The crowd stirred again. One of them was shambling toward the stage, squinting his eyes against the light.

"Zahler, stop," Moz said. "It's like your dogs. Don't show them you're afraid."

"My dogs don't *eat people*!"

I heard more sounds in the darkness behind us. Of course, the peeps weren't just in the audience in front of us. They were all around us. . . .

"Alana Ray's right. We need to keep playing," Minerva said. "We don't want to disappoint the fans." She pulled the microphone to her lips and began to hum.

The eerie melody crept from the amps, a nameless, shapeless tune that we'd made into our slowest song: "A Million Stimuli to Go."

The peeps began to settle down.

Pearl joined Minerva, her fingers spreading across her

keyboards to hold down long, lush chords. Then Moz came in on top, quick notes flirting with Minerva's hummed melody, pushing her toward words.

I began to play, rolling the sticks softly across my paint buckets, breaking into a slow beat. Finally Zahler reluctantly joined us, his bass rumbling through the darkness.

The peeps remained motionless, staring at us, unblinking.

We played the whole song, trying to forget our ghastly audience, but we wound up going faster toward the finish, our fear finally showing in the music. We ended with a brutal thrashing of the same chord again and again, finally rattling into silence.

I looked out into the dark.

There were five times as many of them now.

"Spot the problem," Zahler said.

A ripple went through the ragged army before us. One of them let out a low, hungry moan. A drop of sweat crawled down my back, as cold as the night air.

"We can't stop playing!" I said.

"What?" Zahler hissed. "You want *more* of them to come?"

Moz took a step back, his hands quivering. "Yeah, and what if no worm ever shows up?"

"Boys," Minerva said straight into the microphone, her words echoing through the park, "I don't think we have a choice."

A few of the peeps had begun to advance, teeth glittering in the moonlight, hands flexing into claws.

"Min's right," Pearl murmured.

"'Piece Two'?" Zahler said, and started before anyone could answer.

We all jumped in, playing hard.

Even terrified, I wondered how we sounded to the peeps, whether they really liked the music or whether certain kinds of sound waves calmed them down, like plants and Mozart. They weren't exactly dancing or moshing or singing along. Why were they listening instead of eating us?

I started pushing the tempo, coaxing the others along, almost as fast as a Toxoplasma song—music for insects.

Then Minerva came in, howling her nonsense syllables, setting my vision shimmering, like the glitter of weeping-willow fireworks fading in the air.

Something rippled through the crowd, a sudden wave of motion, and for a terrible moment I wondered if our spell was breaking. But the ragged army didn't rush to attack us; instead the whole mass of them turned together, like a vast flock of birds wheeling as one.

For a second, I thought the peeps were dancing . . . but it was something much better. Or worse, depending on what happened next. The ground had finally begun to shudder.

They were getting ready. They smelled something: the hated worm rising up toward the surface. Sane or not, the parasite inside them knew the scent of its natural enemy.

The rumbling grew, and I pushed the tempo still faster.

The worm broke through just as we hit the first chorus, scattering dirt and black water, tossing a handful of bodies into the air. But these were peeps, not clueless kids in some nightclub, and the crowd didn't panic or run. They came at the beast from every angle, setting upon it with flashing claws, tearing into its pulsing sides with their razor teeth.

The angels didn't stand back and watch. They shot out of the trees, dropping from the amphitheater roof, swords drawn. Jumping into the throng, they fought side by side with the peeps, the great worm screaming and twisting in its trench.

We played and kept playing. When we ran out of verses, we started over without pausing a single beat, the air warping around me. Minerva's voice had a new shape now, shimmering lines of strength that bound peeps and angels into a single force. Zahler's low thumping notes were tendrils reaching down, squeezing the earth shut below the enemy, trapping it here on the surface. I could feel the battle in my muscles, my sticks flashing like the swords below.

Some endless time later the song finally stumbled to a halt, all five of us exhausted, the engine of our music out of steam at last.

I looked down into the park.

The peeps had torn the worm to pieces. Fragments of its huge carcass were spread out across the broken concrete, still twitching as if trying to burrow back into the earth.

A few of the peeps were scrabbling over the remains, *eating* them. . . .

"What now?" Zahler said as the last echoes faded. The army of peeps had grown bigger than the crowd at our first gig—more than a thousand of them summoned by our music and the death cries of the worm.

Most of them still looked hungry.

The handful of angels stood out in the audience, covered with blood and black water. They glanced nervously at the peeps around them, their bloodlust fading.

"Dudes!" Lace yelled up at us. "Keep going!"

So we did.

Altogether we killed five worms that night, playing until dawn began to break at last.

Light filtered across the sky, pink clouds brightening to orange, and finally our grisly audience began to disperse. They faded into the trees, driven back into the dark alleys of the city, sated by the fight.

Up onstage, we collapsed one by one. Zahler's fingers were bleeding, and Minerva had practically croaked her way through our last song. Even the angels looked unsteady on their feet. Covered with black water, blood, and chunks of gelatinous flesh, they cleaned their swords with shaking hands.

I curled up on the concrete stage, shivering in the predawn chill. My hands ached, my body thrummed with echoes, and shimmering hallucinations colored everything I saw.

But I was smiling. About halfway through the concert, my moral hazard had slunk into the darkness.

And *this* felt very real.

EPILOGUE: THE CURE

-MOZ-

Being on tour wasn't all it was cracked up to be.

There were too many long bus trips, we were in a new town almost every night, and I hated living out of suitcases and trailers for months on end. Most hotels didn't have much staff anymore—most didn't have *sheets*. Room service was a thing of the ancient past.

But we did it for the fans.

At every new town they'd give us a heroes' welcome, having hiked in from miles away or squandered their last few gallons of gasoline to drive from farther. They brought their homemade weapons and homemade liquor, ready to fight the enemy and party, to sing along, basically to have a good time. Local angels and regular people, even a few wild peeps wandered in most nights—everyone wanted to see us perform.

We'd become famous after all, even though the old ways of manufacturing fame—television, magazines, movie sound tracks—hardly existed anymore. There was still a lot of radio around, ten thousand backyard stations juiced with solar power, so everyone knew our songs.

They knew our name too, thanks to Pearl, who'd finally come up with the three perfect words to describe us. Even if it is a stupid plural. I mean, it doesn't really make sense without the *s* at the end.

The Last *Day*? Come on. That's as bad as the Desk.

So you probably know how the rest of the story goes:

We toured like crazy, hitting the big cities all over the world, playing one show after another until the local population of the enemy had been destroyed. Then we did our famous Heartland Tour, playing every small town that had ever spotted a worm-sign in the distance and a few that hadn't.

We were just as popular overseas. One good thing about singing in a language that's been dead for seven centuries: nobody feels left out.

Especially not the worms.

Everywhere we and our two dozen superhuman body-guards went, the enemy came, called up from the bowels of the earth by their ancient hunger, unable to resist a thousand tasty humans swaying to Minerva's songs, as tempting as the smell of bacon sizzling in the morning.

Our fans and the angels kept slaying them, until the last few survivors got canny enough to slither back into the depths. The crisis slowly began to subside, the deep-dwelling rats retreating into their unlit warrens, taking the spores of the parasite with them. Thanks, guys, till next time.

Of course, things took a while to get back to normal.

There were cities and societies that had to be rebuilt, and the New Watch still had to mop up the last few untreated peeps. They scoured the wilderness for those that the anathema had pushed into lonely existences, healing the vampires one by one until they became creatures of legend again. And then the Watch itself disappeared back into the shadows.

The earth was cured—or at least we humans thought so.

No one knew what the worms thought, or if they thought anything at all. We'd killed practically all of them . . . except for the most intelligent ones, Cal always pointed out. The ones who somehow figured out that our music was deadly. So the next time the worms rise up, they'll *all* be descendants of those clever enough to escape. They probably get smarter with every invasion of the surface: wormy evolution in action.

Fexcellent.

But the next crisis won't happen for at least a few hundred years, and I'll be too old to tour by then.

Angels don't live forever, after all.

Along the way, Min and I broke up and got back together about fifteen times, and that's if you don't count the breakups that lasted less than two hours. Zahler became a fawesome bass player, and Alana Ray stayed exactly the way she was: ethical, logical, collected. And Pearl is, as you know, running for Mayor of New York again, but that's a whole other story.

By now, we've all been interviewed a million times

about the tour. One of Cal Thompson's books covers it the best; he was there watching our backs the whole way. Most of what he says is true, as far as I can remember.

The only really new thing I can add to all those stories is this:

It happened in a small town outside Tulsa, about halfway through the Heartland Tour. That night's gig had been fawesome, us thrashing through a twenty-minute version of "Piece Two" while the crowd killed the local enemy, a giant bull worm whose death throes tore up that Sears parking lot like a rabid dog does a newspaper.

At the after-party, one of the local angels came up to me. She had short hair, wild makeup, and intense eyes. Her broadsword was strapped across her back like a guitar.

She stood there for a second, eyes flashing in the light of the bonfire. The comforting smell of burning worm-flesh filled the air.

"Hey, good work tonight," I said, raising my hand. "You guys in the Oklahoma Watch are *great*!"

I was sort of expecting her to say, "No, *you're* great!" But she didn't answer, just stared at me.

After a moment, I said, "Tough old worm, though, huh?"

"You owe me a Strat," she said.

I blinked, finally recognizing her.

She was that crazy woman, the one who'd thrown her life out the window onto Sixth Street the night Pearl and I had met. We'd seen the angels taking her away, to New Jersey—or maybe even Montana, because it was that far back—so of course she'd been cured and had become one of them. . . .

I wondered how she'd wound up way out here. Maybe she'd loved New York too much to go back home; the anathema hangs on real hard sometimes. I've seen angels cower at the sight of old friends or flinch when they hear the chorus of a favorite song. Hell, I *still* don't look in mirrors much.

"Wow," I said, starting to smile. "It's you."

Her dark eyes flashed. "You broke it, one of your bodyguards told me. Smashed it on the stage, like you're Jimi Hendrix or something?"

I shook my head. "It wasn't like that. I was going through the anathema."

"That was a nineteen seventy-five Strat with gold pickups and hardware," she said slowly. "Do you know how hard those are to find? Especially these days?"

I knew exactly. I'd been looking for another one since we'd started touring. The last few in existence were so valuable even *I* didn't have enough money for one. Here was me helping save the world, and I couldn't even afford a decent ax. How messed up was that?

But I'd had about enough of her attitude. "Hang on a second. Last thing I saw, you were throwing it out a window!"

"Yeah, well, I was nuts then!"

"So was I when I smashed it!"

"Um, Moz?" It was Pearl walking up, carrying two precious bottles of precrisis beer. She frowned. "Is there a problem here?"

The woman glared at me, then her hands unbent from claws and she shook her head. "No problem."

The acid scent of angels about to get into a fistfight faded from the air.

I let out a sigh, muttering, "She says I owe her a Stratocaster."

Pearl's eyes widened slowly. "Whoa . . . it's *you*." Her face broke into a smile. "Well, I guess you get Moz's beer, then."

The woman snorted, then took the offered bottle. Homemade liquor was common enough by then, but nobody ever turned down the civilized stuff.

I stood there and watched as Pearl told her how fawesome the local Watch had been tonight. Pearl asked if we could tell headquarters about anything they needed, already the politician, effortlessly charming—saving me once again.

Now that I thought about it, I'd always meant to find this woman, at least to say how much the Strat had meant to me, maybe to explain how it had met its end. But I'd never quite gotten around to it.

It was like Zahler said: Pearl was always fixing the things I'd smashed or dropped or just let slip into disrepair. She'd even helped me and Minerva patch things up more than a few times—anything for the good of the band.

Their conversation paused when another hunk of worm was thrown onto the pyre, making a rattling hiss like a radiator in a New York winter, a fresh scattering of sparks spitting forth and lifting into the sky, another round of drunken cheers.

"Thanks," I said to the woman.

"For what?"

"For dropping that guitar at exactly the right moment." I smiled at Pearl. "For bringing us together."

Pearl grinned back at me.

"Well, you've got a funny way of repaying me," the woman said.

"For what it's worth," Pearl said, "I was there, and he *was* bat-shit crazy at the time."

"You only break the things you love," I said.

The woman shook her head slowly. "But don't you get it, Moz? Anathema or not, it wasn't yours to fall in love with."

I swallowed, not knowing what to say, and Pearl came to my rescue again. "We don't always get to choose what we love."

The woman just scowled, sighing heavily as we turned together toward the blaze. It was growing hotter, its center turning blue as the beast's fat and muscle rendered, dripping down into the bonfire's sizzling core. Pearl's fingers wrapped gently around my arm and drew me closer.

The worm kept burning.

In case you haven't noticed, all the chapter titles in *The Last Days* are band names. Some of them are great bands, some lame, and a few I've never actually heard play—I just needed their names for chapter titles, okay? But for your edification, and so that you can see that I didn't just make them up, here's the list of all chapter names, with a little info about each band.

Enjoy.

Chapter 1: The Fall
Prolific not-quite-punk band from Manchester, U.K. Founded 1976.

Chapter 2: Taj Mahal
Ageless bluesman. First album in 1967.

Chapter 3: Poisonblack
Finnish gothic-doom metal. (Yes, *really*.) Founded 2000.

Chapter 4: New Order
Surviving members of Joy Division, Manchester, U.K. Founded 1980.

Chapter 5: Garbage

Madison, Wisconsin–based mega-band. Founded 1994.

Chapter 6: Madness

London ska band. Formed 1976, but not popular until the eighties.

Chapter 7: Stray Cats

Rockabilly band from Massapequa, New York. Formed 1979.

Chapter 8: Cash Money Crew

Old-school hip-hop collective (later a label). Formed late 1970s, NYC.

Chapter 9: Fear

Los Angeles punk band. Formed 1977.

Chapter 10: The Music

Alt-rock band from Leeds, U.K. Formed 1999.

Chapter 11: Sound Dimension

Reggae session band. Formed in Jamaica in the 1970s.

Chapter 12: The Temptations

A Motown singing group—from Detroit, of course. Formed 1960.

Chapter 13: Missing Persons

L.A. electronic pop band. Formed 1980.

Chapter 14: The Replacements

Punk, then alternative, then splintered into solo acts. Formed 1979 in Minneapolis.

Chapter 15: The Need

Queercore duo from Olympia, Washington. Formed 1996.

Chapter 16: Love Bites

All-girl U.K. teen band. Formed 2005.

Chapter 17: Foreign Objects

Melodic death-metal band from West Chester, Pennsylvania. Formed 1995.

Chapter 18: Anonymous 4

Medieval vocal quartet. Formed 1986.

Chapter 19: The Impressions

Drum-oriented group from Melbourne, Australia. Formed 2002.

Chapter 20: Grievous Angels

Canadian alternative country (Northern Ontario). Formed 1986.

Chapter 21: The Runaways

Joan Jett's first band: proto-punk and all-girl. Formed in L.A., 1975.

Chapter 22: Crowded House

Two-thirds Australian, one-third New Zealand pop band. Formed 1986.

Chapter 23: Moral Hazard

Underground band from Ottawa, Canada. Formed 2000.

Chapter 24: 10,000 Maniacs

Jamestown, New York, punk band. Formed 1981.

Chapter 25: Massive Attack

Trip-hop collective from Bristol, U.K. Formed 1991.

Chapter 26: Hunters and Collectors

Band from Melbourne, Australia. Formed 1980.

Chapter 27: Faithless

London trip-hop trio (and sometimes quartet). Formed 1995.

Chapter 28: Doctor

Indie band from Toronto, Canada. Formed 2004.

Chapter 29: The Kills

Minimalist garage duo from London and Florida. Formed roughly 2000.

Epilogue: The Cure

Post-punk band from Sussex, U.K. Formed 1976.

ACKNOWLEDGMENT

Thanks to Morgan Butts and her pals for "fawesome."

ABOUT THE AUTHOR

Texas native Scott Westerfeld has written several acclaimed novels for adults and teens, including *So Yesterday*, *The Risen Empire*, the *Midnighters* sequence, and the *Uglies/Pretties/Specials* trilogy. His books have been named *New York Times* Notable Books of the Year, made the *Times's* essential summer reading list, been awarded the Philip K. Dick Special Citation and the Victoria (Australia) Premier's Prize. Scott and his wife live in New York City and Sydney, Australia.

Visit Scott's Web site at www.scottwesterfeld.com